Above TEMPTATION

Karin Kallmaker

2010

Bella Books, Inc.
P.O. Box 10543
Tallahassee, FL 32302

Printed in the United States of America on acid-free paper
First Edition

Editor: Katherine V. Forrest
Cover Designer: Linda Callaghan

ISBN 13: 978-1-59493-179-6

Also by Karin Kallmaker

Romance:

Stepping Stone
Warming Trend
The Kiss that Counted
Night Vision / The Dawning
Christabel
Finders Keepers
Just Like That
Sugar
One Degree of Separation
Maybe Next Time
Substitute for Love
Frosting on the Cake
Unforgettable
Watermark
Making Up for Lost Time
Embrace in Motion
Wild Things
Painted Moon
Car Pool
Paperback Romance
Touchwood
In Every Port

Erotica:

In Deep Waters: Cruising the Seas
18th & Castro
All the Wrong Places
Tall in the Saddle: New Exploits of Western Lesbians
Stake through the Heart: New Exploits of Twilight Lesbians
Bell, Book and Dyke: New Exploits of Magical Lesbians
Once Upon a Dyke: New Exploits of Fairy Tale Lesbians

visit www.kallmaker.com

Acknowledgments

Dedicated to all the women who set out every day to right wrongs in the real world even when there's no help, time, luck or support. Superwomen are all around us.

For my family and, as always, most of all for my readers. If you didn't exist I would still write. Because you do exist, no one calls me crazy.

Squee! O Glee! We are Twenty-Three!

About the Author

Karin Kallmaker's nearly thirty romances and fantasy-science fiction novels include the award-winning *The Kiss That Counted*, *Just Like That*, *Maybe Next Time* and *Sugar* along with the bestselling *Substitute for Love* and the perennial classic *Painted Moon*. Short stories have appeared in anthologies from publishers like Alyson, Bold Strokes, Circlet and Haworth, as well as novellas and short stories with Bella Books. She began her writing career with the venerable Naiad Press and continues with Bella.

She and her partner are the mothers of two and live in the San Francisco Bay Area. She is descended from Lady Godiva, a fact which she'll share with anyone who will listen. She likes her Internet fast, her iPod loud and her chocolate real.

All of Karin's work can now be found at Bella Books. Details and background about her novels, and her other pen name, Laura Adams, can be found at www.kallmaker.com.

CHAPTER ONE

"Here's the last of the files, Barrett." The clerk hardly paused as he shoehorned two more boxes into her cubicle. "What a waste of paper."

"Wait—take these back. I'm done with them." Kip Barrett wearily lifted four file boxes into the clerk's waiting hands. It was progress, at least. She was finally giving back more than she was getting and it wasn't too often that she felt that way.

She staged the new boxes in the precarious Jenga-like stack crowding her cubicle. She was still trying to figure out how doing her job really well meant she was assigned the mind-shredding task of numbering exhibits. "It has to be right so I want you to do it" from her boss didn't seem like a compliment now, especially when the files in question were actual hard copy, relics of a case from the pre-digital era. A wasteland of manila folders mounded across her desk. The only spots of color were the coded file tags and the printed lettering across each file: CONFIDENTIAL PROPERTY OF STERLING FRAUD INVESTIGATIONS.

It's important work, she told herself. After all, this stack of paper held one critical fact supported with multiple verified source documents. When added to the next fact, and the next, and hundreds of others it meant a failed appeal and Joseph Wyndham III could go on writing his memoir in his minimum security cell.

She swapped her pencil for an indelible fine point marker and wrote numbers on the sheets of paper in the long-used company script. This piece of paper, this fact: $19,929.17 from the account of prosecution witness 4,866, via unauthorized bank transfer initiated in Oregon moving funds through Federal Reserve District 12 from California to a bank domiciled in Zurich.

One mistake, erasures, corrections, *anything* imperfect, and the defense's contention that his innocent, God-fearing, pillar-of-the-community client had been mistakenly prosecuted is bolstered by "shoddy, inconsistent" work by the firm of Sterling Fraud Investigations. There—4,866 files checked. Only 623 to go.

She tried to whip up her flagging energy with the thought of her weekend plans, but that strategy had stopped working two days ago. Just a few more hours, she told herself.

"You want to shut off that alarm?" Her cube neighbor's raspy voice floated over the barrier. "I got plenty of alarms of my own to worry about."

It took her a minute to realize the comment was meant for her. Her tired brain had shut out the persistent tone of an urgent internal e-mail. Ignoring everything around her was a survival skill when confronted with this much to do. Her equally punchy neighbors had been playing a candy bar jingle most of the morning. Someone would rhythmically start it, and it would travel bit by bit along all the cubicles until it was done. It was not nearly so annoying as "Wassup!" and "Who let the dogs out?", the two previous cubicle noise games.

She silenced the e-mail alarm. It was probably from Emilio

Woo, her boss. Please, she thought, any other day I'm happy to do whatever. But not today.

It wasn't from Emilio. She stared at the sender's name and then took a deep breath. What did Tamara Sterling, the woman who stared impassively at her from the covers of SFI annual reports, want with her? Maybe it was a mistake.

It wasn't. The message was brief and to the point: *Come to my office at precisely half past four. Please do not mention this appointment to anyone.*

Her computer put her on hold while her brief confirmation was sent and she allowed herself to wonder what the appointment was about. She'd officially met with Sterling only once since joining the banking specialists staff, though they'd said a casual word or two at meetings, receptions and office functions. A promotion? No, Emilio or his boss would have talked to her about that. There were no openings that she knew about. And from what Kip knew of Tamara Sterling, she didn't need any help finding or balancing her accounts.

Speculation wouldn't get any work done and she needed to finish at least fifty more files before she left for the weekend. She caught her heavy sigh before it escaped from her lungs. She tried to tell herself she hadn't turned into a desk jockey. Field investigations were a lot more interesting, but nobody got to do just the fun stuff. Tracing live digital signals, watching a magician programmer open trap doors for high-tech thieves to fall through, right into their waiting virtual hands—that was so very fun. And all too rare.

Paperwork was killing her, though. After this, she had two trials coming up where she was the lead investigator and end of the month was the report deadline for the last three cases she'd worked on. She was up to her ears in schedules and exhibits with paralegals and lawyers breathing down her neck.

She set her computer alarm to remind her of the appointment and turned back to the manila folders. Time for number 4,867.

There was no sign of Tamara Sterling's assistant when Kip entered the outer sanctum of the CEO's office. She waited a moment or two, then glanced at her watch. She would be late if the legendary Mercedes Houston didn't return.

After another minute ticked away, Kip straightened her shoulders and calmly knocked on the inner door. She glanced down at her favorite ivory blouse and deep plum suit combination, then patted her hair—it was as trim as the rest of her. Though her long black curls could be unruly, the fashionably knotted ponytail was in perfect order. She hoped the tidiness of her attire would mask her exhaustion.

When a low voice called for her to enter, she pushed the door open.

Tamara Sterling was already halfway across the office to greet her. "Please come in, Kip."

She was holding out her hand, so Kip shook it as she looked up at her. The sparkling collar pin at the top button of the crisp white shirt was an inch below eye level for her. That put Sterling at around five-ten. The short brown hair didn't add to her height, but its straight, simple lines echoed the rest of her angular physique. In photographs it appeared dark brown, but the afternoon sunlight revealed a hint of red. The handshake was firm, palm dry, and her expression, while welcoming, was unreadable. The steady gray eyes seemed to be taking note of everything they saw. As usual, when considering her employer's appearance, Kip knew why few people ever forgot meeting Tamara Sterling. She was rarely called attractive. Kip, if asked, would have said *arresting* was the better word.

She mentally kicked herself for having her investigative instincts so engaged that she were describing her boss's boss's boss in her head as if she was a witness or suspect. She badly needed some down time. "What can I do for you, Ms. Sterling?"

She gestured at a chair in front of her desk. "I need to—damn."

Her expression turned so grim as she answered the phone

that Kip hoped she hadn't done anything to jeopardize what she had thought would be a long career. There was simply no other company like SFI.

"Have a seat," she said as she covered the mouthpiece. "I'm sorry, but this will only take a moment."

Kip oozed down into the teak and burgundy leather guest chair and watched surreptitiously as Sterling fired short questions at the person on the other end of the line. The Mount Rushmore face from the Annual Report was in full evidence, and it was easy to believe the rumors that floated around about Sterling's past in intelligence work. She was too memorable to work undercover, and the rumors suggested a more steely-eyed confrontational style—interrogation wasn't hard to believe, though Kip was certain Sterling's own tendency to refer to her past as "Geek with a Badge" was the truth.

To avoid noticeably eavesdropping, Kip stared past Sterling to the iridescent panorama of Seattle and Puget Sound. The normally smoky blue-green waters of the Sound were washed with orange by the late afternoon sun. Across the expanse of Elliott Bay, past the point of Duwamish Head, she could see faint golden lights...probably Winslow. It was one of many spectacular views of the Seattle area and if this were Kip's office, she'd always be staring out the window. Perhaps that was why Tamara Sterling had her back to it.

Today's afternoon rain shower had left the air pure and brisk. Outside the temperature was falling to the high forties. She thought with pleasure of her coming weekend at the cabin. There was no chance of snow and the mountain air rolling down out of the Olympic Mountains would work magic on her tired spirit. A crackling fire, steaming bowl of soup with a good book—heaven, or as close to it as she was ever going to get.

Forcing her concentration inside the room, Kip's brain began tallying up the cost of the office furnishings. She'd had a lot of practice at it. The bookcases, conference table and side chairs were all burnished teak—the real thing, not thin veneer over cheaper wood. The bookcases held books bound in leather that showed signs of actually having been read, and *objets d'art* that she guessed were costly, but not astronomically so. There was no antique commode cabinet worth $20,000 and the carpet had not cost $400 a square yard. The office would have been sterile and impersonal if not for the signed baseball under glass on a bookshelf, an attractive award Kip recognized from the company newsletter as the GLAAD Lesbian of Distinction award, and a framed, signed photo of Sally Ride on the credenza behind Sterling's desk. The reception to honor the GLAAD recipients was one of the times they had officially met. She didn't know if Sterling would even remember her from that event.

The desk was large and also teak and it was a well-used piece of furniture. The surface of the desk sported several large stacks of paperwork, but the collection had an organized look to it. Her practiced eye read file names upside down, but she lacked the memory to be able to recall the coded numbers later. They were definitely SFI client files. Several, however, were names lightly written in pencil—possible new clients?

She was trying to figure out if the Apple laptop was the latest version or one removed when she realized that Sterling had hung up and the ice-gray eyes were intently scrutinizing her.

"You're probably wondering what this is about."

Kip nodded.

"I have a special assignment and you're the person for the job."

"Wouldn't this normally go through channels?"

Her lips twitched. "I don't have to go through channels."

Kip felt herself color. Fortunately, her olive-tinted skin—the legacy of her father's DNA—wouldn't show it. "Of course not. I'm just startled that you selected me."

Sterling opened the file directly in front of her. "You've had the experience I need right now. Before you came to us you graduated top of your class from NYU and then went on to *summa cum laude* honors at Yale with a master's in finance." She glanced up from the file. "You returned to NYU for criminology specialty courses, then you underwent extensive training with the Justice Department."

Kip had schooled herself not to react. "The Secret Service, actually."

"Why?"

"I was following in my grandfather's footsteps."

"And you left after six months because..."

"Personal reasons."

"And they are?"

Kip paused, then said steadily, "Personal."

Sterling stared at her for a moment as if she would press further. The silence stretched but Kip knew it for what it was—people often volunteered information to put an end to a long silence.

Kip could match her, stone for stone.

Finally, Sterling arched one eyebrow as if to say Kip had not outstared her but she found continuing the silence pointless. "The training has stayed with you, I see."

She looked back at the file. "After leaving the government, you joined us as an Internal Controls Consultant. That was four—almost five—years ago, and you've been promoted steadily. Currently you're an Internal Audit Specialist on a team that handles some of our more complicated clients. Your performance appraisals are exemplary and a year ago I authorized a sizeable performance bonus for you after some excellent work tracing transfers for Big Blue here in Seattle."

Kip wasn't sure how to handle this summation of her life. She tried to sound confident as she said, "I hope I've lived up to the expectations of the firm."

Her lips twitched again—not quite a smile. "If you hadn't you'd be gone."

She felt herself flush again but said nothing. She'd only stated the obvious, but apparently making her feel stupid was the game they were playing.

After a moment, Sterling closed the file and leaned back in her chair. Long fingers tapped the folder idly. "I'm hiring you as a consultant."

Kip kept her expression blank, as if her boss's boss's boss

gave her assignments every day. She straightened. "I don't understand."

"I want you to do for me what you did on the McMillan case. Woo's report said that while he took the lead, you were the backbone of the investigation team. Reading the appraisal closely I can see that Woo's been dragging his heels on your next promotion because he doesn't want to lose you from his team."

Kip took a deep breath and let it out slowly. The McMillan investigation had been a guarded, secret commission from the chairman of the board who had suspected that a top executive was embezzling. Discovering the embezzlement had been easy. Figuring out how it was being done had been difficult. Finding where the money had gone and recovering it had been a grueling, nerve-wracking challenge. Ultimately, they'd recovered all but a fraction of the funds, then prepared the documentation for the eventual prosecution of the director of finance.

Kip said carefully, "You want me to investigate embezzlement at SFI? In secrecy and potentially involving one of your direct reports? And you can't ask Woo or Daniels because the guilty party might notice?"

She nodded gravely. "I need you because you're still a low profile. Someone is siphoning cash out of SFI bank accounts. You can start with these." She tossed a stack of papers in her direction.

Kip had examined thousands of bank reconciliations in her years with SFI and the Justice Department. Even in the digital age, bank statements were tick marked by real people for key balances, an essential check against error and fraud. She flipped through the pages and saw the telltale signs of alterations. It was a very good job, though. "How much is missing?"

"Half a million that I've discovered so far. I haven't started looking where the real money is. Someone would notice if I did."

Kip arched an eyebrow. "The trust accounts?"

She got a nod in response. "I was ambivalent about offering the service to clients from the beginning, and this was one of the reasons why."

"We take every precaution," Kip said. "Loss of a client's money would be devastating. It would literally shatter our reputation."

The look she got said she had just stated the obvious again.

Fighting down another flush, Kip changed direction. "I understand why you're asking me. Whoever is doing this might be on the lookout for you or one of the top investigators. But they won't be looking for someone like me. How do you know you can trust me?"

"Because of the Prudential case. If you were susceptible to bribery I think you would have taken the three hundred thousand they offered you. You have no offspring yearning to go to Ivy League schools. You're driving a six-year-old car and you live in a very modest condo. No untoward debts, no unexplained riches."

Sterling had clearly done a cursory background check. Kip tried not to resent the intrusion; it came with the territory. "The condo is modest, maybe, but it cost plenty. Seattle's real estate was through the roof when I bought it." Kip didn't mention the cabin, which she'd been able to buy last year, using her savings and the bonus from the Big Blue case. Nobody knew about the cabin.

"I don't know why you left the government and moved out of D.C., but if the Secret Service brought you in for full training, you must have been screened thoroughly. Though I can't see you as one of those guys that runs alongside the limousine." The gray gaze flicked down Kip's body, then back to her face. It was an impersonal glance, but she knew what Sterling was thinking—she was small for that kind of work. As often as she bemoaned her petite height she was thankful for it. People tended to underestimate small women, a bias she had used to her advantage more than once.

"My ultimate role was going to be advance fieldwork. Investigating the financial status of potential hosts. I was also doing financial investigation of hosts." She saw no reason to tell Sterling that she'd met all the physical requirements, including marksmanship. She wasn't going to explain about the simulators either.

"Their loss was our gain."

Though she found it quite fulfilling chasing white-collar criminals—and there had been so many of them the last several years—she still felt the sting of the failure to serve and protect. As her father routinely sneered, she was the reincarnation of her grandfather.

"And you have no intention of telling me why you left."

It was a statement of fact, so Kip said nothing. The last thing she would do was inform the head of the company why she had been allowed to resign from the Secret Service.

Sterling's vexed sigh was brief, but heartfelt. "There are a few other conditions you should know about before you say yes."

"And they are?"

"You'll have to carry this in addition to your other duties. Woo can't know you're working on something else. I want quick results. If this account is missing a half million, there might be more and whoever it is could be preparing to leave the country and we won't recover a cent. I want the funds back."

"I'll do my best." She said it with all sincerity and the quick nod said she was understood—they had made a pact. At SFI they took agreements very, very seriously. "My resources and investigative reach will be limited if I can't have authorized access to certain kinds of files, however. It will take me longer than a team."

"I understand. Even if all you can do is ETO, it will be a good start. If a senior officer is involved our fidelity bond won't cover the losses, so I'm anxious to know if it's any of them."

Eliminating the Obvious was always the first and easiest step. Kip nodded again.

"Thank you," Sterling said quietly. "After this meeting we shouldn't see each other at the office. If you need to talk to me, leave a message on my private voice mail." She pushed a business card toward her.

"Of course." As she tucked the card in her pocket, she noted the home address and private phone numbers written in standard SFI lettering script.

"I also have a lot of materials to give you. I thought I could do this on my own, but I am traveling too much to do an effective job."

"How can I get them from you?"

"I have to be on a plane out of SeaTac at ten. An appointment in New York came out of the blue, and that's when I realized I needed help. Can you come by my home around eight thirty? I'm on the Hill."

"Eight thirty will work." So much for a leisurely birthday dinner with Jen, Luke and their pals. She could hear the conversation already over birthday cake. Her friends were all starting to sound like her ex.

"Good." Sterling's tone indicated their meeting was over. Kip took the bank statements she'd been given and stood up.

Tamara Sterling rose as well, and came around her desk to shake hands. Her touch was cool. "I think I've made the right decision."

It was Kip's turn to twitch her lips. "It's an SFI motto—hire the best."

"You're not the most modest of people," she said, but for the first time the smile seemed genuine.

Kip arched her eyebrows. "People tend to praise modesty, then overlook you."

She turned to go and could feel the gaze on her back as she walked to the office door. When she got there she turned to salute smartly and made what she hoped was a dignified exit.

Sterling's assistant was still not at her desk, and Kip wondered if the formidable Mercedes Houston was elsewhere so Kip wouldn't be seen coming and going. Probably. A successful investigation was conducted in the utmost secrecy, not that anyone would get anything out of Mercedes Houston. People had tried. They had always failed. Mercedes' considerable wit was company legend. Her boss had IT'S A LAW OF PHYSICS—YOUR FOOT WILL ALWAYS FIT IN YOUR MOUTH tacked to his office wall.

The office door opened just as she reached it. She stepped back to let in the lanky, sandy-haired man. She recognized him immediately and turned the bank reconciliations so the faces were hidden against her chest.

"The old girl in?" He smiled at her with boyish charm. Ted Langhorn was Director of Client Relations and Tamara Sterling's longtime friend. And a suspect until she cleared him. "Where's Mercedes? Are you temping for her?"

Kip was mildly irritated by the question, and peeved by Langhorn's disrespectful use of "old girl" to describe the CEO. He might say it to Sterling's face, but Kip was a subordinate. He'd always struck her as a glib deal-broker. Essential, but incapable of doing the work he was selling to clients.

"Ms. Sterling is in. I was just dropping off something. And picking up." She indicated the stack of papers she was clutching against her stomach.

"Oh, sorry. Don't I know you? You did that Big Blue investigation last year didn't you? Barrett, right? Great work. Clients mention it all the time."

Kip nodded, sorry she hadn't been out of Sterling's office thirty seconds earlier. Besides, she thought she'd been over-praised for that case. Fourteen million dollars was a lot of money, to be sure. But it had been stolen by a clumsy cocaine addict who had drawn a lot of attention to himself with conspicuous spending. He'd even ordered tickets to Brazil in his own name with his company credit card. Kip had seen the transaction on their tap of his credit card records just a few moments after he'd made it. The companion programmer working with her had laughed out loud. Stupid criminals made life easy.

It *had* felt good, arriving at the idiot's office with two agents. They'd done the arresting, and she'd pointed out the evidence they would need to take, including the laptop. That afternoon she'd helped the Fed's forensic accountant hack into the guy's system, though "hacking" didn't really apply when she'd suggested they try his middle name for his password and had been right. Local law enforcement had been delighted to receive the names and phone numbers of several cocaine suppliers. Yes, that *had* felt good, even the tedious preparation for her own testimony. It had been too long since she'd had a moment quite so fulfilling.

Tamara Sterling's office door opened abruptly. "Thought I heard voices. Come on in, Ted." Looking at Kip, she added, "Glad I was able to catch you. There's one more folder for Woo." She looked annoyed that Kip had forgotten something.

Turning back to Ted, she said, "How'd you make out in New York? Oh, and the Seahawks lost a squeaker while you were gone." She waved vaguely at Kip as though she'd already forgotten her existence. Kip made a speedy exit.

"Don't tell me about the Seahawks," Ted was saying as the door closed. "They were supposed to beat the spread..."

In the elevator she looked into the folder she'd been given. A dozen blank sheets of paper. That meant Sterling had waited to find out if Kip was going to be seen leaving. Since Sterling had misled Ted Langhorn about Kip's reason for being there, it meant that she hadn't dismissed Ted as a suspect.

She sat at her desk in a daze, overwhelmed. Her cubicle neighbors were tapping out another homage to the Kit Kat bar. She had to get away this weekend. Everyone, even her, had their limits. She'd been working weekends for so long she wasn't sure what day of the week it was unless she checked her cell phone.

She hunkered down over her work for another hour, carefully double-checking everything because she was so tired. The papers Sterling had given her were tucked into her satchel, out of sight, but to her they were glowing like neon. When the clock told her she had to leave right then or completely miss Jen's birthday party she packed up her running shoes, coffee travel mug, paperback she'd been trying to finish for two months and a half of a banana that was probably going to be her dinner.

Cafe C'est Bon had been chosen by the birthday girl for the crepes, and by the time Kip pulled into the parking lot she was sure that dessert was already flambéed and served. She could linger for thirty minutes. The only break she was catching was that C'est Bon was most of the way to the Queen Anne Hill address Sterling had given her.

On the walk from the parking lot she spied Jen at a table for seven. The chair to Jen's left was conspicuously empty. Jen had cut her long, blond hair—it only brushed her shoulders now. Her boyfriend, Luke, was in his usual black tie on a black shirt, but instead of the customary glower that Kip was used to seeing he was laughing at something Jen had just said.

She threaded her way through the crowded cafe and slid into the empty chair after dropping a kiss onto Jen's forehead. If she had a best friend, Jen was it. "Sorry—work, as usual."

"It's always work with you," Jen muttered. Her schoolteacher you-flunked face was in full evidence.

"It's a living," Kip answered, hoping to change the subject. It was also a calling, something that nobody ever seemed to understand. Certainly not Meena, whose parting words had been, "I moved out two weeks ago and you just noticed."

"Tell us about it," Luke said, tossing a little kindling on the emotional fire. "We've already ordered dessert."

"I'd be honored if Jen would let me have a taste of whatever she ordered," Kip said, trying hard to smile. "I don't deserve more. But if there's coffee I'd kill for some." The last she directed to the hovering waiter, who nodded and sped away.

"A new, important case?" Luke was smiling in that not-a-clue-why-my-girlfriend-tolerates-you way. Kip understood why Jen found him attractive, but the charm of the carefully trimmed beard and moody brown eyes was lost on her. He waited tables to support his career as a bass guitarist in a Goth band, which was fine by Kip except, near as she could tell, the band hadn't gigged in a year. Thirty-something was a little old not to have any kind of plan for the next six decades. Jen deserved better, and she was pretty sure Luke felt the same way about her as Jen's friend.

Before she could answer, Luke added, "Oh, I forgot. You can't say."

"That's right," Kip said brightly. She glanced at Jen and Luke's other friends—two more couples she had met several times and whose names escaped her. They were politely ignoring the undercurrents. She knew Luke had some justification for his feelings. If the other couples had been clients or suspects, she'd remember every last detail. She might not be a bad person, but she was pretty much a bad friend these days.

However, she had her good moments, and hoped this was one of them. Pulling the small wrapped box out of her satchel, she set it next to Jen's plate. "Happy birthday."

The crease between Jen's eyebrows disappeared. They'd been friends since the fifth grade, ever since they'd compared notes and discovered they were both Libras and Jen was only six days older. Jen was the only person outside immediate family who'd met her grandfather. She came closest to understanding why Kip was the way she was. She tapped the bedraggled wrapping paper and ribbon. "How long have you had this?"

"I saw it in a shop window when I was in Munich about five months ago. They wrapped it for me, or else it would be—"

"Wrapped in the funny pages or aluminum foil." Jen laughed. "I know it's not easy—thanks for making time tonight."

Luke's sigh was loud, but fortunately lost in the shredding of the paper. Jen's puzzlement was obvious as she considered the drawing on the outside of the box. She was probably thinking "A miniature china figurine? Me?"

She popped open the box with a smile, though, and pulled out the contents. When the cardboard and bubble wrap finally parted she let out a stunned gasp. "That's amazing. Wow."

She held it up on the palm of her hand so the others could see.

Kip knew she would likely never care much for Luke, but he earned points by saying to Jen, "It's the spitting image of your mom and the cat in your baby pictures!"

"Mr. Peeps," Jen said. "And my mom wore an apron and a blue blouse all the time."

"Can I see it?" One of the other friends held out a hand and Jen passed it along.

If it bothered Luke right then that Kip knew so much about

Jen's past, it didn't show. She got a look that said she might be tolerated a little longer along with an ungrudging, "What a great find."

"It was total chance. The first time I went over to Jen's house her mom was sitting at the window with the cat on her lap—just like that. Her hair was exactly that light shade of blond, too."

"It was before how sick she was really started to show, but..." Jen swallowed. "She was melancholy sometimes, just wanted to sit and think. It's beautiful, Kip."

"Then she made us cookies. Sugar cookies with bits of Hot Tamales. Best cookies I ever had."

"They were the first cookies you ever had." Jen took the figurine back and gazed at it one more time. "Your mom was such a food Nazi."

"True, but remember how much my grandma spoiled me to make up for bulgar and wheat germ salad? Your mom was a great cook too," Kip said. She patted Jen's hand and Jen squeezed back. They didn't have to say aloud that the last cookies Jen's mom had made them had been the day before she'd collapsed and died at home, her bad heart finally giving out. Kip was glad that Jen's own heart was healthy and strong. It had been only another month before Kip's grandfather had also died after a heart attack. There were reasons they were still friends, twenty-odd years later.

Luke didn't miss the silent exchange and was frowning. Nothing Kip could do about that, so she sipped the wonderful, fresh, fragrant, caffeine-infused coffee and joined the conversation as best she could. Jen did let her have a couple of bites of her vanilla gelato and toasted walnut caramel crepe. For a few scant minutes, life was relaxed and easy.

At eight fifteen she excused herself, not free to say she had a business appointment, only that she had to leave.

"I think you must have a hot date," Luke said, after a fake cheek kiss.

"I wish," Kip answered, even though she didn't. She couldn't handle a girlfriend right now.

"You sound like Kip's ex," Jen admonished him.

"He has a point—and so did she." Kip gave Jen one last hug.

"Go get the bad guys," Jen whispered in her ear.

Kip grinned. "I promise."

CHAPTER TWO

"Thanks, Mercedes. Yes, I'll take a jacket. Now go home to your family, would you?"

Tamara Sterling tapped off her mobile, knowing Mercedes wouldn't leave for a few more minutes. The fax to the client in Hawaii would be securely received before she left. That was her job and she was going to do her job and what part of that was so difficult for Tam to understand? Wasn't that why she hired people and paid them so regularly and handsomely? Not a conversation Tam wanted to repeat, certainly not tonight, especially when she knew Mercedes would have the last word because she was, as usual, right.

Even though she was not quite packed for her flight, Tam gave herself three minutes in the living room with a cup of her favorite coffee. She rarely got to linger in front of the view these days. It did little to ease the gnawing heartsick feeling in the pit of her stomach, the feeling she'd had ever since she'd found a photocopy of an SFI bank statement next to the server array. It had been purely accidental. She'd cast a professional eye over it without thinking, and hadn't believed what her instincts had told her: the statement had been altered.

If she started hanging around and peeking into files it might tip off the embezzler. She hoped that the several days she'd waited before seeking help hadn't made matters worse.

The ring of the doorbell drew her away from the window. Speaking of help, she thought. She had known from Kip Barrett's supervisor's reports that she was a capable, experienced investigator, but she hadn't expected her to be so straitlaced. She appeared to have as much sense of humor as a rainy day. Of course, what did humor count for when she had handled that awkward moment with Ted so competently? She either had nerves of steel or no nerves at all.

She suspected the latter and idly wondered if she'd ever know for sure.

"I hope I'm not too late." Barrett slipped into the foyer.

Her watch told her it was eight thirty-one. "Not at all."

She was still in her suit from earlier in the day, but Tam thought she caught a faint aroma of sweets and coffee, as if she'd been to a restaurant. She didn't exactly look like she'd been on a date. None of her business. Everybody needs to eat, she reminded herself.

She started to lead the way to the garage but Barrett froze at her first sight of the view from the living room. Everybody did that.

"Holy wow."

"It *is* lovely, isn't it?" She let her have a good, long look. In her opinion, this ridge on the west side of Queen Anne Hill provided the most spectacular view of Seattle money could buy. The house was small, a custom design dating from the Sixties, and its trim outline was nestled into the height of the ridge, surrounded by trees and sky. The city glowed with mesmerizing activity. Lights pooled to the north and south in all colors. The glow ended abruptly at the shoreline, then began again across the Sound in Bremerton. From the master bedroom, though she'd hardly take an employee there even if the view was spectacular, the Space Needle pierced the sky.

"It's stunning." Barrett pushed her car keys into her pocket. "Friends from New York keep trying to get me to move there, but I'm devoted to Seattle. Views like these are one reason why."

Certain she wouldn't get an answer, but curious about how Barrett would react, she asked, "But you considered living in D.C., didn't you?"

The openness of Barrett's expression turned brittle. She turned away from the view to face her. "You're persistent, Ms. Sterling."

"Call me Tamara, please."

It was a very cool smile. "Personal is personal, Tamara."

She let her smile turn cool as well. There was no mention of why Barrett had left the Secret Service in her file, and the mystery frustrated her. All mysteries frustrated her, a trait that was useful, though Mercedes had told her once that if she ever got answers to all her questions the earth would spin backward. "The boxes are in my trunk. I wasn't sure this morning if I would need to meet you somewhere else."

"You were sure I'd say yes." Barrett's voice was carefully expressionless, but Tam thought she heard a hint of irritation.

"Yes, I was." She glanced at her over her shoulder as she led the way. Barrett looked slightly miffed, but the change of expression on her face was so minor she might have imagined it. Kip Barrett should be playing poker with that face. Attractive—absolutely, especially the luminous blue eyes—but the face was carved in stone. She'd spent years learning to read many different kinds of people, but Kip tested her experience.

She triggered the garage door and opened the back hatch of her Pathfinder. Kip used her key fob to open the trunk of a trim Camry, then came back for a box. Glancing into the trunk, she gave a tiny sigh.

"Too heavy for you?" Tam paused, wondering if the petite Barrett found lifting boxes full of paper a challenge. Based on her Secret Service profile and trim physique, Tam would have thought that she had plenty of physical strength.

"Oh no," Kip said. "I was just wondering where I'd start." She lifted a box out easily and headed for her car.

"I began cataloging, and the box you have has the thumb drive with the worksheet I'd started. I'll get the last one."

As Tam slid the last box into the Camry's trunk, she saw an overnight bag. She was briefly torn again—was Barrett meeting someone? Discussing or conducting work in front of even the most trusted spouse or companion was a breach of their work code. She realized that meant Barrett couldn't work at the office, nor could she work at home if she didn't live alone. Rock and a hard place. "Where are you off to?"

Barrett looked startled, then said, "A weekend near Olympic. There's a place I like to go to breathe. But my laptop's on the backseat, so I'll make a great deal of headway."

Alone then, it sounded like. Could she really trust her? Damn...someone stealing from the company was making her suspect everyone of double meanings and hidden agendas. Just today she'd been second-guessing Ted, wondering if Ted had really laid the groundwork for three very lucrative contracts on his New York trip last week. Ted talked a lot, did bring in clients, but sometimes the smoke was a little thick.

Stupid waste of time, all these suspicions. She managed a smile as she slammed the trunk. "Don't spend the whole weekend on it. Just most of it."

Barrett saluted her again, but this time with a decidedly mocking flip to her hand, and got into her car. So she had a sense of humor after all, but it made the Sahara look like a rainforest.

She watched the taillights until the road curved out of sight. What did Barrett's sense of humor matter when someone was stealing from SFI? The money was a blow, but the betrayal of a staff member felt very personal.

She stiffened her shoulders, aware of the passing minutes.

She didn't have the energy for useless speculation. She'd be in New York before the sun rose there and home again in slightly more than twenty-four hours from when she'd left. She couldn't remember a time as an adult when she'd been more depressed and tired than she was now. A break, like a day on the water, didn't seem likely for several weeks. But she already felt some relief for the burden Barrett had accepted.

Her mobile chirped as she walked back into the house. She answered, expecting Mercedes.

Instead, Nadia's cool voice flowed out of the phone. "I heard you're off to New York."

"Blame your husband," Tamara said lightly. "He arranged the new client."

"You'll be back in time for the fundraiser, won't you?"

"Yes. I'm only gone for a day."

"Sounds exhausting. I could always drop by Sunday and make you a home-cooked meal."

"Since when have you cooked?"

Nadia's low, throaty laugh was one of her most attractive features, and Tam was momentarily glad simply to enjoy it—it was a beautiful sound. "Okay, I admit it. I could bring you dinner from an outside source."

"That won't be necessary, sisterfriend."

"You're no fun, Tam. You never were."

"No, none at all." She abruptly realized she was too tired to keep up with Nadia. "I'm late for the airport."

"Sorry, darling. You will be there Monday night, then?"

"Yes, as I said. And I'll see you Tuesday night too, if you're joining Ted for the client appreciation reception." After Nadia agreed, she clicked off and hurried to the bedroom to finish packing her carry-on.

In the twin beams of her headlights on the asphalt she abruptly saw Nadia Langhorn and Kip Barrett, side-by-side. They were a study in contrasts, in shadow and light. Nadia never approached any goal directly. The friendly call had been about something else and she would know in due time. Kip Barrett, on the other hand, seemed the type to lock sights on the target and take the shortest route.

There was nothing useful to the comparison, so she did what she always did with irrelevancies: she unlocked the door in her mind, put the thought away and turned the key again.

By the time she boarded her flight her head was clear. She read reports until her vision blurred, then fell asleep somewhere over the Great Lakes.

CHAPTER THREE

Universal truth: drunks stink. Kip had just sat down at the counter in the old-fashioned diner and was reaching for a menu when the waft of cheap liquor and ripe body odor made her turn her head. So much for a quick stop.

The drunk—the diner's only other customer at this hour—didn't hear her coming, but then he'd have missed a herd of trumpeting elephants. The waitress wasn't yet truly alarmed by the customer's sudden lunge out of the booth, but from the guy's arc of motion Kip knew—yep, he grabbed the young woman by the forearm. Whatever it was he slurred was meant to be a pick-up line. Middle-aged Caucasian male, medium build and a beer paunch, brown/brown...

The waitress weakly pulled her arm, but the drunk's grasp didn't slip. He let go, however, when Kip peeled his little finger back, then reversed her hold to coil it so the tip pushed violently toward the second knuckle. It wasn't hard enough to snap the bone—yet—but she knew it hurt like hell.

The freed waitress yelped and rubbed the red patch on her forearm. Kip thought it unconscionable that the woman was apparently alone in the diner this late, and with no training to protect herself.

Averting her nose as best she could, Kip said to the man, "With your other hand reach slowly into your pocket, get out your wallet and give me at least a five."

"Okay, okay. Jush wanted a bit of fun. You're gonna break my hand."

"I will if I have to." Kip let up the pressure only slightly. She took the crumpled bill—a ten, good—and handed it to the waitress. "For his coffee."

"I'll get your change." She backed away.

Kip pressed harder on the drunk's little finger.

"Keep it!" He gasped when Kip let him go with a push.

"Now get out of here and go sleep it off," she ordered. "Next time get a woman's permission before you touch her."

He staggered through the door toward his camper, shaking his numb hand in disbelief.

She leaned nonchalantly in the doorway, watching him. She could hear his opinion of her being muttered under his breath. It wasn't anything she hadn't heard before, and like most drunk and disorderly men, he was spectacularly unimaginative. Nevertheless, he scrambled into the back of the road-worn camper and slammed the door. After a few moments it stopped rocking and she guessed that at a minimum, he'd sat down. He'd be asleep before long.

The car clock had displayed eleven o'clock when Kip had pulled off Highway 101 to get coffee and a bite to eat. With another hour en route to Duckabush ahead of her, she'd realized the monotony of her headlights on the road was making her sleepy. She had tried switching from Bach to Santana, even tried to get riled up by listening to the hard core preachin' of brimstone and damnation for gays in the military and unwed mothers, but it hadn't helped. Her heart was certainly pounding now.

She heard the waitress behind her. "Shorty only went home to check on his wife. She's got the flu. I'm not usually here by myself. He'll be back in two-three minutes."

"I'm glad I came along, then."

"You and me both. Dinner is on the house the moment he gets back."

Kip turned to see the waitress—name tag Sherry—blinking back tears. She was willing to bet the young woman hadn't had a moment of self-defense training. "I'll show you how to do that, plus a couple of Let Go defense moves."

"That would be so great. My dad will make me quit if he finds out I got hassled, but I need the money. And Shorty's good to work for. You want coffee?"

Kip hopped up on a bar stool and accepted the steaming cup. "Time of day and location don't really have much to do with getting harassed. Sad fact of life."

Sherry nodded and her skin lost some of its pallor. "Haven't seen you in here before, but I just started a few months ago."

"The old waitress, she's okay?" Kip sipped, then added cream.

"Oh sure. Got a baby on the way, didn't want to work nights."

The back door of the diner slammed. Sherry called out, "Shorty! Filet, medium-rare. With shrooms and onions."

Kip grinned. "I'm really not that hungry."

"You can take it with you—be dandy for breakfast. No pecan pie today, but there's apple. I think we've got some caramel ice cream."

"Okay, now that's sounding very appealing."

"You drive here from Seattle tonight? Kind of late, isn't it?" The question was asked as if Seattle were on the other side of the planet, not just two hours by road.

"At least there's no traffic once you're south of Tacoma. Olympia had already rolled up the sidewalks when I went through. I had a late meeting. Work, you know."

"Yeah, can't live with it and can't eat without it." Sherry busied herself at the carousel where homemade pies were gleaming with sugar and glazes.

"We have a few minutes. Let me show you a basic move to break someone's grip on your arm."

Sherry was a quick learner. Kip enjoyed their impromptu lesson. Enjoyed, too, the warm human contact, especially with a woman. Hopping up onto her bar stool again when her dinner was served, she admitted that her batteries were just about run dry, and her social life had to be a wasteland when putting a chokehold on Sherry was the closest thing to a hug she'd had in months. And there was little hope that would change.

Fall mornings dawned crisp and clean on the Olympic Peninsula. Seventy-foot pines swayed in the light wind, and the thin roar greeted Kip as she opened her eyes. It could almost be the sea. She could almost be on vacation. No work, no ex-girlfriends, no regrets.

She rolled out of the loft bed and pulled on her robe and socks. The wood floor was cold and she knew from experience that it was hard to climb down the ladder from the loft if she was shivering. Had she not arrived so late last night she'd have left a fire banked in the stove to help take some of the chill off. Instead, she'd only managed to get the groceries and boxes brought in before crashing.

The sky outside was dotted with puffed clouds against the blue, but the light was darkening. Rain later, perhaps. Now was the perfect time for the hike she couldn't afford to take. She felt the urge to pummel something. Sure she was flattered by Tamara Sterling's request, but a day she'd planned to spend in the dogged pursuit of nothing at all was now wall-to-wall work.

She loved her job. There was no job she'd rather have. Well, no job she'd rather have that she *could* have. Secret Service and its simulators be damned.

Pulling on an old sweatshirt and jeans, she went outside for wood. The cold morning air snapped her awake better than any coffee ever could. After reheated filet for breakfast she decided that work or no work, there was not enough split wood ready for winter visits.

She felt a lot better after a half hour of swinging an ax. The rhythmic thump of ax into wood, punctuated with the crack of splitting pine, became its own kind of music. She pictured the face of the supervisor who had told her she could either take a routine Justice Department job or resign the Service altogether. He'd just been delivering the news. It wasn't his policy. No final score on the simulator, no career.

She drove the ax into the image of his face and grimaced. After all these years, it still hurt, apparently. Tamara Sterling's questions had poked the scar.

Breathing hard, she stopped to stack for a while, letting the ache in her shoulders ease. She was out of shape from a job that had too much time at a desk.

She did love her work. The bigger the investigation, though, the more paperwork. Preparing for testimony was time-consuming. Few people thought about the painstaking effort it took to catalog work papers and itemize evidentiary statements. Sure, a trainee could do part of it, but it was still a big pain in the ass.

She pictured her boss's face on the next log as she prepared to swing the ax. She liked Emilio, a lot. It felt really good to chop him to bits.

Too much paper. Too much documenting.

Not enough thinking, puzzling, solving.

Not enough laughing, not enough fun, not enough jogging, sailing or tae kwon do. She was dull. Dull and boring. A bad friend, most of the time. A bad daughter, a distant sibling—well, that wasn't entirely her fault.

And lonely. She pushed that unwelcome thought away.

She pictured Tamara Sterling's face, the woman who had ruined her first weekend off in months. What an arresting, intriguing, dominating, driven, self-assured, brilliant, annoying woman. She planted the image of that chiseled face on the log and drove the ax into it as hard as she could, splitting the chunk of pine evenly in two.

Showered and sated with peanut butter and jelly, which tasted all the better for the exercise and mountain air, Kip unpacked the first of the boxes from her trunk. In short order the small dining area was covered with folders and paperwork. She gave the sofa a longing look. It was positioned perfectly for reading, dozing and gazing out the window at the forest. The tartan throw folded on one end had been a fine nap companion more than once. But not today.

Okay, she had to hand it to Sterling. The worksheet she'd started was plain as day as to where she'd left off and what accounts she'd already checked. Kip had to check them herself again, but the paperwork was tagged and arranged by the SFI book, making the task easier.

Rain dripped, then drummed on the shingle roof as the laptop's drive spun on. She'd timed her outdoor chores well. Some people would no doubt think it strange that she was in the remote woods, listening to the rain and working on a laptop computer no heftier than a magazine. It wasn't the first time, though. She was grateful for the technology that let her work so far from home. Of course that same technology made the very crimes she tracked down all the easier to commit.

Win some, lose some, she thought. Meanwhile, the solitude of the trees, the steady patter of the rain...it felt very, very good. The cabin had no phone land line, and with a delicious sense of being bad, she switched off her cell phone and didn't launch her e-mail program. There. Alone at last.

With a regretful sigh, she opened her electronic diary and made a few summary comments about the assignment, the times and places she'd met her client—Sterling *was* just another client—

and recorded the paperwork she'd received. Keeping such a log was an SFI requirement and she was making a concerted effort to treat this assignment like any other. Her summary made, she turned to the actual work. First she had to discern the scope of the problem. Then she'd work on ETO—eliminating the obvious.

She'd been at it only a half-hour when she found another account that was missing funds. Sixty thousand dollars and some change. The copy of the bank statement had been expertly doctored, but a ghost of ink betrayed the effort, and a close-up look at the staff auditor's initials revealed that they, too, were likely forged. She munched away at a pile of carrot sticks while she methodically examined the staff auditor's work. To her, it looked as if the staff auditors were comparing the print version of the bank statements to the online record, which verified that the printed version was in fact authentic. After they initialed the comparison, someone was substituting fake statements so that the reconciliation staff thought they had the real ones, and everything balanced.

It was actually a lot to keep track of—the embezzler was essentially running his or her own set of books to falsify the statements going back two months to avoid detection for as long as possible. Ultimately, the thief would miss something in the minutiae and alarm bells would sound. Sterling had found it early, and so far the thief had no clue. That meant they had a good shot at recovering the funds.

By late afternoon, she had found another four accounts and the total cash missing was taking an alarming turn. Sterling had found a half-million missing, and she had found at least six times that, and most of it from the SFI investment accounts and some from pension accounts.

Increasingly anxious, she turned to the largest of the trust accounts. Bad enough their own and their employees' funds were missing—a client's money would be the death knell for SFI's unparalleled reputation.

As she worked, grateful to turn over page after page and finding nothing amiss, the rain stopped and watery sunlight peeked in through the windows. Hunger made her leave the pile of paperwork for a northward drive to tiny Brinnon where a bona fide, greasy spoon, full fat with bacon burger was calling to her. She was a long way from the city, no reason to check her rearview mirror or worry about her billfold visible on the seat of the car. She ate at a splintery picnic table, watching the daylight fade on the other side of the Sound. Just to the north a cluster of lights marked the naval base where Trident submarines launched, but otherwise, this finger of Puget Sound was quiet as dark approached.

The evening was so peaceful she decided to drive further north to her favorite vista point at Seal Rock on Dabob Bay. She owed herself some fresh air and her work would be the better for it.

It was her favorite time of an autumn day. The ancient pines were falling into winter shadows of steel gray. The sun had dipped below the mountains of the Olympic National Forest. Streaks of pink- and orange-painted clouds stretched toward Seattle. If she'd had a whole day to herself she might have hiked on the Mount Baker glacier in the morning and spent the afternoon walking through the Hoh Rain Forest. Only the Olympic Peninsula offered such extremes in a single day's drive.

She rolled down the windows to let the crisp air whip around her ears, inhaling the rich salt brine coming off Dabob Bay. She should spend her next vacation someplace where she could sail. She'd loved sailing with her grandfather. Thrilled to the spray on her face, tugging against the sail, his voice insisting it didn't matter how small she was, or that she was only nine, she could do *anything*. His voice was always there in her head, urging her on, telling her she could overcome anything if she tried hard enough.

If only that were true.

"Damn." She rolled to a stop in the scenic overlook and switched off the engine. The wind in the high trees behind her combined with the *shush* of waves against the shore ahead of her, creating a quiet that breathed, slow and steady. She closed her eyes to listen, and wished her heart could find that strong, unhurried rhythm.

She had no more success than usual. Dollar amounts and bank statements danced behind her eyelids. Swirling around all of it was the jarring memory of all her lost hopes—every time Tamara Sterling asked about it she felt an ache in that familiar, deep wound.

This is a waste of energy, she warned herself, but she couldn't stop thinking about it. From the time she was twelve she'd been filling out her Secret Service application in her head. As the years went by she'd mentally added her degree, and on the actual day—so important—the names of her immediate family and their occupations. She'd been so proud to put in her grandfather's name—Rudyard Kipling Barrett, twenty-six years service, deceased. She felt as if she was immortalizing him by following in his footsteps. For a while, she'd certainly appeared to be a chip off the old block.

There was just one thing she couldn't do, one choice she couldn't make. Every time it had come up in the simulation she'd hesitated. Her focus and aim had wavered.

Her supervisor had told her, over and over, "You're not going to be in the field, Barrett, it's just a machine. Shoot the suspect and get the heck out of training."

She tried to tell herself it had no meaning. Just a computer game, like hundreds she'd played. A computer game with a real gun, real bullets—but the bad guys weren't real and if she made a mistake, no one would get hurt.

She inhaled fresh sea air with the pungent tang of pine, trying to clear her memory of the sweltering warehouse with lung-choking clouds of gasoline fumes and electricity-tinged smoke. Shoot, then ask. Just do it. It's not real. Just a game. Just a test. Pass the test. Just pull the trigger.

She pivoted on her heel, leaving the peaceful vista behind. Some Xena, some superhero she was. She couldn't do what needed to be done, plain and simple. So she could handle a drunk—big effing deal. She wasn't capable of acting on instinct. Her brain always wanted facts before taking action.

On her good days she told herself that the simulator had indeed served its purpose. She wasn't fit to protect the President of the United States. Best to know that before a real situation erupted in her face.

"I'm not ashamed," she told a fallen tree. "But what a way to find out."

All her hopes and dreams gone, and a life rebuilt in spite of the disappointment. Plenty of bad guys to catch.

"You don't always get what you want, Barrett." She kicked a rock into the undergrowth and went back to the car, vexed that she was dwelling on a past she couldn't change and, in honest moments, knew she wouldn't even if she had that power.

When she got back to the cabin she lit the woodstove, and then settled down to continue her methodical work, more than halfway through the papers Tamara Sterling had given her.

She would find out who was stealing from SFI, and she would bring him, or her, or them to justice. It would be a challenge and if she was a little tired right now, that didn't matter. SFI's code of ethics was well-known and absolutely necessary to make sure that clients had full trust in the integrity and abilities of every SFI staff member. White-collar criminals who stole millions from everyday people so often went free, as if financial losses didn't take a real toll or cause tremendous damage to every victim. Underpaid, overworked prosecutors counted on SFI to be rock solid on the witness stand.

This thief was one of their own, and had broken their code and endangered the path of justice. She would get back every dime she could lay her hands on and then she would present the culprit and the cash to Tamara Sterling on a silver platter.

"Another red?" The steward paused next to Tamara's seat with the napkin-wrapped bottle in one hand.

"No—not a good idea." She was depressed enough as it was

to be heading for home without accomplishing one useful bit of work. She'd had just enough time at her hotel this morning to shower and change, only to get a call from the SFI local office head that the meeting had been canceled. She'd turned around, checked out and headed back to the airport. At least she'd managed to get on a slightly earlier flight.

"It's twice as powerful at altitude," he admitted. "Can I clear away your dinner then?"

She nodded and turned her attention back to the reports she'd carried all the way from Seattle. Reading them would be something useful for the time she'd wasted on this trip. She hated flying coast-to-coast in less than twenty-four hours.

At least she would see her own bed before midnight. The New York office manager, Hank Jefferson, had been equally appalled that Tam had wasted the trip, and he'd promised to get to the bottom of it. They both hoped it wasn't a case of the client deciding to sleep in on a Saturday morning instead. Weekend meetings usually meant something serious was suspected.

Somewhere over North Dakota she initialed the last report and slid it into her briefcase. Nothing but reports, meetings and more reports leading to more meetings. She liked running her own firm, but in the most perverse way, she had been almost relieved to find an investigation right under her nose, and had at first thought she could run it all by herself.

Not that she was glad there was an embezzler on their staff. But once her initial disbelief had eased, she'd felt the old and familiar thrill of a puzzle to solve. Now she delegated puzzles to other people. She didn't miss working for the Feds, but she missed the thrill of seeing if she could outwit a criminal on a one-to-one basis.

You're not a kid anymore, she told herself, and you're pushing forty. *You have responsibilities. You love this work.* If only she'd get a good night's sleep she knew she'd feel better in the morning.

Her depression led from one bleak thought to another. Had Nadia's laugh on the phone been the last pleasant thing she could remember? She could still hear it. She would have eventually recognized Nadia, she was certain, but hearing that unforgettable laugh in an English class in college had made her scan the rows of the lecture hall until she found the source. Nadia had recognized her, too. They hadn't become the best of friends, but there were binding ties that had nothing to do with friendship that they both respected.

She closed her eyes and saw Ted's face in the Student Union Lair, that night fifteen years ago when he and Nadia had met. One-of-a-kind love story, that one. She'd known Ted from mutual computer science classes. He'd taken one look at Nadia and it was all over. His eyes were mirrors of his every thought.

Nadia had tossed her hair back with a look that said she knew he was already hers. "Tam, seriously, how did you not mention that such an attractive man was in your classes?"

"I'm not on Tam's radar," Ted had said.

Nadia had laughed, showing off that lovely voice. "Well now you're on mine."

Just like that, and three months later they were married. They credited Tam with their introduction. Nadia had made sure that Tam caught the bouquet, but fifteen-plus years later that magic hadn't happened. She'd rarely gotten to a second date and never to a sixth. Not being able to talk about her work limited the conversation. A few women understood that it wasn't lack of trust, but the rules. Most, however, failed to make another date. One woman had summed it up with, "If I'd wanted a mystery for dinner, I'd have ordered a book."

She let her gaze drift over the clouds outside the airplane, exhausted and worried. Clouds shaped like horses and dragons, angels even, failed to distract her until in the depths of one she saw Kip Barrett's eyes, full of conscious intent and disciplined fervor. She liked that trait in people. It would have been fun to work with her on this mystery, to see how her mind worked out the complexities.

"Would you like anything else before we land?"

Tam couldn't hold back a startled gasp.

The steward looked chagrined. "I'm sorry, I woke you just as you were dozing off, didn't I?"

"No... I was just daydreaming," Tam said. "I'm fine." Tam handed her empty water cup to him and realized he was leaning a little closer to her than duty called for.

"Do you live in the Seattle area?" At her nod, he went on, "Maybe you could recommend a restaurant or two? I've got an extended layover and I'll be on my own."

Oh, please, she thought, do I really have to come out at 38,000 feet? Fortunately, a sharp downdraft, followed by a crash from the galley, sent the steward scurrying up the aisle. When he came back, Tam's eyes were closed.

She wished the sleep weren't feigned, but she was too caught up in brooding for the comfort of sleep. She wondered if Kip Barrett was making progress. She ought to have asked explicitly for her to contact her with a progress update tomorrow, even if it was a Sunday.

By the time her plane touched down at SeaTac it was close to midnight. Groggy from lack of sleep, Tam nevertheless had made up her mind. The office should be quiet on a Sunday with only the people on deadlines working. She'd sleep in, then take the stack of approved reports into the office. If the coast was clear she'd do a little poking around. It would beat sitting on her hands and wondering if Kip Barrett was getting anywhere.

CHAPTER FOUR

Kip was weary from the long drive home, but still refreshed enough not to think a short stop at the office late on a Sunday afternoon much of a burden. There would only be a few people around and she wanted a peek into a couple of the accounting files, if she could get access to the area.

The accounting floor of the SFI offices seemed deserted when she peeked through the safety glass alongside the door from the elevators. She swiped her ID card through the magnetic reader, entered the access code she used for the doors on her own floor and got a green light to enter. It had been a risk—if she'd been red lighted it might have generated an error message to building security. If challenged, she'd been planning to claim being too tired not to realize she wasn't at her usual floor. They did all look a lot alike. Flimsy, but nobody had a reason not to believe her.

She could point out the visible dribble of coffee across the front of her sweatshirt as testimony to her fatigue.

When this was all over she'd point out that she—and everyone else with no relationship to accounting—ought not to be able to enter the area. That green light had been too easy, which didn't seem right.

She had her hand on the accounting file room door before she realized someone was already in there, moving quietly. Just as she was moving quietly. A suspicious person would call it furtive.

Kip was a suspicious person. Her ex thought it was a character flaw, but SFI thought it a marketable skill.

She slowly pulled the door open, telling herself that her abruptly pounding heart wouldn't be audible to anyone else. Another inch and she would be able to see who was there. Maybe it was a staff auditor, catching up on a backlog. But maybe not. Another inch... Quietly, quietly she told herself.

When she recognized the intruder her heart stopped but her mind did not.

Explanation one was that she was trying to help. And that was just not going to happen. *Clients* did not help SFI investigators. It ruined the chain of evidence and muddied the clarity of the investigation. It did not matter that Tamara Sterling was more qualified than Kip was to handle the case.

Explanation two, and far more sinister, was that Tamara Sterling had hired her as a blind to cover up her own guilt. It had been tried before by clients who thought they were exceedingly clever. Sterling could be hoping to use Kip's reports to determine how long she had until she needed to leave the jurisdiction.

She didn't want to believe Sterling was the embezzler. It made little sense. But she hadn't yet ruled it out. She watched, fighting an enormous sense of betrayal, as Sterling slipped a few pieces of paper into the inside pocket of her jacket.

She let the door fall shut behind her. The quiet click seemed as loud as a gun shot. Sterling whirled to face her.

She held out her hand. "I'll take those papers." Her voice was glacial.

Sterling started to put her hand in her jacket but Kip quickly added, "Hold the jacket out from your side and reach in with two fingers."

A dull flush climbed slowly up Sterling's throat. "I realize how this looks," she said. She slowly and carefully removed the papers and then held them out.

Kip waited for her to say more. But instead of protestations of innocence and fumbling explanations, she said, "I'm starved. Why don't you update me over dinner?"

Kip couldn't hold back a laugh of disbelief. "Do you really think I don't deserve an explanation of why you're here?"

The flush that had seemed to mark Sterling's guilt faded. Her mouth twitched to one side. "I know a restaurant that serves crow. Isn't that what bosses who don't believe anyone will do the job as well as themselves should eat?"

Kip thought she was making too light of what was a serious matter. But she'd humor her and see if she slipped up. The need to study Sterling as a suspect was her only motivation for a light tone and smile. "Do you like your crow baked or boiled?"

"Southern-fried, with Tabasco. Shall we?" She indicated the door.

"Give me a few minutes to get what I came in for."

Kip quickly photocopied the reconciled bank statements she wanted and slipped them into her windcheater's inner pocket, alongside the papers Tamara had given up. Ninety seconds with a high-capacity disk in the PC connected to the mainframe gained her the cash general ledger. She knew it was encrypted, but she had a few guesses as to how she could read the data anyway. She preceded Sterling out of the area and into the elevator. "An interim note to my client," she said quietly. She tapped the disk in her pocket. "This was too easy for me to do. I expected to be locked out."

"You're right. When this is over, I'll order an overhaul of our internal security. Maybe that's been tampered with. Now let's get out of here before someone sees us here—and together."

Tam's thoughts were in a whirl. Coming here and searching through the files after she'd turned the job over to Kip had been stupid. She was too tired and too hungry because her brain didn't seem to want to work. Now the most important thing in the world seemed to be getting out of the building together without being seen. No matter who saw them it would start gossip, and gossip would reach the ears of their embezzler.

Just as she relaxed, the elevator stopped two floors down—another SFI floor. She heard Kip mutter a four-letter word. Acting purely on impulse, she seized Kip, forced her into the corner and inclined her back as if they were in the throes of passion. It was a cheap, desperate move.

Kip fought her for a moment, then stiffened as the doors opened. Tam ran her hands over the faded sweatshirt, momentarily surprised at the well-developed muscles her fingertips encountered, muscles that yielded to softness at her ribs. She did her best to engulf Kip completely, hiding her from view. Better someone should think the boss was having a torrid affair than guess the truth. And she was pretty sure Kip couldn't be recognized from this angle.

She heard the shuffle of papers and someone's quick intake of breath, but not the sounds of someone entering the elevator yet. For good measure, she pressed her lips to Kip's.

A sardonic voice said, "I guess I'll catch the next one."

Damn, it sounded like Ted. But the elevator doors closed again and she and Kip were still alone.

About to voice an apology, she let go of Kip so she could check the floor indicator as they descended. She turned back to Kip. "That was a close—"

For the fortieth or fiftieth time, Kip said, "I'm sorry. It was pure instinct. For a minute I couldn't breathe—it felt like you intended to smother me."

"Forget about it," Tam's voice was muffled by the ice bag Kip had produced from her medicine cabinet and filled with cubes. The ibuprofen tablets she'd given her had not kicked in yet. "I should have known better."

"I suppose it was quick thinking." It sounded like a reluctant admission to Tam.

The doorbell rang.

"Saved by the bell," Kip muttered.

She came back into the kitchen carrying a bag of something that smelled delectable. In spite of the raging pain in her face, Tam's stomach growled.

"I must be alive. I'm still hungry."

"Just keep the ice on it and chew on the right side of your mouth."

Egg rolls had never tasted so good. Tamara munched gingerly on one, then said, "I didn't realize you were a southpaw."

"I'm not," Kip said. "That was just my left jab."

Damn her, but she sounded more than a little smug. She had seemed genuinely sorry that she'd nearly KO'd her. Now Tam wasn't so sure. "Don't do me any favors," she muttered.

Kip paused with her chopsticks sunk into one of the containers. "Would you like a plate? Living alone has given me horrible manners."

In spite of what felt like a broken jaw, she managed a smile. So Kip did live alone. "I thought the point of takeout was no dishes."

Kip extracted a water chestnut from the container and popped it into her mouth. After chewing thoughtfully, she said, "Well, we're in agreement on two things, then."

She frowned. It made her cheek ache more. "What?"

"Not doing extra dishes and—" she enunciated very clearly, "It's really stupid for the client to try to help the professional she's hired to do a job."

Tam winced. If she'd stayed home and caught up on her sleep

she'd still have use of her right eye. "Actually, it's three things we agree on."

"What's the third?"

"It's really stupid to grab a woman in an elevator." The memory of Kip's body and the moments their lips had been pressed together had thankfully faded behind the throb of her eye.

Kip stopped in mid-crunch of a stir-fried string bean, then cleared her throat. She swallowed, then sipped some tea. "Well, if you're unhappy with me now, wait until you hear my report," she told her quietly.

"Give me the worst." She braced herself.

"I went to the office to check on a couple more bank statements, but I'm pretty sure the total is six point eight million. Five point three million and change is from the pension accounts, the rest from operating accounts. The good news is that I think the trust accounts are fine. It's just SFI money. But there are nearly twenty-five accounts involved so far, invested through six banks and I don't have information on all of them. There's a small group of signers, but I may not have a comprehensive list."

"That's what you took away from me, the list of approved signers. I was going to give it to you."

Kip arched an eyebrow and looked at her.

"Right," she mumbled. "That's your job."

"Thank you for remembering that. And just because I'm feeding you doesn't mean I've written you off as a suspect."

She glared. Kip, with her curly black hair down and the casualness of an old Seahawks sweatshirt, looked like a completely different person. And she was being...impudent. She really hadn't thought her capable of it. "Okay by me. Do this by the book," she said. "Any idea of how?"

"Yes," she said, her tone pert and satisfied. "I can't discuss that with you in detail, of course. I could quote you the chapter and verse of the SFI Handbook."

Her glare deepened. Kip was enjoying herself far too much. "Any idea of who?"

The silence stretched, then Kip slowly said, "That's another thing I shouldn't discuss with the client at this stage."

Her voice was taut as she said, "I think you could make an exception in this case." She expected a fiery retort. She could see it bubbling around Kip's lips.

But then her mouth curved into a surprising smile. "Well, the head of the company gives me my marching orders and she just told me to do this by the book," she said as lightly as she could manage. "She'll have my head if I even bend a rule."

So she was being inconsistent, but she didn't appreciate having that pointed out to her. Tam surprised herself by laughing, though. She set the ice bag down and tucked into the chicken lo mein. "I don't know how you could work for someone like that."

"She pays well," Kip said, her voice tinged with sarcasm.

Tam was feeling better with every bite. "Excellent choice," she said, indicating the lo mein. "What's in there?" She prodded a large Styrofoam cup.

"Hot and sour soup."

She was definitely feeling better. "I think separate bowls would be appropriate."

Kip grinned and fetched two bowls and spoons. Tam ladled out her portion and inhaled the steam from the soup. She couldn't believe she was sitting in Kip Barrett's immaculate kitchen, chowing down on Chinese food and mostly sanguine about seven million dollars. The kitchen looked immaculate from lack of use rather than any neatness of habit, but the glimpse she'd had of the living room said Kip was either exceedingly tidy or never home long enough to disturb anything.

Focus, she told herself. Almost seven million dollars was missing. "You've made considerable progress. Thank you."

"It's all included in the service," Kip said. Her light air faded as she said soberly, "I'm far enough along to do some fieldwork, so I may call in sick tomorrow so I can get to the local banks. I need to ETO the signature cards."

"When this is done, I'll make sure you get your leave back, and some time off to boot."

"That will be very welcome. I'll head back to the mountains.

They did me a world of good this weekend."

She rubbed her cheekbone. "I wouldn't say that." Actually, she would. It wasn't just the faded sweatshirt. There was color in her face and a sense of humor was evident. The shirt was far from shapeless and she found herself easily recalling the soft, melting firmness of Kip Barrett's body. She stopped that train of thought, but remained surprised that she'd even had it. There were lots of attractive women in the world. She admired, but it wasn't like her to ogle.

Kip crumbled her fortune cookie and read, "'Watch out for turning tables.' Well, that's always good advice."

Tam smoothed the pink slip of paper she'd extracted from her cookie. "'To conquer temptation you must yield to it.' Mothers everywhere would disagree."

"Mine certainly would have," Kip said. "And my grandfather had quite explicit ideas about that, too." She added softly, "He really *was* one of those guys who ran alongside the limo."

"So your file says." Damn it all, she thought. "Look, you don't have to tell me why and I'm not going to ask anymore."

Kip had stiffened. Their gazes locked across the table.

Just when she thought Kip wasn't going to respond, she said softly, "It's not relevant to any work I may ever have to do for SFI."

Disappointed, but not surprised, Tam gestured at the food. "Thank you for this."

"You're welcome." She glanced down at her food and Tam puzzled at what might have been a faint flush over her cheeks.

"And thank you for the update. I know you're working with limited access to information but go ahead with the ETO, full speed, and when you need more help we'll get it."

"Will do," Kip said. She gave Tam a cheerful smile but something in her expression was not the least bit nonchalant. It didn't seem the time to probe and after a little more conversation, she made her excuses and headed home. When she found it difficult to relax and sleep she blamed it on her black eye and seven million dollars missing.

When Kip locked her door behind Sterling, she leaned her forehead against it. "Stupid, stupid fool," she muttered. She cradled her aching left hand against her stomach. Tamara had seemed too bemused to notice Kip hadn't used it for much. Thank goodness she'd used her left or she'd never have been able to handle the chopsticks. She picked up the ice bag Tamara had discarded and put it on her aching knuckles.

Once again, she was proven to be a *papier mâché* superhero. One jab and she'd trashed her hand.

She sank down into a chair and stared into space. She was tired and, having gobbled dinner, she was also drowsy. There was more work she could do tonight, she told herself, so she went down to the parking garage for the boxes and her laptop.

It was difficult with one aching hand, but she managed to carry everything up and stow her laptop on her desk. Since she spent a lot of time working there, the cherry wood desk had the best window at the far end of the high-ceilinged living room. The view from her second-floor window was of treetops in the park across the street. Pleasant enough, but no comparison to the view that would greet Tamara Sterling when she reached home.

Not that she wondered what Tamara Sterling would do with the rest of her evening. Sterling had never made any secret of her sexuality, so it wasn't a total surprise that she'd use making out with a woman as a cover ploy. But her private life was zipped up tight, and Kip had no idea if Sterling was in a relationship or not.

Not that it was her concern—unless Sterling was her suspect, she reminded herself. Yes, she was merely focused on Sterling's private life because she might be involved in the embezzlement, and if she wasn't, it was Kip's job to clear her of suspicion.

Glad to have sorted out her meandering thoughts, she almost switched the laptop on, then shook her head. Now she was too tired to work. Sleep would be better and she'd be more efficient for it in the morning.

Only when she settled into bed did she acknowledge that she was badly shaken by the incident in the elevator. When they'd entered it, she'd been on her guard for attack. Though her instincts said Tamara was not the embezzler, she had caught the woman in the midst of taking evidence. Thinking herself prepared had been false, though, since she'd still been caught off guard when Tamara had grabbed her, using height and strength to stifle her. It should have never gotten that far, but a flare of something Kip couldn't even describe had slowed her reflexes. Maybe that was a good thing. She was pretty sure she hadn't been recognized, and that was important. Another stupid mistake, she scolded herself. She ought to have suggested separate elevators.

She'd understood the purpose of the grab, and the kiss, but her mind and body had gone separate ways. There hadn't been any reason to take a swing at her boss's boss's boss, but she'd panicked.

Palms grasping at her ribs, thumbs sliding down her stomach, fingers caressing the small of her back—it had felt good. Too good. She'd been on the verge of inviting a more thorough kiss when Tamara had set her free. Completely idiotic, stupid, inappropriate, you-really-need-to-date-again response, she told herself.

If Tamara Sterling *was* the embezzler Kip couldn't afford to let her know that Kip's defenses seemed to have some weaknesses. And if Sterling wasn't the embezzler she was still her boss's boss's boss, and there was no fraternization at SFI. Zero tolerance. Anyone wanting to get involved with a colleague had to find a new job.

End of story, Kip told herself firmly and she proceeded to lay awake for half the night.

"Don't even ask." Tam tried to forestall the inevitable question she could see forming on Mercedes' lips. "I don't want to talk about it."

Mercedes fixed her with the look Tam was sure she used on her kids. Her large, expressive eyes were fully equipped with you-don't-fool-me laser beams. "Uh-huh. That's right. You don't tell me what happened on your interesting weekend. You go right ahead as if your face weren't black and blue. Don't you say a word."

"I had an accident."

"No, no." Mercedes waved her eloquent hands. Her southern origins revealed themselves in her tone. "Don't tell me about it even though that accident must have involved running into someone else's fist. I don't want to know. I wouldn't listen if you did tell me."

Tamara slumped into her chair and tried to summon her dignity. "New York was a bust."

Mercedes became all work. "I heard—I'm so sorry. You must be exhausted."

"It certainly wasn't your fault," Tam said emphatically. "What's on after the Monday morning staff meeting?"

Mercedes glanced at her book, and Tam was glad that the southern belle—rare in Seattle and charmingly incongruous with her Amer-African-Asian features—had disappeared. "You already know about the conference call at nine. Richardson at Seattle National Bank moved the meeting back a half hour. Tonight is that fundraiser for the new wing of the library. Nadia Langhorn called to make sure you'll be there. Today's report review is stiff. I've got five on my desk already and at least two on the way."

"You're tying to kill me, aren't you?" Tam idly thought that her estimation of men was taken down a notch by the fact that Mercedes was single. She was curvy in the right places, had impeccable fashion sense, and given the passion she showed for her work Tam had no doubt she would show passion at other times.

"Yes," she said emphatically. "I want you dead because I enjoy the unemployment line." She glanced at Tam over the top of her gold-rimmed glasses. "I can farm a couple of them to Diane. She wants to see you at two anyway. But you know as well as I do that she'll want to know what happened to your face. If I knew I could prepare her, then she wouldn't pester you so much. But of course I don't know, now do I?"

Tam should have known Mercedes wouldn't give up until she had the whole story. "I did something I shouldn't have and the someone who didn't appreciate it had a very direct way of explaining her displeasure."

"Her?" Mercedes eyebrows disappeared under her page-boy bangs.

Tam mentally groaned. Mercedes thought the best thing for her would be a wife who would take on mothering her full-time. As if she needed full-time mothering. She couldn't for the life of her imagine Kip Barrett mothering anyone. She started to smile, then realized she'd thought of wives and Kip Barrett way too close together. What was wrong with her today? Oh—exhaustion. Sleep deprivation. Anxiety. The memory of a soft sweatshirt.

Mercedes coughed loudly and rapped her book with her pencil again.

"Someday soon I'll explain everything. I promise."

"Uh-huh. I'm sure it's complicated. That's right, you keep it to yourself. I don't need to know a thing. You keep your secret. You be Ms. Secret Woman if you want. And I'll keep my secrets, too. We'll be just one big secret around here. That'll help productivity." She sniffed and closed her book. "I'll go back to my desk, but I'm not telling what I'll work on next."

The door of her office clicked loudly behind her and Tamara couldn't help but laugh. Mercedes was an absolute gem of an assistant and even when she decided to have an attitude it was usually to teach Tam a lesson she needed. But she couldn't tell Mercedes about Kip Barrett. Not until it was all over.

Kip couldn't lie to Emilio Woo about being sick, but she'd worked for him long enough and hard enough to ask for a sick day for no particular reason.

"Put it down to mental health," she said. "I spent the weekend in the mountains and I just haven't come back to earth. I've got some reading I can do at home to get over the Monday blahs." Everything she had said was true, but it was far from the whole truth. "The exhibit numbering will still be done on time."

Emilio sighed, but she could tell he wasn't upset. "You've earned it. I'll see you tomorrow."

She dressed as she would for the office and stocked her slim leather briefcase with business cards, an SFI employee roster, and one set of statements for each bank she would visit. She presented herself at the main branch of First Nation Federal Savings Bank shortly after it opened.

"I have an appointment to examine our account records," she said to the Asian woman at the new accounts desk as she handed her a business card.

The new accounts officer gazed at her in chagrin. "Oh, it must have been made with the branch manager, but she's out today. I hope I can help you."

"Oh, that's all right." Kip was relieved she wasn't going to have to pretend a nonexistent assistant had forgotten to make an appointment for her. "I'm just going to review our signature cards. This would be so much easier if someone on our end would photocopy the signature cards before they turned them over to you, but somehow they never do. So we routinely check to make sure they're up-to-date."

She gestured at her copy of an SFI bank statement from First Nation to further prove that she did indeed have a relationship with the company. The young woman glanced at them and seemed to make up her mind to be helpful.

It was relatively easy to see a company's bank records. All it took was a business card from the company and a plausible reason. Approving transactions was a great deal harder, or at least it was supposed to be. The digital age had changed some of the basic assumptions about security and banks.

She gave the officer a short list of account numbers and asked for the signature cards. The woman returned after some delay, bringing a stack of copies and the original signature cards with her. "I made you copies of the cards," she said, "front and back."

Kip beamed at her. "Thanks! That will save me some writing. I'll need to see the originals, though."

Under the account officer's watchful eye, she verified that the copies made by the account officer were indeed accurate, and that she had all the copies she needed to take with her. Each card had the signatures she expected them to have—no surprises. It took a great deal less time than writing everything down. Within a half hour she was at the next bank.

As noon approached and the branches became more crowded, she spent more time writing information out because the officers were busy. Some of them even left her alone with the cards. She could have replaced them with a set she'd signed herself. It was exactly that kind of laxity that she was confirming hadn't already happened.

The task at hand occupied only part of her attention, so the rest of her mind turned over the question of how the money was being moved out of the accounts. An embezzler just didn't cash a check for fifty thousand dollars these days. Instead, the banks were electronically transferring money from SFI accounts to other banks where SFI had no accounts. Those instructions could be presented two ways: as signed authorizations such as a letter or bank-specific form, or as a computer instruction that successfully presented itself as authorized to the bank's software. The first took chutzpah, the second took varying degrees of a hacker's mindset and skill.

As soon as she finished eliminating the obvious, Kip knew she would be hip deep in investigating the receiving accounts and who had set them up, another way to triangulate in on the culprit. Normally, she'd be working with a team and someone else would already be doing that work. And they'd have a warrant to make it even easier, but as soon as the money went offshore, more subtle methods would be necessary. There was a time and place for law enforcement. Calling them too early might have a zealous investigator, whose priorities didn't include recovering the stolen money, taking important evidence out of Kip's hands. Law enforcement also tended to move loudly, and their very activity on the case could tip off the thief that the embezzlement had been noticed.

The local FBI agents assigned to federal statute fraud and embezzlement were no real exception. She had no doubt that they were as committed as she was to finding the truth and turning suspects over for appropriate justice. However, she'd worked with them briefly about six months ago and was pretty certain that her diplomatic skills hadn't been at their best when they'd attempted to bump her out of the investigative loop. She'd gone over their heads and their boss had overruled them. She hadn't made friends by being the one who held all the codes and keys when their forensic hacker had asked.

She and the computer nerd had gotten on just fine, leaving the tall men in the well-filled out blue suits and dark glasses to stare at each other. She had no reason to think they wouldn't make her go over their heads again, so she would wait until as late as possible before involving them. A clever thief who realized their crime had been noticed would immediately send the money off to harder-to-reach places or convert it to non-cash, like bearer bonds, and then fall off the grid, beyond her reach.

If she could discover how, it would help figure out who, and figuring out who would help discern how. She still didn't even have enough information to know if this case would be simple or complex.

As overwhelmed as she felt by the extra work, she was thrilled to be actually doing what she was best at: gathering evidence and looking for the clues that uncovered a crime. She wished it weren't for SFI, though. Her own reputation would be compromised at trial if SFI became embroiled in a scandal. If Tamara Sterling was involved they were all compromised.

She felt a chill. Tamara Sterling had been a computer hacker for the FBI, and she'd been brilliant at it. She had all the means and opportunity to be the embezzler, and the brains to confuse and mislead an investigator like her.

Surely, Kip thought, there was someone else at SFI with the same skills. She just didn't want to believe it was Tamara. Last night, in her kitchen, she had seemed too genuine to be a thief. Well, first thing she was going to do when she got home was the ETO.

As if her thoughts had conjured her up, Tamara Sterling walked into the bank, was greeted by the branch manager and disappeared into an inner office. Kip blinked. It had been her, with that unmistakable height and bearing. She swore colorfully under her breath. What was she trying to do? After last night, she'd have thought Sterling wouldn't get within a mile of her.

She wrapped up what she was doing in record time, thanked the account officer, then hurried outside the branch. She waited at the best vantage point to watch both doors in what felt like a subzero wind tunnel. By the time Tamara Sterling appeared she was thoroughly chilled and almost mad enough to unleash her right hook.

"May I speak with you, *ma'am*?" Kip seized Sterling's elbow and guided her into the lee of a building. Her nose began to thaw, but her temper didn't diminish. "What do you think you're doing? Have you any idea what the bank might do if we both asked for account records on the same day? They might call SFI to verify me and they might tip off the very person we're trying to catch. You put me in charge of this investigation and I don't need any help. And I don't need anyone checking up on me!"

Sterling jerked her elbow out of Kip's grasp. "Are you through?"

Kip's temper began to abate. "Yes. I'm through."

"For your information, I was there on routine SFI business having nothing to do with your investigation."

Kip swallowed as the gray eyes favored her with a gaze colder than the wind. "Such as?"

"Discussing the possibility of financing for construction of our own building."

The unmistakable bruising along her cheekbone and jaw further unsettled Kip. Nice job, slug the boss, then yell at her in the street. She took a deep breath as her inner voices gibbered with embarrassment. "Maybe I jumped to a conclusion. If you were me—"

"I'd have asked my client before I accused—"

Furiously, she admitted, "You tried it once already. And you're my boss. It's making me a little hypersensitive."

One eyebrow lifted. "A little?"

"Okay, a lot." Kip tried to summon her best Secret Service stare to cover her discomfiture, but she knew she wasn't having much luck. Damn Sterling for making her feel short, inexperienced—flustered. She should have never let her into her kitchen. "I apologize," she snapped.

"Apology accepted." Tamara wasn't having any trouble maintaining her Mount Rushmore facade. "Since we're having this meeting, how is it going?"

Kip flushed hard enough that she could only hope it didn't show through cheeks already reddened by the sharp wind. "Fine. I could have a status report on what I've ruled out late tonight."

"I won't be home. Call me tomorrow—no, that won't work either. And I do want to give you some room to work. Let's make it Wednesday evening for a full preliminary report."

"Yes ma'am. I think that will give me enough time." Kip struggled to choose the right words and she set aside any thoughts about what her boss was doing with her evenings that made her unavailable. That is *so* inappropriate, Barrett, she told herself. "I'm sorry I jumped to a conclusion. I usually don't. Maybe it was guilt. I've been telling little lies all day and then when you came in I was sure I'd be caught, even though you have every reason not to impede me."

Her gaze softened slightly. "Again, apology accepted. I didn't see you when I went in. If I had I'd have ignored you."

"I'll remember that if we stumble across each other again. I hope we don't." Kip stopped suddenly, her internal guilt meter having gone off. She'd just told another lie. Oh, this just wasn't fair. Even in the cold weather, Tamara Sterling looked as steady as a mountain. A fascinating mountain. Damn, damn and *damn*.

Now was not the time to think about how long it had been since she'd been on a date. Telling herself to go get laid wasn't useful either because she didn't have the first clue how to do a one-night thing, and that's what made Tamara Sterling and her strong hands so unfair, that and her uncanny ability to bring out the gibbering fool lurking inside her.

"I have another appointment," Tamara said, "or we could talk over lunch. If you don't hit me first I'd even buy." Her eyes warmed along with a rare smile.

Kip smiled dumbly back, then found her voice. "Wednesday evening will be better. I'll have a list of most probable suspects by then and I should also know method."

"Good." Her expression was abruptly cold.

Taken aback, Kip could think of nothing to say. When it was plain Tamara Sterling was done speaking to her, she turned away, humiliated. One minute smiling, the next glacial.

"Diane! What brings you here?"

Sterling's voice startled her and she turned in time to see a hearty embrace between Tamara Sterling and Diane Morales, who managed operations in California and Illinois. Was Diane the afternoon and evening appointment?

The two were still embracing, though Kip could see there was nothing more than an embrace. Still...damn and damn, she thought. Collusion makes embezzlement so simple.

She stomped away, her head full of unwelcome personal and professional speculations.

CHAPTER FIVE

She grabbed lunch at a soup and salad bar far from the SFI offices. It was still crowded, but she found a seat at the high counter. She was almost finished when someone at her elbow said quietly, "Heya, Kip."

It took just a moment to recognize the voice. "Hi, Meena."

"How ya doing?" Her ex was as quietly handsome as always, thick, brown hair slightly tousled, collar of a crisp white button-up open to show off a simple gold chain against her tanned throat. At the moment there was no sign of the chip on her shoulder labeled *Kip Barrett, lousy girlfriend.*

"I'm doing great." It had been nine months, she thought, or maybe more. How quickly they had passed. "How are you?"

"Equally great. It was a surprise to see you out in the daylight." It sounded a little bitchy, but Meena's tone wasn't overly arch.

"I'm actually between appointments." There was an awkward silence and Kip fumbled for a topic. "How's your mom?"

"Also great, and I'm not just saying that. Um... I'm getting married. Mom's over the moon as you can imagine."

"Oh. Congratulations."

"My girlfriend has a job waiting in Iowa, so we're going to settle there and we can get married, so..."

"Sincerely, all my best wishes." Kip rose to give Meena an awkward hug. "You deserve the best." And that sure wasn't me, she added to herself.

"Thank you. I'm glad I ran into you. I think I was mean when I left."

"Well, I know I was thoughtless."

"It's the job," Meena began, then she raised a hand. "No need to go down that road. It was good to see you." She walked away without looking back.

Kip finished her salad in an odd funk she knew would pass. But for a few minutes she had visions of a house and a white picket fence and two women living there who made each other their priority. What was wrong with that? Nothing at all. So why didn't she want it?

There were no answers forthcoming, and she didn't really have the luxury of time to puzzle about it. That's right, she told herself, if you keep up this work pace you won't have time to figure out that you don't have time to be happy.

She left the cafe and realized she didn't even recall what she'd eaten. A glance at her watch told her she had just enough time to finish at the two remaining banks.

She finished up at the last bank before its old-fashioned three o'clock closing. At home again she spread out her notes and copies and fired up her laptop. She logged her activity, the documents she'd gained and wrote a quick summary of her impressions to date.

Formalities tended to, she began her real work by comparing the statement copies she'd collected from the banks to the copies attached to the internal reconciliations. She worked on the largest accounts first and noted the dates and codes for any transactions that had been altered before the accounts were reconciled at SFI.

She absentmindedly tore open a frozen low-fat dinner and popped it in the microwave. Her back ached from hunching over the paperwork, so she did jumping jacks to get her blood going. She supposed a grown woman should feel a little silly doing jumping jacks, but it was her own kitchen and she was used to doing as she liked on her own turf.

She ignored the little voice that said she wasn't getting any younger and before too long, she'd be so set in her ways there wouldn't be room for anyone else. Her stubborn adherence to her own ways of doing things had been one of the reasons she and Meena had cooled to each other from the moment Meena had moved in. She had tried to change—but, she knew, only to a point.

She devoured the steaming dinner and rewarded her virtuous meal with a bag of M&Ms, sorted by color. She now had a good list—an all-inclusive one she hoped—of the accounts that were missing funds. The doctored bank statements had been changed in two ways: balance summaries changed and electronic funds transfers that had been altered to smaller amounts or obliterated. The statement in her hand was a prime example, and she hoped represented the thief's methodology. On the 5th, 13th, 21st and 28th days of every month there were standing withdrawals from several sweep accounts, bringing money into the account. She could then trace the money out to payroll accounts in New York, Illinois and California. Standard stuff.

But last month the very next transaction after each authorized one she couldn't trace to its landing place—the amount in question disappeared to a destination not listed in SFI's general asset ledger. The amounts varied and weren't singly very large. They added up, though.

If she had to guess—and she didn't like guessing—their thief had appended additional instructions to the existing, already approved withdrawal demand, then made sure the transactions weren't discovered during account reconciliation. It *could* be one person doing both. It *could* be one or more people at SFI—someone with the authority to sign a transaction order that would fool the bank, and someone with ready access to the account statements.

It was time for ETO. Time to eliminate the obvious hows and whos.

She typed in her list of signatories for each account, then sorted by last name. The list of people who were signatories on every affected sweep account was short—only four. It should be simple to eliminate them as suspects who acted alone, at least. If she cleared them all, it meant focusing on the next most obvious how and who: any of these people working together or with an accomplice she didn't yet have on a suspect list.

ETO number one was Tamara Rebekkah Sterling. She privately owned SFI as a limited liability corporation of which she was the only shareholder. All net worth was her personal asset and she could draw any amount she liked from several company accounts and need not pay it back. Of course the IRS would want her to pay taxes on the income, but the money was hers. But she couldn't touch the pension accounts for her personal use. Why would she? There was plenty of cash elsewhere and easily hers with a signed check. Why steal it?

Well, her devil's advocate argued, to get it tax free, or to possibly recover an insurance payoff in its place. She'd seen that plenty of times. But she had no inkling that SFI—or Sterling—needed a cash infusion. Corporate fraud investigation was a growth industry.

Ted Langhorn was next on her list. Along with the other suspects, Ted was a member of the operating board. The directors were all employees in charge of various areas of responsibility.

Langhorn's responsibility was client development. He had a small staff, of which he was the most visible. SFI didn't advertise, but Ted Langhorn attended conferences and symposiums and often taught small how-to-spot-fraud seminars for senior managers. The job required charm, intelligence and the ability to stand endlessly at cocktail parties, smiling and appearing to enjoy any and all topics of discussion. Kip lasted about ten minutes at "networking" events, so she admired Ted Langhorn's ability to make small talk. He certainly brought in the clients.

Running into him outside Tamara's office was the first time she'd been that close to him, but she had spent several minutes talking to his wife at the last company picnic. Nadia Langhorn was as cool as Ted was warm. She'd chatted politely, looking impossibly elegant in a simple white linen shirt and jeans. Her perfect tan was visible through a fashionable rip in her jeans high on the outside of one thigh. It was chic, but Kip couldn't help thinking they were suited to a woman ten years younger. There was also one tidbit of office gossip, that before she'd married Ted, Nadia and Tamara Sterling had been an item.

Next up, Cary Innes was in charge of finance, and that put her ahead of Ted on the list, but right behind Tamara. Cary had the final say on where the pension funds were invested. She would be intimately involved in balance management. She was relatively new to SFI, having been hired away from a client. Perhaps as a new employee she'd seen opportunities to steal that established employees might miss, such as a weakness in their banking protocol software. Innes also reviewed the bank statements for the largest accounts, but in keeping with their internal controls, she didn't review reconciliations for accounts where she had signatory authority.

Because Innes had access, most of her work was conducted in a fish bowl and her authority was heavily constrained. Multiple reviews of her signed agreements, no authority to authorize even petty cash and so on. Everything she signed was reviewed by a senior staff member—they were fraud investigators and knew how to control their assets. That was why embezzlement at SFI looked so bad. If anyone should be able to prevent it, it was them.

After Innes came Diane Morales, who managed the offices in California and Illinois. She had been with SFI since its founding, one of the first managers Tamara had brought on. She was a busy woman who traveled a great deal. For that alone, Kip ruled her out as a suspect acting on her own. Or would be able to if she could get a record of when Diane's ID card had been swiped at the Seattle office. It just didn't seem as if Diane could count on being in Seattle at the precise times she needed to be to do the statement doctoring.

Her laptop's drive whirring, she used her SFI login at a private credit reporting agency and pulled credit, driving and employment histories on her four suspects. Embezzlers were invariably neck deep in debt. As their debts piled up, they blamed their inadequate salaries which became "justification" to steal from their employer. She'd heard the excuses often enough. She dished herself some blackberry sorbet while her printer chunked out the reports.

For each of her suspects she learned physical characteristics, marital status, names of all dependents, automobile license numbers, driving records, home address and phone, schools they'd claimed they'd attended, their largest creditor payments and their full credit history right down to the names of the banks they dealt with. No matter that she often relied on gathering information this way, the availability of all that data so quickly and so cheaply was disconcerting. Her scruples were mollified by the fact that she was looking for a thief and that she was responsible with the information she collected.

She started to read Tamara's profile, but the letters literally danced in front of her eyes. She used what was left of her concentration to update her work log with her findings to date and to back up all her computer files quickly onto a thumb drive.

It had been a long day, and she couldn't help but feel that she wasn't really getting anywhere. This job was difficult working alone. A team would have probably singled out a prime suspect by now. It wasn't that uncommon for SFI to open and close a case in forty-eight hours. She couldn't call in sick again tomorrow without a real malady to show Emilio, so she'd need another long stint tomorrow night before she was ready to make a coherent report.

As she settled into bed, she recalled that she was to report to Tamara Wednesday evening. It should have made her anxious, but instead she slipped into welcome sleep.

"I want your office," Diane said as she closed Tam's office door behind her. "You can work somewhere else."

Tam grinned as she rose to give Diane a welcoming hug. "Sorry I couldn't join you for lunch. I had to get back."

"Sure you did." Diane's tone was dry. "That shiner is turning purple."

Tam retreated to her chair, still grateful that Diane hadn't realized that Tam had been talking to Kip when she'd waved from across the street. "Don't ask."

"As if. When Mercedes sent me in she told me not to ask too."

"It was an accident. Really." She hoped Diane would let it go. Their friendship went back to just before she'd left the Feds to open SFI. Diane had been briefly under investigation by Tam's unit. She was exonerated, but they remembered each other when they'd found themselves waiting in the same airline boarding area. That conversation had led to a wonderful, positive collaboration.

She patted the bruise. "Someday I will tell you all about it, I promise. Mercedes isn't speaking to me because I won't spill the story."

Diane dropped into a guest chair and stretched her legs. "I suppose I can wait. Just not too long. I'd drag it out of you, but there's this to go over." She boosted her briefcase onto the desk. "I've got two final reports. Mercedes gave me two more." She pursed her lips. "But first, we need to talk about something Hank faxed me. He wasn't sure you'd want Mercedes to see it." She handed Tam a memo on the New York office director's stationery.

Tam glanced through the contents as Diane continued, "He said you would make sense of it for me."

Hank wrote that he was getting a polite "Your services aren't needed" when he followed up on the mysterious meeting cancellation on Saturday morning. Since then, two meetings with clients in the final stages of contract approval had been canceled. Looking back, Hank had also found a pattern among NY clients. The cancellations for himself and his own staff had started as long as three weeks ago.

Diane listened to the account of the New York fiasco, then said, "I'll ask Eric in Los Angeles and Melanie in Chicago to keep an eye out for anything like this happening. I'll take care of San Francisco myself. First thing when I get back there on Wednesday morning."

"If there's a wide pattern you know what that means, don't you?"

Diane nodded. "A rumor. A rumor that SFI has troubles."

Tam could only agree. She wanted in the worst way to tell Diane about the embezzlement—it even seemed likely there was a correlation, though at the moment she couldn't see what it might be. But it was more important she tell Kip Barrett about the situation, because that would make the embezzlement possibly the part of a larger plan, and greed not the only motive.

As she and Diane discussed the reports and caseloads in the regional offices a part of Tam's brain was spinning in overtime. Who? Why? And how soon before some kind of rumor surfaced in business trades?

A cocktail party fundraiser was the last way she wanted to spend her evening, but incurring Nadia's wrath was something she didn't need to do right now. She really had no choice but to settle down to working on reports with Diane, going to the silly party and trusting that Kip Barrett was making headway.

CHAPTER SIX

It wasn't humanly possible to label exhibits and work on another investigation at the same time, especially if every aspect of that investigation was secret. On Tuesday morning, Kip's cubicle was still buried in paper files and she had until the end of the week to finish the last several hundred. Even if there had been room, spreading SFI bank statements and the personal histories of SFI directors out on top of that mess felt like setting off an everybody-come-have-a-look flare. Every time she made an attempt to read the reports someone showed up to talk.

By late afternoon all the jumping like a guilty child when the phone rang or someone walked by her cubicle was getting old. But even her cursory attempts to filter through all the paper she'd gathered had eliminated Morales and Langhorn of the capability of acting alone as the embezzler. As soon as she had a travel record for Sterling and a keycard use record for Innes she could clear them as well. From the personal dossiers, none of the SFI directors appeared to have a monetary motive for embezzlement, either.

Two steps forward was also one step back. It was also true that all of the SFI directors had the means to hire a hacker of the highest caliber. Only Sterling and Innes had the access with their physical presence—Langhorn and Morales traveled far too much—to support the work of the hacker by doctoring the paper account records. Sterling had the skill to actually *be* the hacker. There were black holes in her personal history that meant she, or the Feds, had put some of her employment history behind a claim of national security. Her precise assignment with the government was blank, her security clearance—blank again. There was nothing in Sterling's dossier Kip couldn't have learned from the annual report.

With one exception, she reminded herself. She had been very surprised to learn that Tamara had been born in what was then East Berlin. When she'd relocated to the United States, and with whom, even the names of her parents, wasn't in the publicly accessible paperwork Kip had pulled. Not that the missing data was relevant. Still, she disliked blanks and either the Feds had seen to the computer version of redacting the data when she'd been in their employ, or Tamara Sterling had done it herself—she had the skills for it.

She wanted the travel and keycard records in the worst way, because that would resolve the first level of the ETO. It really made no sense to go on suspecting Tamara, but every time she told herself she was certain, an inner voice would warn her she was acting without evidence. And there was another little voice that reminded her that Sterling made her anxious and scared in not entirely unwelcome ways.

She ignored both little voices and forged ahead with her other thoughts. One of the directors acting alone was a long shot, and colluding among themselves equally unlikely. No, she was most likely looking for a paid hacker and an accomplice within SFI—and that could be one of the directors, she accepted that. The accomplice could also be just about anyone with a keycard, it seemed, given how easily she'd walked into the records area. She suspected security protocols had been tampered with. Pinpointing when might be a helpful bit of information, but hardly her priority. She was faced with literally hundreds of suspects as accomplices.

Okay, so she could finish the highest level ETO with the keycard swipe records, so how was she going to get them without going through regular channels? Even Sterling couldn't just ask for them without a number of people wondering why. She had no doubt that Sterling could get them by herself though. But that meant the list was worthless. She couldn't accept as truthful any evidence supplied by someone who was technically still a suspect.

Two people paused near the entrance of her cube, talking about football. She quickly shoved some of her paperwork in a drawer, and cursed herself for being so jittery. She had looked forward to a tidy explanation, a neat report for Tamara Sterling. But now she was going to have to admit she—they—might be in over their heads.

She went back to tagging exhibits until her cube neighbor, Michael, knocked on her cubicle frame.

"Just making the rounds. I'm going to miss working with you," he said.

"Goodness! Is today the day?" Kip rose to hug him. "I want to hear how the other half lives."

"It won't be nearly as much fun, I'm sure."

They chatted a bit more and she hugged him again when he moved on to the next person. Michael was a good member of the team, but he and another colleague had started dating. They'd been wise not to hide it for long—the last time someone had kept quiet and hoped not to be discovered both parties had been quickly fired. Once Michael and his girlfriend had disclosed their relationship they'd both been given the same choice. Michael was the one who had decided to resign. At first he'd been a little bitter about it, even though he knew he'd signed the same code of conduct agreement that everyone else had. She hoped his new job with First National's Internet Fraud group worked out.

Nearly an hour later her desk phone shrilled, breaking Kip out of an exhibit-numbering focused zone. She let voice mail pick up the call. It was the very end of the workday and if it was Emilio he'd come looking for her if he really needed her.

The phone rang again, went to voice mail, then rang again. Kip's heart sank. She could think of only one person with that kind of persistence.

"I was just checking in." Tamara was trying to sound relaxed, Kip thought, but her voice was strained. "I did manage to leave you alone for more than twenty-four hours."

"I have made some progress," she said, aware that her voice, too, was noticeably strained. She couldn't help it. "But not as much as I had hoped, or as you would like, I'm sure." It could be Tamara, she reminded herself. Don't relax. Maybe she wants to know if you've figured out the method yet. Stay vigilant, Barrett.

"I think I'll have everything in shape tomorrow night as we discussed," she continued. "I can't imagine it taking until Thursday." She felt as if she were standing on quicksand. How could she play this out if Tamara was guilty? But it was so likely that she wasn't... But what if...? Why did not knowing make her feel sick to her stomach? Maybe it was the flu, and if it was, someone else would have to ride this seesaw.

Way to go in the intestinal fortitude department, she scolded herself, wishing your problems on someone else.

"Why don't we say tomorrow night—come on in, Di."

Kip could hear a woman on the other end saying she'd come back, but Tamara told her to have a seat. Was that Diane Morales with her? Still?

"If I'm ready, I'll leave you a message. I really think I'll be ready."

"All right then, talk to you tomorrow." As she hung up, Kip could hear the other woman saying something about dinner.

Was it Diane Morales? And if so, what did she and Tamara have to talk about again?

Stop it, Kip, she told herself. You are getting needlessly paranoid. Tamara and Diane must have a thousand things to discuss about business. If they were colluding Tamara wouldn't be so foolish as to let you know she was in touch with Diane. Besides, there was the no-fraternization rule, and they would both be violating it. Well, if they were embezzlers, why would they care?

She was officially spinning in circles. She was momentarily too dizzy to stand up. Too much data, too much pressure. It was terrifying, after her years of experience, not to know what to do next.

Tam surreptitiously glanced at her watch. She didn't know how Diane could stand small talk. She'd been the picture of congeniality last night at the library donor cocktail party and tonight she was glad-handing as successfully as Ted with Seattle's top financial managers. Two nights in a row standing around being polite, but she looked as if she was having the time of her life. Mercedes, who had planned the client appreciation event, was also making effortless chitchat with clients, and if her feet hurt in those elegant suede pumps it didn't show.

Everyone, in fact, looked as if they were enjoying themselves. She hoped that her own morose frame of mind was going unnoticed. She couldn't concentrate on peeled shrimp and eight kinds of artisan cheese.

Diane had found that both the Los Angeles and Chicago offices had had mysterious cancellations but, like Hank, she had so far been given no real answers as to why. Tamara knew it had something to do with the embezzlement and she longed to tell Diane about it, but she knew it compromised Kip's effectiveness and would rob her of the focus from her primary goals: recovering funds and identifying the thief. Tam had only her own suspicion, even if the link seemed obvious to her.

She touched her face, far less swollen this evening than on Sunday. The bruising was hidden by more makeup than she would normally wear in a year. She trusted Kip Barrett, maybe because the blow hadn't been a limp slap but an unvarnished, honest message: respect me or pay the consequences.

Kip had sounded tired and tense when she'd spoken with her. She had put a heavy burden on such petite shoulders but every time she wondered if the burden was too much, her face told her that *petite* didn't mean *weak*.

She pulled her thoughts up short. Kip was an employee, and on assignment. She thought of Kip far too often in other ways, including those brief moments in the elevator when *petite* was the last adjective she would have used. Others were much better, like *warm* and *strong*. It wasn't the thing to do just because she was bored stiff and she longed for a good night's sleep. A wrong number had woken her up last night at two in the morning. After that she'd kept startling awake, thinking the phone was ringing again.

"Tamara, sweetie, who is she?"

Nadia Langhorn slipped into the circle of Tam's arms, leaving Tam little choice but to look down at her. She was aware that the brilliant blue eyes that were the most arresting feature in a delicate, heart-shaped face owed some of their luminous quality to tinted contact lenses, but that was Nadia. She gilded her lily beautifully.

"Who's who?"

"Ted saw you on Sunday. Don't be coy." She looked up at her with a toss of her lustrous black hair. "I was going to ask last night, but not in front of the library people, of course. He said it looked as if you'd been with some snow bunny for the weekend. Did you take her up to your office to impress her? What else did you do up there?"

Tam hid her relief that Ted hadn't recognized Kip. "It would be exceedingly ungallant of me to discuss it."

"You and your pigheaded chivalry," Nadia said. "I hate you for it, you know." Her tone was casual, but she leaned into Tam's side and an affectionate stroke of Tam's face became sudden pressure on her bruised cheekbone. Tam jerked her head away from the jab of pain.

"I didn't get a chance to ask you about that, either, last night. Did she do that to you? Are you into that sort of fun now? Dungeons are all the rage. You should come out as a bondage devotee. Sex always trends on Twitter."

She extricated herself from the entangling arm with a frown of annoyance. "There are clients here, so please stop the snuggling act. No wonder those rumors about us never stop. The bruise was an accident." That was true enough. She had had no idea that if she grabbed Kip Barrett she'd get punched. Next time she'd get permission first. Next time? What was she thinking about?

Nadia brushed nonexistent lint from the shoulders of Tam's jacket. "Come back, come back, wherever you are," she said.

"Sorry, I was thinking about how much I don't want to be a trending topic on Twitter."

Nadia pouted. Sometimes Tam didn't like Nadia at all. But their bond made liking or not liking each other irrelevant.

"Get me something to eat while I powder my nose, would you?"

Tam bowed meekly and headed for the buffet table. She was aware that Nadia's perfume clung to her, and she found it more cloying than usual. Kip Barrett didn't wear perfume. She smelled like...Kip.

She drew her breath in sharply. These thoughts had to stop.

Diane appeared at her side, and she swatted the shoulder where Nadia's face had rested. "She got makeup on your jacket."

"It'll come out," she said.

Diane wrinkled her nose. "Thank goodness. I know she's not under your skin. She just acts like she is and that annoys me."

Diane was giving her a speculative look, her gaze focused mostly on the well-hidden bruise. Before Diane could do any more speculating about it, Tam quickly said, "Let's focus on the clients."

Nadia arrived to claim the drink. She and Diane made polite small talk that didn't really hide the fact that they didn't like each other and quickly moved away in opposite directions. Thank goodness, Tam thought. She was tired of both of them giving her too much scrutiny.

She sipped her drink and took a deep breath. Time to clear her mind of Kip Barrett. She even went so far as to picture putting thoughts of her in a safety deposit box and throwing away the key. Not that it helped.

Having a large double-shot mocha may not have been the wisest decision, given that Kip was already jumpy as heck, but tipping in just the right amount of sweetener and nonfat milk, stirring, tasting, adding a dusting of cinnamon followed by more stirring and tasting all served to calm her nerves. It was likely to be the closest she came to cooking anything all day.

She told herself it wasn't so much that her stomach clenched every time she considered that Tamara Sterling might be playing cat and mouse with her, but rather that she couldn't put together any kind of decent report for her very important client. Hours of work and she still didn't have a sound ETO formulated, plus she had no plan on what to do next other than involve more people.

But she didn't have to feel so desperate, did she?

But wasn't desperation a path to inspiration? Desperate measures and all that?

Well, if she was desperate there was one phone number to call, that is, if it still worked. She never knew with Buck.

He answered on the seventh ring. "I'm busy, Barrett."

"I have a cash bonus." She gritted her teeth.

"And you'll send me a 1099, like I want to pay taxes."

"I can fix it so you don't get a 1099. Interested or not?"

"You can stop by. I want the cash upfront."

"Half upfront. If you do what I want quickly, you'll have it all tonight."

He whined, then whined for a change, then moved up to more whining until Kip's head was aching. She didn't say anything because she knew it that would just slow down his inevitable capitulation. "Oh fine, whatever, have it your way. But don't be one minute after seven."

She glanced at her watch. "Fine."

She headed for the nearest cash machine.

"Six hundred? You've got to be kidding me!"

Buck kept her standing in his dimly lit doorway. Only a few inches taller than her, he was a walking stereotype of paranoid twitches and geek slovenliness, except instead of his mother's leaky basement, he lived apparently by himself in a duplex with a white picket fence and well-tended hedges. His bright red hair was cut short, but he'd let his beard fill out since the last time she'd seen him.

"Actually, it'll be five-ninty-nine. That way I don't have to send you a 1099. I told you I could fix it so you didn't get one. If you cheat on your taxes, that's up to you, but I'm not playing."

"I'm not doing anything for a lousy six hundred bucks." His Green Day T-shirt testified to the recent consumption of pizza.

"I'll have you paid the usual SFI rate for the job. The six hundred is from me, not SFI, so you do it *now*."

He glared at her. "By Friday."

"Now."

"Tomorrow."

"Now." She sighed. "I can do this all night, but you'll get rid of me faster if you stop complaining."

"I have a life—forget it. Fine. Whatever." He opened the door just wide enough for her to enter. "Don't move from that spot."

She rolled her eyes as he leaned out to peer up and down the deserted street. He wanted to be a character in a movie, like Snake Plissken or Neo, but the baby boy cheeks and freckles undercut the persona, even with the beard trying to cover them up.

He locked the front door five different ways. "What do you want?"

She handed him the names of the SFI board. "I have standard workups already. I want to know if these people are interconnected financially, if their names show up on the same charities, two or more used credit cards in the same hotel on the same week, that sort of stuff, and the sorts of details that are standard redactions for former federal law enforcement types. And you can't breathe a word of it. If you do I will find you. I know where you live." She smiled and attempted to twinkle as if she were joking, which she wasn't and Buck knew it.

"Sterling herself? What's she involved in?"

"As far as I know absolutely nothing, but I want to be unshakably certain. You're just part of the research."

"And I'm going to get standard rates?"

"Yes, and here's three hundred. I'll bring you the rest later tonight."

He pouted, then said, "Ten o'clock. And I'm going to bed at five after."

She refrained from commenting on his night life plans. It wasn't as if hers were any better. Great, her social life was that of an escapee from *Revenge of the Nerds*. It made it worse that Buck was probably perfectly happy with his social life. She was the one who knew she'd be happier with a little more than she had and was doing absolutely nothing about it. And how could she? She wasn't heading for an exciting, romantic tête-à-tête with a gorgeous half-dressed woman. Her agenda was a drive-through taco and then back to her cubicle.

That's what you get for living in the real world, she told herself, as she mopped hot sauce off her lap.

Stomach not entirely happy, she plowed through as many exhibit assignments as humanly possible. With Buck bolstering her reach with his research, her brain was finally able to efficiently tackle the tedium. She had less than four hundred files to go now.

At nine thirty she went down to her car in the garage. It was late, so after the elevator doors closed she paused to listen. No sounds of running engines, no suddenly ceased footsteps. There were basic survival skills she wouldn't ever forget, and thank you Grandpa and Uncle Sam for the training.

She pushed away the bitter edge of that thought. She was

grateful for everything she'd learned during her Secret Service training. It made her wary without sapping her of confidence. She decided to prove to herself she'd lost none of her stuff by driving to Buck's via a roundabout route and keeping an eye on the headlights in her rearview mirror. She was not being followed, just like every night she'd ever kept track.

Meena had hated it when Kip played The Secret Service Game. She said it made her feel as if Kip was never one hundred percent focused on her. Maybe Meena had a point—vigilance for no good reason was distracting. Maybe it had been easier to be distracted than deal with the fact that she and Meena weren't really suited to each other, and their experimental cohabitation had been a mistake. Either way, she was now safely arrived on Buck's street and could park her car and head for his house just like any other neighbor.

She knocked, and when he cracked the door open to peer out, said, "The silent dog lies panting in the oceanic sun."

"You are so full of shit, Barrett. Here." He cracked open the door to thrust a large manila envelope at her. "Boring people. With boring lives and boring money."

She rifled through the contents and was satisfied that he had done what she'd asked. One stapled collection was flagged with a yellow sticky. "What's the note for?"

"Only oddball thing in the bunch. There's a lot of bio info on Sterling that's just not there. I don't mean it's there and I can't get it. I mean it's not there to get."

"What does that mean?"

"Well, I'm not accusing anybody of anything, so I still want to get paid."

"What does it mean?" She gave Buck her finest steely-eyed look.

"The only time I've ever run across those kinds of holes was when the profile was a cover."

"A cover? You mean like a false identity?" Kip's stomach did a queasy roll.

"Hey, you *did* go to college. I want my other three hundred bucks."

"Here's two-ninety-nine. Remember the tax reporting issue? I'm not screwing with the IRS." She held out the roll of bills.

He said a very bad word and cast aspersions on her parentage before jabbing her with, "I scrubbed your records down with a brillo pad and you've been such a naughty girl, all those parking tickets in college. Really stuck it to the man there, didn't you? Oh that's right, you actually *paid* those tickets and never put a foot wrong since. Really living a meaningful life, aren't you, Ms. Anarchist?"

She let him finish his snitty little rant, then said, "I love you too, Buck."

She was stopped at the corner to make a right turn before she realized how angry Buck's comments had made her. Since when was playing by the rules a meaningless life? Why were people who exercised their gun rights by shooting up a school some kind of hero, and people who tried to protect those lives and prevent that violence the ones in league with the forces of doomsday? Buck had some screwed up priorities. Would he like her if he knew she'd had a few drinks before legal age? Tried pot and shoplifted CDs?

Okay, she hadn't.

That wasn't the point, she told herself.

She was trying to make a difference, and thieves who stole from everyday folks, the moms and dads who thought they were putting their money in a safe place, should pay. She didn't think a minimum security prison for a few years was nearly enough, either. She thought they should have to paint the houses and mow the lawns for the people they'd ripped off and actually *work* off the debt. Someone like Joseph Wyndham III should be scrubbing toilets in public parks for ten years, and actually do something that improved the quality of other people's lives.

Which was why she was an investigator and not a judge, she supposed.

She was nearly home when it came back to her with a clang of alarm that Buck was suggesting that "Tamara Sterling," her boss's boss's boss, wasn't a real person.

Sitting at her kitchen table, in the chair Tamara had occupied only two nights earlier, she looked at the report he'd flagged. Tamara's passport application provided data but that information had no matching verification in the government files where it ought to have been. Buck was right about that—blocked from his access was one thing. But data actually missing was another. One piece of missing data could perhaps be an oversight. But names of German birth parents missing? There were American adoptive parents listed, but their birth places and the office that had issued their Social Security cards was missing. Immigration departure point in Germany and arrival point in the U.S. was blank. No residences prior to the age of twelve recorded for Sterling, and looking in her adoptive parents' records didn't turn up that information either.

There could be a simple explanation. There probably was. Given her work and how often defense attorneys would have loved to have cast doubt on Tamara Sterling's credibility, it seemed improbable Buck was the first person to find these anomalies. Perhaps they were a recent glitch of some kind.

It made no sense. She got more information on Google about Tamara Sterling, CEO of Sterling Fraud Investigations, than Buck had found about Tamara Sterling, native of Berlin, Germany, who had become an American citizen at twelve. It wasn't odd that a child's residence couldn't be easily traced, but those American adoptive parents had no residences or credit histories before the adoption. The adoptive parents had no deceased flags with Social Security, so they ought to exist *somewhere*.

She flipped through the rest of the paperwork on Sterling. Buck had not been able to discern what federal departments Tamara had worked for, though one of the few dates left indicated she'd had a government-paid physical exam while she was in college. But which agency authorized it—blank.

It was all simply bizarre. Instead of making her life simpler, this lack of information took her back to square one. Was Tamara Sterling the embezzler she was looking for? How could she prove she wasn't if she didn't know who Tamara Sterling actually was?

CHAPTER SEVEN

Tam was early to the office in spite of a night too late with a little too much wine, talking shop with Diane and uselessly spinning her wheels about the cancellations from clients that were plaguing all of their offices.

She knew the moment she opened the door to Mercedes' sanctum that something was wrong. Mercedes had an odd look on her face as she spoke into her phone.

"There is no comment at this time. I will give Ms. Sterling your message. I'm not going to speculate on when that might be." She listened as she gestured at Tam to linger. "I'm sorry, I'm not going to speculate on any of your questions. I must return to my work now. Yes, I wrote down the number."

"What the heck was that about?" Tam watched as Mercedes mimed wiping her hands of something smelly.

"That was a reporter with that sleazy gossip show SLY. They

want confirmation that you flew all the way to New York to have breakfast with Wren Cantu."

"Who?"

"I looked up the name while we talked." Mercedes glanced at her monitor. "Some lesbian supermodel, all the hot topic in New York, I gather."

Tam blinked. "Huh?" She looked at the door, Mercedes' desk, the carpet. She appeared to be in the universe where she belonged. "I don't get it."

"Neither do I. But they knew you'd been on flights there and back and they knew which ones. Well, they knew the return flight you'd been booked on, but not the one you actually took."

"I spent five hours in the Admiral Club at JFK waiting to jump flights, using the wireless."

"I know." Mercedes gestured at the phone. "Do you want me to call them back? This snotty guy said they tape in less than thirty minutes for tonight's program. Haven't you seen it—bunch of people with no life except chasing celebrities sit around and make snide comments they think are clever. The kind of people who see a celebrity woman eating a hot dog and joke about oral sex. And they call it *journalism*."

"I don't have a clue how my name has been linked into this. This isn't how I planned to start my day."

"And Hank Jefferson called twice."

Tam headed for her office. "I'll take care of this reporter, then call him back. Would you let him know?"

She took a moment to compose her thoughts, then dialed the number Mercedes had written down. She introduced herself to the man who answered the phone, then asked, "Can you provide me with some assurance that you represent this program?"

He rattled off credentials and with a few quick Web searches she decided to believe he was who he said he was. Even if he wasn't, she wasn't going to tell him anything useful.

"So my source tells me that you flew to New York last Friday on a red-eye, had breakfast with Wren Cantu, then flew home later that day."

"Not to insult Ms. Cantu, but until my assistant gave me your message I'd not heard of her and to my knowledge I've never met her."

"So you deny that you flew to New York last Friday—"

"I deny knowing Ms. Cantu. Since that's what you're inquiring about, I've answered your question."

"So you didn't have breakfast with her?"

"I don't know her."

"That doesn't answer my question."

"It does. It's called a logical chain of events."

"But I can still say you didn't deny having breakfast with her."

"Are you in the habit of having meals with people you don't know and have never met? I'm not."

"So that's a denial of having breakfast with her?"

"Asked and answered. Unless you have a different question, I'll go back to my work now."

She had no sooner hung up than Mercedes buzzed to say that Nadia Langhorn was on the phone. Tam sighed and took the call.

"Ted's got the flu," Nadia said. "Since we were all together last night I thought I'd check on you. Thank goodness it's the flu and not food poisoning."

"Ouch—that's a little cold, and from his wife, no less."

She laughed. "Just being pragmatic. Can you imagine, all those clients sick from the food?"

"Okay, I grant you that. If Ted must be sick, I'm glad it's the flu and not food poisoning too. I'm fine. Haven't heard of anyone else with it, either."

"That's a relief then. Do you have time for dinner with me tonight? He's such a bear when he's sick and I could use a quiet meal. You don't chatter. I've always liked that about you."

"You make it sound tempting," Tam said, recalling her after-work hope to meet with Kip. Even though Nadia could be wicked and fun, Kip was her first priority. Just business, she hastily added to herself. "I've got way too much work. A dinner meeting is tentatively scheduled on a new case. I couldn't."

"Fine. Be that way," Nadia said without rancor. "If you end up at a loose end, take pity on me."

Tam sat for a moment, hand still on the phone. Right, just business to put a chance meeting with Kip ahead of a welcome diversion with a friend.

Quelling the sudden butterflies in her stomach, she called Hank back. She was so lucky in her colleagues. Hank was as devoted to the company as she was. The New York office was huge and growing every year, but the knack for managing and motivating people that she'd admired in him when they'd both worked for the FBI kept the chaos organized. He was far more subtle than most people expected. Like with Diane, it was a successful collaboration.

She must have sounded odd to him, because the first thing he said was, "Who already put salt in your milk? That's my job today."

She quickly explained about the gossip reporter.

"I know the Cantu woman—well, of her," Hank said. "She was at the fundraiser we co-sponsored for the New York Public Library. We were introduced but I quickly knew I was not of consequence to her. You've been linked romantically?"

"Never met her."

"I know. It's just strange. And I doubt it's a coincidence. Here the *Journal* isn't jumping on rumors of client losses and staff leaving yet, but the scandal rags can't wait to blog up you and a model."

"I know it has to be connected. I just don't know how. Anyway, why am I on your list this morning?"

"I've got a letter from our contact at Big Blue. The New York office is canceling our contract."

"Big Blue?" Her fingertips went numb. "Some of the biggest corporate butt we've ever pulled out of the fire?"

"That Big Blue. I've worked with Avery Jessup for so long that I've talked him into dinner tonight. I want answers—this makes no sense to me. Nobody else will give me the time of day. It's like SFI suddenly has bad breath."

"Diane says the other offices are having cancellations too. We think there's a rumor about us circulating."

"What does Ted think?"

"Good question. I think if he'd heard something he would have said something, though. He's got the flu. I'll ask him, though." She could ask Nadia to relay the question, but that would mean Nadia knowing more than she should about company business.

"Well, I think it's a rumor. A rumor bad enough for someone like Avery to pull the plug on us without talking first. He's a pretty straight-and-narrow guy, conservative. I'm shocked he wouldn't at least call me first, ask a few questions."

She ought to tell him about the embezzlement—just like she ought to have told Diane. But she would wait until she got the report from Kip tonight before doing so.

"I appreciate what you're doing, Hank."

"Hey, don't thank me yet. Besides, your ass is my ass. Okay, plus fifty pounds."

Tam didn't know how she could laugh, but picturing Hank's broad-shouldered ex-football physique compared to her too-tall, too-thin frame struck her funny bone. "We're in this together, aren't we?"

"Always have been, boss. I'll call you later."

Kip sat up with a gasp. A page of Buck's reports was stuck to her cheek. She'd fallen asleep at the table. She could have sworn she heard her bones creak as she peeled the paper off her face.

The days of all-nighters and bouncing to a class to ace a test were behind her, obviously. She felt a hundred years old as she loaded the stacks of printouts into her satchel.

She had no idea what she was going to do about Tamara Sterling. About anything.

Not the least bit refreshed by a hot shower and a triple-shot mocha, she arrived at her desk to find a note from Emilio asking her to spend an hour with a colleague tracing a transaction through a series of banks and accounting codes. The projected hour became three. By the time she felt as if she'd found her feet for the day it was pushing noon and her stomach wanted lunch. She told it to shut up.

How was she going to make any kind of report to Tamara if she believed Tamara was a viable suspect? She had to deliver on promises to her client, but in doing so she could be telling key investigation points to a suspect. Or believed that Tamara had secrets of her own, and somehow Kip was part of keeping those secrets intact? She had never been in this position before. People higher up than her usually dealt with the rocks and hard places.

She threw herself into more exhibit checking and labeling. Following the same procedures, over and over, might clear her mind. But no matter how many case files she looked at and numbers she printed, she couldn't forget for more than a minute that Tamara Sterling was expecting to hear from her by the end of the day.

As the workday ticked toward its end, she knew she had to contact Tamara. If Tamara was guilty, she'd find her failure to get in touch suspicious. If she wasn't, she'd find it incompetent.

At five minutes to five she called the private voice mail number written on Tamara's business card. She hoped she sounded brisk, and not freaked out, as she left her cryptic message. "I would like to get together and share details. This evening, if you're free. You have my number." She hoped any colleague nearby would presume it was a date of some kind.

There was no immediate return call, so at six thirty she packed up her things and headed for home. What she was going to do there she hadn't a clue. Her empty stomach wanted a big, fat slice of pizza with two inches of gooey cheese and pounds of pepperoni, but her brain sent back queasy signals at the mere thought. She'd open a can of soup at home.

She had just unlocked her front door when her cell phone rang.

"I hope I'm not interrupting your dinner," Tamara said in her ear.

"Not at all. I haven't had a chance to start it," she responded.

"It can wait, depending on your schedule. I think it would be better to meet in person." It was the truth, even if she did experience a swooping feeling in the pit of her stomach. It was just nerves, she told herself.

"I have a thought, if you'll take pity on me," Tamara said. "I haven't had lunch or supper, and dinner last night was those dreadful hors d'oeuvres that would be dinner if you had fifty of them. If I don't eat I won't be able to listen to a word you say. If you'll let me order us dinner—"

Kip cut her off, surprised to be laughing and horrified to be pleased. "Dinner I don't have to make sounds too good to be true. Where should I meet you?"

"I have a sailboat docked at Gas Works Marina. Just give your name to the attendant who'll tell you where to park."

Kip was momentarily delighted...to be on a boat, even one docked, was a thrill. Her delight was short-lived. Down girl, she told herself. You are meeting a client. Your boss's boss's boss. A suspect. Someone who might not be who she says she is.

She sedately agreed to be there in a half hour. A handful of almonds quelled her stomach, though every time she thought of asking Tamara "So who are you really?" she felt nauseous.

The weather had remained clear and sunny throughout the day, but the temperature had plummeted as the sun had set. She changed into long underwear under jeans, thick socks and deck shoes, and a tightly knit shepherd's sweater. Traffic on the George Washington Bridge was light so she arrived on the north side of Lake Union a little early. She scooted into Il Pattiserie for a couple of slices of their Triple Sin cake. She hoped Tamara liked chocolate. If she didn't, then that was another tick mark in the "bad guy" column for her.

She was shimmying out of the tight parking space before the irony of repeating "This is not a date" to herself and at the same time singing along with a silly love song on the radio hit home. *You are making a report to her and investigating her at the same time. Don't forget*, she scolded herself. This was a business dinner and a chance for her to further the investigation. Whether the client/suspect liked chocolate was irrelevant. Tamara was *not* good-looking, her touch had not thrown Kip into a panic, and for all Kip knew she already had somebody in her life, like Diane Morales, in defiance of company policy. *She could be a fraud, a cheat and a liar.*

There, she thought, that was better. Cheat and liar.

With a firm grip on her nerves she turned into the marina parking lot and was directed to Tamara's berth. There was no sign of Tamara as she walked down the floating pier toward the lithe sailboat. The graceful vessel—20-24 footer she guessed—gleamed with white paint, teak decking and sails wrapped in dark green. The polished brass of the porthole frames glinted like pure gold in the last of the autumn sunlight. The *Emerald Petral* was lovely.

Cheat and liar... The refrain was getting weaker.

"Ahoy, captain," she called.

There was a muffled reply and then Tamara came up from below deck. A worn University of Washington sweatshirt and jeans accented her angular hips and shoulders. "I was just setting up the table downstairs, but the wind has died. Can you manage sitting up here if I switch on the deck heater?"

"I can handle it if it gets chilly, but the night air is perfect right now." She let the Il Patisserie box dangle into her view. "Dessert," she said.

Tamara smiled at her with a relaxed blink. "I hope there's some chocolate in that bag."

Kip's heart went *thump-thump-thump*, stupid heart, no brains at all, unreliable, foolish thing. Her voice sounded unnaturally high as she said, "Absolutely."

"Good," Tamara said as she disappeared down the hatch. "The harbor restaurant only had coconut-lemon something. I'm sure it's quite good, but it's not chocolate."

Kip set down what she was carrying. She attributed the slight sense of vertigo she felt to the mild drift of the boat against its moorings. *Cheat and liar...* Nope, that wasn't working at all now. She felt a flutter of panic as she called down, "Can I help?"

Tamara handed up a picnic hamper emblazoned with the port's coat of arms. "Would you like wine?"

"I really don't drink," Kip said. She'd never acquired a taste for it, and her father's problems had only made her more of a teetotaler.

"I should drink less than I do. Can I interest you in some hot cranberry juice?"

Kip wrinkled her nose. "That sounds a little weird, but I'm willing."

Tamara looked over her shoulder from the steps. "Trust me." She disappeared into the galley.

I do trust her. Kip froze as the unbidden thought sank in. She knew she had to fight it. She knew she shouldn't trust anyone she was investigating. She knew better.

Feeling on autopilot, Kip set out the dinner—it looked like chilled salmon filets in a light orange sauce. When she sniffed the contents of a bowl of linguini salad her stomach did a little dance. Seed rolls and butter were at the bottom of the box, but after she lifted them out she found a tray of antipasto. Mortadella, salami, tapenade... *Mmm.*

She heard Tamara emerge onto the deck. "This all smells delicious." She warily accepted the steaming mug and cautiously sipped. Her eyes widened.

"Like it?" Tamara was warming her hands around her own mug. "I find it very refreshing and it chases away colds."

Kip nodded and sipped the hot cranberry juice again. It was like a tart, sweet tea. "It is refreshing. And unusual. Thanks."

Tamara pressed the deck heater's ignition lighter and a soft glow suffused the table, followed by a wave of heat. "I hope the food is up to their usual high standards. I just told them to double the fresh catch order."

She does this often, then. Kip felt a wave of disappointment, then mentally booted herself. *This is not a date, you dope!* "I was just hoping you wouldn't think I was a pig if I helped you devour every ounce."

"I am hoping you'll be as devoted to enjoying the dinner as

you are to your work." Tam's tone matched the twinkle of good humor in her eyes.

Kip was glad the low light hid her blush. Stop flirting, she told herself and she turned her attention to the meal.

They made short work of the food while they bantered back and forth about sailing experiences and favorite meals. The salmon was obviously freshly caught and Kip's tongue wanted to melt from the exquisite parmesan garlic sauce on the linguini salad. It had real Greek olives stirred into it. She'd forgotten how good they were. Her daily cuisine was boring, she realized. Boring because she didn't spend any time planning it. She made a mental note to put more energy into her menus in the future, then glumly erased it. Sure, she told herself. You'll have time for that just after this case is over, and then you'll get another case and you'll be right back to eating out of boxes and buckets.

Tamara restacked the dishes and bowls in the hamper and Kip handed her one of the takeaway containers of Triple Sin cake.

"We really shouldn't," Tamara said. She peered at Kip's slice. "How come I get the smaller piece?"

Kip grinned—who knew that Tamara Sterling could pout? "Big baby. Here." She lifted the chocolate curl from her slice and put it on Tamara's. "Better?"

"Yes, thank you." Tam's smile was open and for just a moment Kip saw a woman who could relax at the beach or set out for a day's sailing just because the lake was beautiful. "You've been very kind. I was starving and in a lousy mood. This has been very relaxing."

Kip tried to strike a light note. "It's all part of the service."

"No, it's not." Tamara looked at her seriously for a moment, then stared down at the cake. "I'm sure... You must have other places you'd rather be. People you'd rather be with. I appreciate your giving your time to me."

Kip didn't know what to say. She could hardly tell her boss's boss's boss she hadn't dated anyone in months and months, nor would it sound right to say she lived for her work. "You're welcome," seemed the only correct answer.

They were silent for a few minutes, savoring the cake. Finally, all the chocolate licked from her fork, Kip reluctantly reached for her paperwork.

Tamara sighed and got up to bring a deck lantern closer to the table, adding to the soft glow from the deck heater. "I suppose we should get down to business."

Kip passed her a single sheet of paper. "These are officially the affected accounts and the amounts missing as of Monday."

She went very still. "Six million nine. How?"

"It's all being done in concurrence with pre-authorized transfers and the next one is Friday. We need to move fast because—"

"Because a lot of thieves leave town when they hit a major milestone. The perp could be aiming for seven million—but it could also be ten million."

Kip nodded. "Our thief started small only two months ago, just after our last quarterly audit. In the last four weeks, the amounts have been larger. If I were them, I'd be alert for investigation and ready to leave at a moment's notice. And I'd have already picked a day to leave anyway, whether it appeared anyone suspected me or not."

"So how are the transfer orders being sent?" Despite the lantern's glow, she couldn't really see Tamara's eyes, but the tone was overly nonchalant.

Kip had had a lot of experience making cogent presentations. She took a calming breath, hoping it would save her now. "As you know, a number of our largest clients pay their retainers on a quarterly basis. The financial firms in particular pay by pre-arranged wire. The wires come into several sweep accounts. Four times a month there are transfers out of those accounts. Most of the balances are transferred to payroll accounts for the California, New York and Illinois payroll systems. A variety of other payments are made to the overhead accounts at the various offices for premises expenses like rent. Our malpractice insurance premium gets paid that way as well." Tamara probably knew this, but the background was important.

Kip absently scratched behind one ear. "Our thief apparently knows all of these details. He or she simply adds another destination account on to the instructions to transfer money to an account we don't control."

Tamara had been leaning back in her chair, but now she sat forward, bringing her face into the light. "That's pretty sophisticated computer work. Not many people could do it."

"I know." Kip desperately tried to appear nonchalant, as if she didn't have a reasonable investigator's suspicion that the woman across the table from her could be the mastermind. "It's easy to cover up if you can doctor the bank statements. It's equally easy for me to discover it. But there's no paper trail other than the statements."

"I don't understand."

"Neither did I at first. But I can only come up with one explanation," Kip said. "If this was being done the usual way, which is falsified paperwork, the paperwork we sent to the bank, with the extra instructions, would be in our files. But our paperwork is fine."

"So why is the bank processing the extra instructions?"

"I think because computers do what they're told."

Tamara took a deep breath. "Someone's hacking into our instructions before they hit the bank? I did the protection system myself and... Let's say it's nearly impossible. Those systems are tight."

"Tighter than a bank's own security protocol?"

"Yes, I think so."

"Well, there's only two explanations," Kip said slowly. "If it wasn't done on SFI's mainframe, then it was done on the banks' systems."

Tamara was shaking her head. "That seems equally impossible."

"Yes," Kip said, nodding. "I know. But I checked a few of the SFI mainframe files. It wasn't that hard to open them for reading only."

"You didn't find the originals," Tamara said confidently. "Those were copies and meant to be accessible."

"Well, if those are valid copies, our ledger files appear intact and unedited. I'm not an expert, though."

"I'd be able to tell," Tamara said. "Damn—my day is incredibly busy tomorrow and I won't get the chance."

"That wouldn't be a good idea," Kip said sharply.

"You want to call in someone else to do it? I wrote the safeguards myself... Oh. I get it." Her face was like stone. "Later someone might say I used the opportunity to erase my work."

Kip could not stop her lips from trembling. She felt like she was riding a seesaw blindfolded, up and down with no ability to predict or control the motion. She believed Tamara and her heart—stupid thing—sang. Then she thought Tamara was guilty and she ached with betrayal. Up and down, up and down, with the ground never under her feet.

Tamara was looking at her questioningly. "Do you think that's what I meant to do?"

Kip lowered her gaze to the bleak landscape of papers. "We're looking for someone who can do the impossible on a computer. I don't think it would look good at all for you to go—"

"Kip."

She had to look at her. She could not trust her. "We're looking for someone who can break into a bank computer, find the legitimate transaction entered properly and append an additional line of instructions. Without setting off alarms and without messing up the processing totals."

"You didn't answer my question."

"No," she said softly. "I didn't."

In the soft lantern light, Tamara's eyes were oceans deep, unreadable. Kip knew it wasn't the same with her. She could not find The Stare, could not even blink and look away.

"You're a good investigator," Tamara said finally, and she finally broke their intense gaze, leaving Kip feeling as if she had nevertheless disappointed her. "Since I know I'm innocent, however, you'll have to excuse me if I proceed on that basis."

Kip didn't respond to that comment. Instead she said, "There's a further complication."

Tamara pursed her lips and looked at her through lowered lashes. "How does this get more complicated?"

"So far, I've listed thirty-five destination accounts. This is a talented thief, so those accounts are likely already closed, making the traces complex."

She sighed again. "I can't believe this is happening at SFI."

"Even the best of people can be tempted."

Tamara shook her head. "No, the best people aren't tempted, and they can't be bought. If I didn't believe that, I'd close up shop tomorrow."

Kip said quietly, "I believe that too. But we have both worked cases where people thought above suspicion gave in to the lure of money. Sometimes for a loved one's sake. Sometimes for all the best reasons to do a wrong thing." She wanted to ask Tamara if she had a reason like that, but couldn't make herself do it.

"For love and country," Tamara said, her face turned again toward the shadow. "McVeigh truly thought he was saving America when he blew up all those people in Oklahoma City."

There's something she's not telling me, Kip thought. A secret—like so many she's keeping, apparently. "Patriotism can be played out in the strangest ways, yes."

"Your grandfather was a patriot." She seemed almost relieved to shift the topic.

"He was," she agreed. "Loyal to the office of the President, therefore to the Constitution. Like something out of a Jimmy Stewart movie."

"Did you know that even a sophisticated data search doesn't turn up your service file?" Tamara asked the question casually, but the hand on the table was tensed.

Kip bit back a gasp of anger. "You had no right—"

"I hate mysteries," she said.

"Why I left the Service has nothing to do with working for you." Kip stood up, clenching and unclenching her fists.

Tamara looked up at her. "I thought you personally had some sort of indiscretion and I got cold feet. So I checked you out on my own this afternoon. I have to know how far I can trust you."

Kip's heart was pounding. "I think that stinks."

"How many innocent people do you investigate before you find the guilty one?" She was standing now, slowly moving to her side of the table.

"Dozens. And it stinks, too. I don't like probing into people's lives when they've done nothing wrong. Ted Langhorn and Diane Morales have done nothing to deserve my prying through their financials. Besides, I'm not a suspect being investigated. You were just curious." Her voice faded away as she considered that she was, once again, not using the wisest tone with her client.

How ironic, she thought. *I don't know if I can trust her, and yet it stings to know there was a moment when she didn't trust me.* Maybe, her devil's advocate argued, she checked up on you to see if you could be bought.

"I'm trusting you with everything that matters to me," Tam said quietly. "I'm sorry I blurted it out like that. I did feel guilty afterward."

Kip swallowed noisily. "We're even because I don't know how to tell you all the little things I know about you that you probably wish I didn't."

Tam's expression clouded slightly with wariness. "Such as...?"

There was nothing for it. "Nobody knows where your adoptive parents were born. The data on your passport application can't be verified. There's no record of when you immigrated to the U.S. And so on."

Tamara's breath caught—it was almost a gasp. "How...?" She pressed her lips together, staring at Kip intensely.

She felt ensnared by Tamara's eyes, but her fight-or-fly instincts weren't engaged. She was terrified, but not because she felt in physical danger. "I hired some very good help who suggested that Tamara Sterling was a cover."

"And if it was, it's blown."

Kip nodded. She ought to be on alert. Tamara could snap her neck and toss her overboard with no one the wiser until at least morning, perhaps longer. Nobody knew she was even here. But her body refused to feel threatened. What could it possibly know that she didn't?

"What do you think?"

That I don't know and it's killing me, Kip wanted to say. Instead, she spoke another truth. "I don't know what to think."

"It concerns what some might think an odd matter, but I will say it's very, very private."

"Who were your adoptive parents, then? Their last name wasn't Sterling."

"No. But then as you've guessed," Tam said coolly, "they didn't exist."

She drew in a sharp breath with a needle of anxiety jabbing under her ribs. "I truly don't understand."

Tamara shrugged. "I'm surprised to learn that my passport didn't pass close scrutiny. It used to. I've been Tamara Sterling for twenty-five years. Who I was before that really doesn't have anything to do with any of this."

Kip blurted out, "I can't clear you as a suspect."

Tamara's answer was a quiet, "I know."

"I want to." She admitted it before she could stop herself. "I do believe some people are above temptation."

Tamara nodded. "I know you do. You're like me. You know yourself. You know if you're above temptation other people can be as well."

Kip had to lower her gaze. There was a flare of something in those gray eyes that was too dangerous and she could no longer ignore the warning alarms in her head. Her arms were trembling with the effort it took to keep them at her sides. A good investigator always stood in the middle of the evidence. Leaning too soon one way or the other was a sure way to lose her balance. It was too soon and too risky to lean.

"Kip?" Tamara took a deep breath. She had been calm only moments before, but now tension was written all over her body—shoulders bunched, nervous flexing of her fingers. "Do you really think I'm guilty?"

The abrupt question startled Kip out of her reverie. Her

heart told her to say no, she didn't think she was guilty. All the earlier camaraderie they'd shared during dinner was gone. You fool, Kip railed at herself, you fool. She felt her Secret Service mask descend on her face. "I wouldn't tell you if I did."

Tamara finally said, "You're tough, Kip Barrett."

"I have to be."

She shifted again out of the light. "All day, every day?"

Kip found herself missing the feeling of Tamara's gaze on her. The feeling that Tamara wasn't telling her something relevant was pronounced. She got to her feet and gathered up her papers. "I don't know what to do next. I need to directly gather the keycard user data, which I can't do without your help. And you can't help. I think no matter what I do, I'm going to tip off the thief."

Tamara was silent. There were too many shadows, and not just because of the low light. For the first time, Kip felt a shiver of physical fear whisper over the back of her neck.

She needlessly added, "Lots of puzzle pieces but not enough to see any kind of picture. There are things I just don't know." She let the unspoken question dangle in the air.

Finally, turning away from the railing, Tamara said, "I might be able to add some pieces to the puzzle. I'm not sure they fit at all. And I have no proof for any of it but my own word unless we bring in some of the other directors."

She nodded, her heart pounding in her chest.

"For the last three weeks we've had an unusual number of potential clients cancel pitch meetings, including one that looked like a sure thing. Big rush, secret meeting—canceled without explanation. It's happening in all of the offices. The office directors are looking into it. This morning we lost the standing contract from the New York office of a major client. I expect to find the same for the office here any day."

Kip considered the information. "A rumor do you think?"

"Yes, Diane and I thought so."

She digested the casual intimacy of "Diane and I" and refused to let it unsettle her. "It's almost as if..." She paused, not wanting to sound stupid.

"As if what?"

"Well..." She swallowed and summed up her thoughts. "Embezzlement is theft. But we both know that theft is sometimes motivated not by greed but the desire to steal from a particular person or company. If this was about money alone, someone with that kind of talent could go after an oil company, grab seven *hundred* million, not the penny ante quantities in SFI's accounts. If it's not about money, then it's directed at SFI for other reasons. An attack."

Tamara cocked her head. "These rumors certainly feel like an attack. But why?"

Kip shrugged. "Thinking horses, not zebras, it's aimed at you or SFI, which are sometimes one and the same. Lots of people would love to see our credibility jeopardized. We must have close to a hundred pending cases on dockets all over the country. A little high-end cybercrime combined with malicious gossip..."

Tam was nodding. "And presto! SFI isn't the company it once was. We become the same pariah as an accounting firm caught faking its audits, then trying to testify to the veracity of our findings."

"Exactly."

"An attack." Tamara nodded slowly. "They'd have to have an accomplice inside to doctor the statements."

"And that could be nearly anybody. I think the security attached to keycards was tampered with."

"Child's play for this kind of hacker."

The relief in Tamara's voice was plain. Not a trusted, close associate. If a disabling attack by a hired gun was the why and who, Kip told herself, that meant who Tamara Sterling is, or was, really didn't matter.

It did, though. It deeply mattered to her.

"The bank hacking—that's not cheap or easy," Kip pointed out.

"I can only think of a handful who could do it."

"Including you?"

Tam stilled and drew back until her face was shadowed again. "Including me."

For a moment there was only the sound of water lapping against the dock.

Finally, Tam asked, "Do you really still think it could be me?"

With all her heart Kip wanted to say *no*. But what did her heart understand? Nothing, that's what. She had to do her job. Would Tamara Sterling respect anything else?

Her hesitation was her answer.

Her tone crisp and cold, Tamara asked, "Is that your full report?"

Kip returned the papers to her briefcase, feeling two inches tall. "That's all."

Tamara said nothing as Kip closed her case and turned to the gangplank. As she stepped over the lip to leave the deck, Kip skidded a little, nearly losing her grip on her briefcase.

Tamara steadied her with a firm grasp on her wrist.

"I'm fine," Kip muttered.

Tamara's words seemed wrenched from her throat. "I'm not."

Kip gazed up at her, her breath coming in short gasps. There was no light in the gray eyes, only a dark hunger that both frightened and inflamed her. She could not want her and yet she knew she did. She looked down at where Tamara's hand circled her wrist. It was a conscious decision to turn her palm over so she was no longer captive, and their contact was now obviously by her choice as well.

Her briefcase clattered to the deck as Tam pulled her close with a throaty groan. The power of her grasp was surprisingly strong—Kip had the feeling Tam would have no trouble lifting her off her feet. The thought was forgotten as Tam's rough gasp of surprise and desire was matched by her own.

She arched against her, heedless of the alarms that went off in her head. Her brain wasn't in control anymore. Her arms wrapped around Tam's shoulders of their own accord, and her mouth opened to the demanding pressure. The sweatshirt did not mask the pounding of Tam's heart and Kip felt hers match the ever-quickening beat.

Kip groaned when they broke that long, incredible kiss, then she kissed her again, hard and quick. Tam's hands were caressing her back and ribs as if she wanted to commit the feel of her body to memory.

This was wrong—her boss, it was wrong, a *suspect*, it was so wrong. All her hard-fought adherence to a code of ethics did not allow for this passion to exist, but it did. She buried her face in Tam's neck as cool hands slipped under her sweater. She didn't know how she could compromise herself this way and hope to have any honor left. She wanted Tam no matter what she might have done, yet having her was as painful as not having her.

The Tamara Sterling that Kip wanted so badly to believe existed couldn't respect Kip for this moment even if Tamara Sterling the woman was enjoying it.

Tam whispered, "Don't cry," before Kip realized she was whimpering. "I'm sorry. This was my fault."

"It's not just you," she whispered. "But this isn't going to happen." She knew if they didn't stop now she would be asking for more than kisses. The cold air chilled her tears on her lashes as she stooped to recover her briefcase.

"No, it isn't." Tam said nothing more.

She managed to stride down the pier, her head up as if tears weren't again spilling over her cheeks. She even managed a mocking salute when she reached her car, not sure it could been seen. She could not make out Tam's body in the darkness but her own body told her Tam was still there, still watching her.

CHAPTER EIGHT

Tam watched Kip's taillights disappear at the top of the marina ramp. She stayed in the frigid air for several more minutes, trying to make it the equivalent of the cold shower she badly needed. What had she been thinking? Had she wanted comfort from Kip so badly that she'd been willing to compromise her to get it? Kip had cried—she could still feel her tears on her neck.

Dinner had been both a pleasure and a torment. She could see that Kip doubted her and it had at first stung, then burned. She'd wanted to erase the doubts, but—damn, she'd been a fool.

Her fingers clenched on the rail. She should not have expected Kip to dismiss her as a suspect on her say-so. She should not have expected Kip to be less than she was. So why was she shaken by Kip's lack of trust? Intellectually, she understood why Kip was suspicious of her—it was her job. Her excellence at her job was why Tam had picked her and respected her. Then she had taken all of that and forgotten it in order to hold Kip close and feel her warmth.

As her thoughts turned over and over she forced herself back to the things she could do something about. Someone had expertly helped themselves to almost seven million of SFI's dollars and if Kip Barrett thought it a possibility that she had done it, others would too. Well, she knew it wasn't her. She needed to look at their upcoming dockets and find the most likely people on trial with the scruples to try to bring down SFI to save themselves jail time for their crimes. The answer was there, and thanks to Kip—lovely, tenacious, honor-bound Kip—she at least had an idea where to start looking.

Whoever had tampered with the security settings to allow more people into the secure accounting area had probably left tracks on pathways that Tam knew very well. Plus, a simple printout of personnel not assigned to accounting that had accessed the accounting area with their keycards could spot the inside accomplice. She could pull that data without anyone knowing. Inadmissible, true, but she didn't need admissible data to form her own theory of the crime.

She glanced at her watch—it was just past nine. There was time to do a good night's work.

It took an act of will to lock up the boat and leave. She wanted a stiff drink, badly. Kip Barrett was not allowed, not the reality of her, not even the idea of her. Kip had her job to do and it was difficult enough without kisses getting in the way. The work, she told herself. The work is all that matters.

At first Kip simply drove. She turned randomly and found herself crossing the GW Bridge, then onto Westlake. Aurora would be faster, but all she could do was drive.

Her body trusted Tam, so did her heart. Giving into the moonlight or the chocolate or whatever that was—her head didn't agree it was okay. Her mind, in fact, was hopping mad at her arms, wrapping so eagerly around a *suspect.*

Where's your sense, girl? She could remember every word of the only time her grandfather had scolded her. He would know what to do—and she didn't even need to ask. She knew what to do about her body and heart, and that was control them. She wasn't an adolescent, and just because she was burning didn't mean she got to play with fire.

After several blocks, she sped up for a green light and decided to turn. She wouldn't have noticed the headlights that made the same turn if not for the slight squeal of the heavy sedan's tires.

She made a couple more turns and ended back on Westlake. She thought she saw the same headlights come into her rearview mirror. The left-hand low beam was directed slightly more groundward than the right. Even as she told herself not to be paranoid she was turning off Westlake, this time going all the way over to Aurora. The lopsided headlights followed. They followed her all the way south to Broad Street, where she zipped onto Westlake again. The hair on her arms stood up. It looked like a late-model sedan from here, tan or white.

She didn't think it was in the least paranoid to link this pursuit to her investigation, but who could know about it? Who would be scrutinizing her and Tamara? Again, horses not zebras. It was far more likely that a couple of punks had spotted a woman driving alone and thought they'd have some fun scaring her or worse. The sedan gained on her at each stop sign—not exactly threatening, but not falling back. They'd have to know she knew they were there by now, but they hadn't tried to trick her. They must think she was stupid enough to lead them home.

She sedately drove down from the peak of First Hill. At a less tense moment she would have savored the glitter of lights stretching below her. She made a couple of quick turns and pulled into a mall parking lot, still disgorging the last shoppers of the day. She abruptly turned right down a row and zipped past a car in the process of backing out, earning an angry honk and gesture from the driver. The driver resumed backing out—no room for the sedan to get by. Kip hooted at her success.

Kip quickly pulled back onto Boren, then floored it to make the next light. It was a split second from red when she went through, but there was no cross-traffic. She kept up her speed until she made the next light, then she knew from experience that a steady 41 mph would take her all the way to Ranier without stopping. Unless the sedan was willing to run a lot of red lights, they'd never catch her. Punks usually looked for easier prey than she had turned out to be.

She meandered down Ranier, then headed back to Broad Street and home. There was no sign of the sedan as the Camry glided into the parking garage under her building. She made sure the security gate closed completely behind her before she got out of the car. There was no traffic on the street outside, no idling motors or footsteps. Kip relaxed and gathered up her briefcase and laptop.

Though she was tired there was work to do. She followed her work habits, even though she was no longer sure she was on the case. She updated her log, noting the gist of her report to Tamara, the day and time again, and what they'd discussed. She made no mention of the delectable meal, the chocolate and the resolve-melting passion that had erupted as she was leaving. She would kick herself for that later. Paperwork completed, she decided she should look through the reports Buck had provided her one more time.

She had scarcely removed them from her briefcase when her cell phone rang. Speak of the devil.

"I have one of your reports," Buck announced.

"You do? But I have what I asked for."

"One of those guys was married, so I did the wife too."

"Oh—Nadia Langhorn?"

"Yeah, her. I want to be paid for her too."

"Fine. I'll get it in the morning on my way to work. Was there anything unusual about it?"

"Yeah—that's why I'm even bothering, plus, I do want to get paid. But there was something weird. Nadia Rachel Belize, now Langhorn, was adopted the day before Tamara Sterling was, in a town about a hundred miles east. She has the same holes surrounding birth parents as Sterling. Also born in Germany."

"Are they related?" The most bizarre explanations occurred to her first—they had both been kidnapped as children, white slavers, some kind of child porn ring moving kids around. Stop, think and listen, she told herself. That was when the Berlin Wall fell—refugees from behind the Iron Curtain?

"How would I know? Their adoption decrees won't track back to any databases and Langhorn's passport app has the same lack of verification that Sterling's does."

"They can't both be in some kind of deep cover situation." Buck was just being paranoid. She felt a chill when she remembered that Tam had admitted the adoptive parents weren't real.

She had fallen from one mystery that was still a familiar pattern and into another that was beyond her experience. Right now, with her nerves shattered, her heart pounding and her body acting out some kind of hormonal lust fantasy, she knew which mystery she wanted to solve more. It was the one that was none of her business.

After a poor night's sleep, Kip woke with a start. She had barely opened her eyes when the alarm went off. She forced herself through her morning routine, with the exception of coffee. There wasn't enough caffeine in the world and she already had the jitters.

Though her composure was in tatters, she dressed with care. A black suit with a mixed animal print blouse came close to stylish. She even opted for a skirt and medium-height heels instead of trousers and more comfortable slides. It seemed important. She didn't feel like a professional but at least she could look like one.

After last night's business with the car on her tail, she kept track of cars behind her on her way to Buck's, where she paused long enough to retrieve an envelope he heaved out the door in response to her knock. Proceeding to work, she saw nothing out of the ordinary in her rearview mirror. It had been a bunch of punks, she assured herself. Nevertheless, she was glad to get to the secure parking garage. She felt stretched like a balloon over too many worries.

Still, it felt bizarre to sit down at her desk as if nothing had happened last night between her and Tamara. As if she had nothing else to do but work on exhibits and numbering.

She waited until it seemed like most of her colleagues had settled into their own work before she pulled the report on Nadia Langhorn out of the envelope. Buck had been accurate. Mrs. Langhorn's missing data weirdly matched up with Tamara Sterling's. She'd taught Italian out of college before abandoning her teaching career in favor of marriage. In spite of the southern Italian looks, she'd also been born in Germany, popped into existence in the U.S. at the age of eleven and adopted by parents Kip had to assume didn't exist any more than Tam's did.

She told herself that it had nothing to do with anything that affected the case or her life or her heart or—

She shoved the papers into her briefcase. She didn't know what to do next, and Tamara hadn't given her any prompting, either. She prodded a pesky folder back into a stack only to have the whole pile unbalance and swirl across the only open place on her desk, knocking over knickknacks and what was fortunately an empty water bottle.

She caught sight of the picture she kept on her desk of her and her grandfather, after a day's sailing. She pulled it from under the disarray. She wished she'd spent more time at Jen's birthday celebration. She had missed all of the summer, again. There were blue skies, somewhere, but no sign of them here, in her crowded cubicle.

Normally, she would have said she was a calm, cool, collected type, but when her boss cleared his throat behind her she shot to her feet.

"Sorry," Emilio said immediately. "Planning your next vacation?"

She glanced at the picture still in her hand. "More like wishing

I was already there." She set the frame down where it wouldn't get knocked over by the files again. "What can I do for you?"

"I just took a call from a new client. We haven't worked for them before. They're looking for a quick job. Pierce a corporate veil of a takeover threat. Shouldn't take more than a couple of hours."

"Um...I'm not quite done with checking the exhibits. I've still got about four hundred."

"Is that all? I seriously thought you wouldn't be done until next week."

The deadline you gave me was tomorrow, she wanted to say. Nothing for it then. She took the note from him.

"Call for more information."

She glanced at the note. "Well, I'll certainly see what I can dig up."

Emilio slapped her playfully on the shoulder. "Just do your best. You'll have my job before too long."

"As if I want it," Kip retorted at Emilio's retreating back. She leaned out of her cubicle and called after him, "All that sitting around in the Jacuzzi, sipping mimosas and pulling the strings of the poor plebes who report to you. I don't think I could take it."

Emilio gave her a simple but eloquent hand gesture in response just as he turned the corner. It meant he loved her right back.

She called the client, took notes on the various players in the competing companies, then spent the next two hours pulling credit and corporate filing information. It was more tedious than not, but she eventually wound her way to the top dog in the corporate chain, a vast holding company for a consortium of venture capitalists. One of them was on the board of the company facing takeover—oh, the intrigues of business. She typed up her notes and e-mailed the report to Emilio.

She felt pretty good. She hadn't even thought about Tamara. Much. She would just go on with her work and wait for Tamara to decide what next. If she didn't hear from her by tonight, she would make contact herself.

She was down to nearly three hundred files left to go when her desk phone rang. Without lifting her gaze from the numbers she was copying, she snatched it up and said, "Barrett."

"One would think you hadn't eaten last night."

"Sorry, I'm trying to meet a deadline." Tell me what you want, Kip wanted to say. Give me a clue, anything, so my heart can beat steadily again.

"I have some information for you. And before you ask, no, it's nothing you can trust without question since I did it myself."

"Could you tell me more about that, please?" Kip tried to use an ordinary tone in case any of her near neighbors could hear her.

"Our keycard security *was* hacked, and I picked up a few traces of the programmer's style. Just little things, the order of the steps, the coding of the workaround that kept the security protocols from issuing reports, but whoever did it probably learned their trade in North America."

"You can tell that?"

Tamara's answer was immediate and confident. "Yes, within a reasonable doubt. An Eastern bloc hacker does things one way, those out of southern Europe another, the Indonesian hackers have their own stamp too. It's like accents."

"That doesn't narrow down our list much, does it?"

"Actually it does. There's only three North American-based people who can do what's being done at the banks, and I'll assume this is all the work of the same person, given the security I had in place. Two are freelancers, and both have happily worked for various employers with ties to organized crimes."

"The third?"

There was a pause, then, "That would be me."

"Oh." It's not her, Kip thought. It just can't be. "Was there anything else?"

"Yes. I have the lists of employees who weren't supposed to be in the accounting file room but were. That list is distressingly long—nearly fifty."

"Ouch."

Tamara made a noise of displeasure. "You said it. Fifty people and not one staffer found it odd. I'm not happy."

If this was the truth, and not all made up, it moved Kip substantially along her ETO. An outside-hire hacker and inside collaborator as a theory of the crime worked well. It would leave Tamara, in particular, in the clear. Except—oh why did there have to be an *except*? Except Tamara could *still* be responsible for the whole thing.

Just as she asked again, "Anything else?" a shadow fell across her desk.

Emilio leaned in, started to speak, then motioned he'd wait until she ended her call.

Kip knew she was blushing. He couldn't know who was on the phone, but she felt as if he'd caught her red-handed. She put the mouthpiece against her shoulder. "Yes, boss?"

"I just wanted to say beautiful work on that job this morning. Client's *very* happy."

"Thanks. It was pretty easy."

He left her to her phone call and when she put the receiver back up to her ear, Tamara said, "That's everything I have."

"Thank you. I need to think." It was absolutely true. The next steps would take a careful tiptoe act. That is, if she wanted to treat this new information as reliable.

"I understand. Tomorrow?"

"Yes, I'll be in touch."

She stared at her phone, brain ticking. She was stuck at the same crossroads. One road Tamara was innocent, the other guilty. The "innocent" road was much easier. Much more plausible. Decisions and swift action could happen on that road.

The other road was dark, difficult. It ended in betrayal and pain. She didn't want to go down that road, not in the least.

But she still could not forget, no matter how much her heart wanted her to, that the dark road existed.

"You look like hell, Tam. Let me run out and get you a big plate of something hot." Mercedes stacked several files as she picked them up from Tam's desk. "Don't think I didn't notice you skipped lunch yesterday. And I'll bet you're going to work this weekend."

Tamara smiled her gratitude. Mercedes' stated job duties did not include Mother Hen, but she liked to play the role. And she was right. Other than meals with Kip and Diane, she hadn't been eating properly. "Order something in for both of us and we'll keep working on this report."

Mercedes grinned with approval, having almost forgiven her for not spilling details about the rapidly fading bruise. "I'll be right back. While I'm gone, you think of something relaxing to do this weekend. You need a break. It's only Thursday. Not too late to get theater tickets or something else fun." She was still making suggestions as she closed the office door behind her.

A moment later the intercom beeped. "Hank Jefferson is on two. Do you feel like cole slaw?"

"I'll take it and I'd love cole slaw."

Mercedes chuckled and hung up.

"What do you hear, Hank?"

"I hear things that are not too good." Hank's usually easy-going tone was noticeably absent. "I'm also sending you an expense claim you're not going to believe. It took a lot of drinks and lunch at Morimoto to get Avery Jessup to tell me why Big Blue canceled."

"I'll sign it," Tamara said. "What did you find out?"

"Well, I'll just be blunt because this is all the biggest load of bull I've ever heard. You are stealing from the company to pay for a jet-set lifestyle including drugs, ladies like that model Cantu, plus gambling. You're also an overbearing tyrant and most of your senior staff is on the verge of quitting."

Tamara found she couldn't swallow. She managed a couple of quick breaths, then said hoarsely, "Let's take that from the top."

"I'm not kidding. Somewhere someone started what is getting to be a viable rumor—it'll be in the *Journal*'s 'On the Street' column any day now. It's bull. I told the client so, but he insisted he got it from a very, very reliable source. An *inside* source."

Tamara closed her eyes. This rumor had to have something to do with the embezzling. The same person or persons. It was time to trust someone. She and Hank went back to the Bureau. They'd worked long hours together and she'd never been uncertain of his loyalty or ethics. If she couldn't trust Hank, of all people, she was in deeper trouble than she knew.

"You there, Tam?"

"There's more to this than I've told you," Tamara began. "Someone is stealing from us." She succinctly filled in what Kip had unearthed.

"Wow," Hank said when Tamara was done. "You think the theft and these rumors are related?"

"Yes—I think I am, or SFI in general is, the target of both. Think about it. Why would someone who could do this think so small? And they've carefully avoided the trust accounts, which could borrow trouble with unexpected parties. It's us—me—they're out to destroy."

"If their goal is to destroy your credibility and take SFI out of the picture, this would do it. Is there anything I can do to help?"

"Start reminding your press contacts that there are some people who would stop at nothing to assassinate my character. Or to make sure I wasn't credible as a witness." That could well be it, she thought. She would have Mercedes pull together a list of open dockets. She should have already taken care of getting that done.

"I don't know if it'll help, but I'll do it right away. Diane up to speed on this?"

"She doesn't know about the embezzlement. I'll tell her when she gets back in town. She's back up here tomorrow night, I think. She's dealing with her own rumors."

Hank promised frequent updates, leaving Tam to pull her wits together. Hank hadn't said it, but if that bad press unloaded on her, every time her name was mentioned the word *lesbian* would be appended in some way, milking homophobia until a full scale witch hunt was underway. She had no desire to be known as the Swinging Sapphic CEO.

She triaged the work she and Mercedes had to get through tonight, or people would notice. It didn't feel as if she could hold things together much longer. Hank's unequivocal support was a welcome balm to her spirit. Her people trusted her, and would stand by her. But if she was going down anyway, she didn't want to pull them under with her.

The best solution was not to sink.

Mercedes knocked and bustled in with a white sack that oozed out delectable aromas. "Soul food, that's what you need."

"You got Dave's."

She grinned. "I got Dave's." She slid the covered plates out of the bag and handed the top one to Tam. "Eat a bit, and then we'll get to work again."

By the middle of the wedge of corn bread Tam thought she might survive. She flashed on last night's dinner. It had been so relaxed, so easy.

"So who is she?"

Mercedes' question caught Tam by surprise. She lifted an eyebrow.

"A little bird told me you were necking with some girl in the elevator on Sunday. 'Course most people don't know the next day you had a black eye. And now you're smiling like you've just seen a rainbow." She forked up some link sausage, but her gaze remained on Tam's face.

She shouldn't have underestimated Mercedes' intelligence-gathering network. "Let's put the reports aside for a bit. Can you stay a little late?"

"Sure. My mom will get the kids to bed. What do you need?"

"I need a report of the client cases in prosecution phase where someone on our staff would testify in the next... Let's say the next two to six weeks. Start there."

"That shouldn't be hard. Ray is—"

"You can't ask Ray or anyone else. Has to be you."

"Okay. Do I get to know what's up yet? Hank is your best friend lately."

Tam savored a mouthful of smoky ham, feeling an inordinate amount of gratitude for smoke, ham and Mercedes. She wanted to share this meal with Kip while they were out on the lake some sunny summer afternoon. She didn't want to be here, dealing with this.

She hoped Mercedes would understand. "What you don't know you won't have to deny knowing."

"But something's up. Hank and Diane know. Ted?"

She shook her head. "Flu. Just as well."

"Cary?"

She shook her head again. "Not her bailiwick." She thought wryly that her head of finance was just about the only accounting-related person who *hadn't* been in the file room in the last two months, which was as it should be.

"You want me to put that list together for you first? It'll take me some time. I don't know my way around the tracking system like I should."

"I know. I would normally expect you to delegate this so you can bring me my lunch." She found a grin. "Dinner in this case."

"You spoiled Yankee," Mercedes said. She mopped up the last of her baked beans with her biscuit. "Let me get going."

As soon as Mercedes left the room, Tam reached for her phone. When Kip didn't answer her mobile, she tried her desk extension. She listened to it ring, two, three times, then Kip answered.

"I have more—"

"Hi, Carol," Kip interrupted. "This isn't a good time. Can I get back to you?"

She could hear a hubbub near Kip—sounded like someone's birthday. "Yes. A call here isn't wise. Why don't I call you on your mobile later tonight?"

"Yes, that will be fine."

A raucous chorus of *Happy Birthday*—the Beatles' version—started up before the line went dead.

She turned her attention to reports, but could not recall the last time she'd celebrated her birthday with a party. Probably because she wasn't exactly sure when her birthday was.

CHAPTER NINE

When Tam pushed the last report away with her final notes she realized how late it was. Nearly eight o'clock. Mercedes had been gone for an hour, finally leaving what met Mercedes' standards as an acceptable report on their cases currently being prosecuted.

She checked her voice mail, but there was no message from Kip, not that she expected one. She slipped Mercedes' report into her briefcase and went all the way to her car before calling Kip. She answered on the second ring.

"I'm sorry to be so late."

"No, not at all." Kip sounded weary.

"I have additional information for you. You need to hear it."

"I'm ready."

"It's..." Tam knew she could tell Kip over the phone, except she wanted to see Kip's face when she explained there was a rumor that Tam was living the high life with other women. After the kiss that should have never happened, and the awareness that Kip still thought she might be a suspect, she wanted to plead her innocence in person. She craved Kip's trust. And she shouldn't, she knew that, but telling herself so wasn't making a bit of difference.

"Do you need to tell me in person?" Kip's voice softened. "I'm not sure that's such a good idea."

"It's essential." Was that the truth? Tam wasn't sure.

There was a long pause, then Kip said finally, "Then I suppose you had better come by."

"I'll be about twenty minutes," she said.

She stared into the dark for a few minutes, knowing what she ought to do, which was call Kip back and tell her the information over the phone, then go home to a tall whiskey and her cold bed.

Kip stared at the phone for several minutes. She didn't want to see Tamara and yet parts of her were scrambling around in what-should-I-wear mode. Right—what did those parts know that she didn't?

She needed time to think. It had annoyed Meena that Kip so often would pull back from a decision and work through permutations. She'd complained, "It feels like you weigh everything on those scales of justice in your head—and I'm never on the winning side."

Maybe it was a personality flaw. Looking at the world from arm's length made her critical of her best friend's mostly unemployed boyfriend and her shiftless father because she never got close enough to see any positive traits they might have. But it was a strength, too. With distance she could dispassionately examine complicated scenarios and find the black-and-white realities amidst the shades of gray. No amount of closeness would change the fact that her father was an unrepentant alcoholic whose promises were as sturdy as pie crust.

She had amazing focus, and she used it. So why in this case was it so hard?

She knew she shouldn't, but she unwrapped and took several bites of the slice of birthday cake everyone had insisted she bring home. How screwed was that? She'd forgotten it was her own birthday. If not for her cubicle neighbors she might not have remembered until Saturday, when her calendar would remind her that she was due at Jen's for dinner. Hello thirty-four.

Tamara would be here soon and she probably ought to stop eating just the frosting. A sugar buzz wasn't helping. Her cell phone rang, which at least stopped her from the face-plant in the cake. She hoped that thinking of her father hadn't caused him to call. It was always about money.

It wasn't her father, but definitely a pest.

"Barrett, you owe me. You really do. I went the extra mile for you."

"What is it now, Buck?"

"I had put a query into a couple of State Department databases—"

"I'm not sure I wanted to know that."

"It's public stuff. What do you take me for?"

She didn't answer.

"Anyway, they lag bad on keeping up to date, and today some new listings of American nationals applying for waivers to open foreign corporations were posted. Your girl's been busy."

"Could you be a little more detailed?"

"I'm gonna get paid, right?"

He was as annoying as her father about money, but he at least was working for it. "Yes."

"She and Wren Cantu—some crack-thin supermodel—opened a corporation in the Bahamas six weeks ago."

Kip was speechless. Her mouth tasted of acid.

"Did you hear me?"

"Yes. Can you get copies?"

"Sure—public record for SFI of the Bahamas. You could have it in the morning."

"I want a workup on Cantu, like the others."

"Okay." Buck sounded positively gleeful. "I did good?"

"Yeah." Kip felt dead inside. "You did great. I appreciate it."

Tamara was on her way. A confrontation seemed inevitable because Kip knew she would be unable to pretend everything was fine.

She willed her heart to start beating and her hands to stop shaking.

An offshore corporation in a country where hiding money was the only goal, where bank transfers in and out were some of the easiest in the world? Even if in the remote chance there was a legitimate reason for it to exist, Tamara should have told her about it.

Wren Cantu? Kip had seen her in a commercial for a fashion design reality TV show. A fitting companion, together they would make a striking couple.

Her lips burned at the memory of that kiss on the gangplank.

She wasn't sure how long she'd been drumming her fingers on the table, but when the buzz came from downstairs she nearly jumped out of her skin. A deep breath was not the least bit calming.

Tamara looked tired. Exhausted even—it wasn't just the poor light in the entryway. There were large circles under her eyes and deep lines grooved around her mouth. Stress obviously, but from guilt or innocence?

Kip was glad her tone was perfectly normal as she offered coffee, but Tam shook her head. "Let me hang up your coat at least," she offered.

"Oh, thanks," Tamara said absently, shrugging out of the thick Burberry tweed.

She felt surreptitiously in the pockets as she carefully hung it on the coat rack just inside her front door. No gun. No large packets of money. No spy style portable keyboard or any other hacker gadgets—what had she expected? A card printed with, "I did it"?

Tamara glanced into the kitchen. "Cake? I heard the singing, earlier, over the phone. Whose birthday was it?"

"Mine," Kip said. "I had forgotten. I guess that explains why I'm single." She led Tamara to the living room and took a seat in one of the two side chairs.

Tamara settled on the sofa opposite her, coiled tightly with her elbows on her knees. "So where are you?"

"You first," Kip said. "What new information do you have?"

"The rumors have gotten worse and they're specifically aimed at me."

"What's changed?"

"To be specific, all the senior managers are on the verge of leaving because I'm a tyrant and I'm stealing from the company."

Kip sat like a stone. Was this disclosure just inoculating Kip in case she stumbled across those rumors? "Why would you do that?"

"To support a lifestyle that includes designer drugs and designer women."

And there it was. Kip didn't believe Tamara was a drug user. She had none of the signs. That part of the rumor was laughable. If that part was untrue, then maybe it was all a lie. But there was that small matter of a corporation in the Bahamas and Wren Cantu certainly seemed the epitome of a "designer" woman. If Buck hadn't called she'd be ready to declare Tamara a non-suspect. But now... It was a good strategy: invent a big lie so nobody notices the part that's the truth in plain sight. "And what do you say to that?"

Tamara's face froze. Kip wished they were seated closer together, but knew she would still not be certain Tamara's eyes were telling her any kind of truth.

Finally, Tamara said, "It's a lie. I don't have the time that kind of lifestyle takes. I hardly have time for work, let alone play. I don't even have the time it takes to find the person who's stealing from me." Her voice rose. "Don't you see, Kip? This highly personal rumor would take me out of a witness box. This entire scheme is about neutralizing me."

She nodded. There were too many unwise words crowding in her mouth to speak.

"I have a list of the cases. The next three where I was going to give expert testimony are where we should focus. I would have started there anyway, but now we don't have to waste time with anyone else's cases."

Kip rose long enough to take the sheaf of papers. Three were circled. Her numb brain read the lines without taking in more than the case names. She read them aloud. "Markoff, Sheames, Riley. I did a little work on Riley—some of the transfer traces. I wouldn't have said he had connections like this."

Tam nodded. "Of those three, Vernon Markoff's the one with the shady associates. And still-deep pockets because only his U.S. assets were frozen. We know he had Swiss funds, but those were gone before we got cooperation from Swiss authorities."

"So he's bought off an employee to do the inside doctoring—but that couldn't be just anybody. Those were good fake jobs on the statements. Careful attention to detail."

"An accountant or investigator seems likely. A cursory search could turn up large cash deposits in their account, or relatives with shiny new cars, mothers with debts paid, that sort of thing. And if that someone is one of the fifty people who shouldn't have been in the accounting file room and was, then we're getting to some solid ground, finally."

Kip nodded.

"This means we're close to finding the accomplice and the person who paid for it to be done. But not the money." Tamara leaned forward. "Kip?"

"If I were reporting to my client," she said slowly, "I would present this as a viable theory of the crime, yes."

"But?" Tamara's expression was openly puzzled.

Her tone was like lead. Tamara had said nothing about the

corporation in the Bahamas. "I haven't cleared you of suspicion."

She gave absolutely no reaction for several moments, as if she hadn't heard what Kip had said. Then she got up and went to the door.

Kip followed her, hurrying a little. "Tam? Did you hear me?"

She swung back abruptly. "Yes. Yes, I heard you. I heard everything you didn't say, too." She grabbed the papers from Kip's hand. "You're thinking this could all be an elaborate fake."

Her voice rising, Kip protested, "It's what I do. It's what you pay me for."

"Yes." Tamara's voice was thick with disappointment. "It's what I pay you for."

"You can't... It's not fair for you to imply that I'm in the wrong for doing *exactly* what you require of your employees. You can't blame me for not forgetting that's what I am."

"You're right. I was hoping for faith and that's not part of the equation with you."

Kip failed to keep her voice from trembling. "Faith isn't part of this job. That's why we're who we are. That's why our reputation is spotless. Facts." She gestured at the papers in Tamara's hand. "A chain of evidence. Those papers are not useful to me right now. They're tainted because they're provided by a suspect and I have to vet them. I don't have the means to vet them, so they're just confusing everything."

"They cleared things up for me, because I know I'm innocent," Tam retorted.

"Well it doesn't for me." Why did Tam have to be so tall? It was a disadvantage, having to tip her head back so far, but Kip stood her ground. She had never envisioned that she would be arguing about ethics in her own entryway with Tamara Sterling.

"I guess that means I'll just keep gathering information for my own use, and fix this myself." She snatched her coat off the rack.

"Don't you dare!" Kip swelled with anger. "You'll make it impossible to prosecute the real thief!"

"So you *do* think it's someone else—not me."

Caught by her hasty words, Kip said, "And you make it impossible for me to prove it's you, how convenient."

"If that's what I'm doing then why am I here? I could have covered my own tracks a dozen ways by now. Why bother trying to trick you?"

"For fun, maybe."

"Kip." The fight left Tamara's eyes. "You're not just...It's not..."

"Who is Wren Cantu to you?" She hoped she didn't sound as hurt as she felt.

Tamara's jaw dropped. "Is that what this is about? That stupid gossip program?"

"Gossip program?"

"It was some minor story on SLY, I guess. She was at a fundraiser we arranged in New York. I've never met the woman."

"I'm not talking about gossip." Kip was lightheaded.

"Then what? She's nothing to me. I don't know her. I didn't fly to New York just to have breakfast with her, either."

"I'm not talking about any of that. I'm talking about the corporation in the Bahamas you two opened six weeks ago."

Kip may have felt faint, but now Tamara looked it. She put her coat back on the rack and leaned heavily on it.

"Run that by me again?"

Kip knew she was looking at someone shocked to the core—but was it in overwhelmed innocence or the guilt of discovery? *I can't afford to trust her*. But how could she be so drawn to someone she couldn't trust? Someone who wasn't who she said she was, who offered nothing as proof of her innocence but tainted sources?

"You, or whoever Tamara Sterling is," she added bitterly, "and someone named Wren Cantu, opened an offshore corporation in the Bahamas six weeks ago. That's according to the Department of State. I'll have copies of the documents in the morning, and from an independent source."

"I did no such thing," Tamara said. "The Bahamas? Really, their banking is digital live now to law enforcement. Anyone wanting to hide their business would go to a dozen other jurisdictions." She took a furious breath. "And I *am* Tamara Sterling."

"The same way that Nadia Rachel Belize, now Nadia Langhorn, is who she says she is?"

Tamara flushed with annoyance. "Nadia's not part of this. And her childhood history is no more relevant than mine."

She supposed she shouldn't be surprised that Tamara would defend someone rumored to be her ex-lover. "How am I supposed to believe you?"

"That's why I'm leaving. You're not supposed to."

"I'll have the report in the morning. We can talk about it after that."

"I suppose." She pulled on her coat. "I'm not going to sit idly and wait."

"You don't have a choice. You want to be cleared and you want the money back. Let me try to eliminate you as a suspect and then... Then we'll see."

Tamara put her hand on the doorknob, but didn't turn it.

Kip reached to turn it herself and their fingertips touched. "I'm sorry," she whispered.

"For what?" Tamara pulled her hand away from their contact.

"My lack of faith."

"I really could use it. But you have faith in the evidence, and I guess I need that too."

Kip could hardly hear for the alarm bells in her head. She prided herself on knowing through her intellect, through study and focus. She denied her heart any reasoning powers and had learned to ignore it. But it was her heart that brought her fingertips to Tamara's chin. "There is one thing I can give you."

She kissed her tenderly, quietly. Tam tasted of cinnamon and Kip abandoned herself to the moment. She would think later.

Tam said her name as their lips parted, then raised her head and whispered it again. Her arms tightened as Kip inclined forward for another kiss, but her mouth said, "No."

Kip turned her head and nestled her ear to Tam's chest just long enough to hear her heart pound once, twice, three times.

Then she let go.

Tam said something, then the door was closed and she was gone, leaving Kip with her head and heart at war.

She didn't go after Tam. She didn't call or text. She did what any heartsick woman of sense would do: she finished the cake, cried into a cup of tea and flicked through channels of late-night television until she fell asleep on her cold, hard sofa.

The city lights twinkled with false cheer and warmth, but the beauty of the panorama from her window failed to move Tam. She made herself study the empty expanse of black where the shoreline ended. In daylight it was Puget Sound. In the deepest part of night it was a void that existed because of what it wasn't. Unlit, silent, like secrets. She found the darkness outside easier to contemplate because the one inside her was too intimate.

She put one hand to her lips, living the memory of Kip's kiss, playing it over and over. Sweet and impetuous, nothing like the woman who'd walked into her office—could it be only a week ago? Her mind was playing tricks. It seemed like so much longer. That her knowledge of Kip's warmth had been part of her for years.

This was a waste of time. She had other priorities. Just one more time, one more recollection of the way Kip's eyes could spark with light when she was roused, then she would focus on what she could actually do something about. It was time for that whiskey and some creative intrusion into a few databases.

Halfway down the glass she found the resolve to place the bundle of light that was Kip's smile, the smell of her, the blue eyes, the shrug of her shoulders, the curl of her ponytail, the curve of a hand lifted to accent her words—she put all of Kip into a ball and pictured locking it away. She visualized turning the key in the lock. She had done this a thousand times, and it kept negativity and distractions at bay.

She finished the whiskey with a slight burn in her throat, but she didn't feel the alcohol. That wasn't the point. She opened her eyes and waited for the mental clarity and peace of mind that the process always triggered.

CHAPTER TEN

When Kip came fully awake she realized two things simultaneously. Since she wasn't asleep in the bedroom she hadn't heard her alarm, which meant her day was going to get off to a rough start. The light seeping around the blinds suggested it was well after eight.

She also realized her cell phone was ringing.

"Why aren't you answering your phone? You don't pay me enough to hunt you down, Barrett."

She cut off Buck's whining. "My reports are ready? Give me the highlights."

"SFI of the Bahamas—your girl Tamara filed the State Department waiver as the principal of the foreign corporation. Wren Cantu is listed as secretary/treasurer. Too early for tax returns of course. But I found a dozen bank accounts in Nassau with that corporate identification number."

"Couldn't all of this have been done by anyone with brains and WiFi?"

"Some of the declarations are notarized."

Kip rolled her eyes. How many notary stamps had she examined in the last few years that had proven to be courtesy of Photoshop? "Did you get copies?"

"I have several of them. These are just forms. If a determined person had the basic biographic information—social security number, et cetera, it would be easy to do it without her."

Kip's mind was running at hyperspeed. Maybe she wasn't falling for a thief and in the process shredding her own self-identity and sense of morality. Maybe this was a setup. Or was she just hoping that was so? See, she wailed inwardly, this is why investigators shouldn't have attachments to their clients. Second-guessing the instincts and deductive abilities she'd trusted all her life was shattering her confidence.

"Was there anything unusual about Cantu?"

"Not really. She owes a bunch of people money—or rather, Wren Cantu Incorporated owes a lot of people money. But it's not bad, I mean, she makes a mint, too."

She focused on what she could control. "I'll be at your place in forty minutes or less. Add to the report a call list for these phone numbers." She rattled off Tam's private line and cell phone.

"That would be illegal. Where's the warrant? What happened to the Girl Scout? You know, trustworthy, loyal—"

"That's the Boy Scouts, and if you hadn't noticed, I'm not a boy."

A lightning-fast shower was followed by a scramble into a pinstriped pantsuit, leaving her no time to dwell on her impetuous decision to kiss Tamara last night. It hadn't felt impetuous, though. Part of her had been very deliberate about it. That fact made other parts of her anxious, and still other parts really angry.

She scraped her wet hair back into a severe ponytail, grabbed up a light jacket at the last minute and pulled up in front of Buck's in slightly over the forty minutes she'd allotted. He pushed an envelope out through the smallest possible opening in the door.

It was accompanied by the aroma of strawberry Pop Tarts. Her stomach growled.

Kip flipped through the pages at stoplights. Like most of the other evidence, a third party could have filled out and signed the original documents, but they could have also been executed by Tam herself, with Cantu's help. Tamara had never called the Bahamas from her private line, but she had called one number there numerous times in the last twenty days from her cell phone. This puzzled Kip because Tamara knew better than anybody that cellular phones weren't secure. She knew it was possible for a sophisticated electronics wizard to listen in or even use the phone line for their own purposes. Someone else could have placed these calls. They did conveniently begin just after Tamara's last phone bill was posted by the carrier so Tamara would have only seen them if she'd made an extra effort to look at her usage since then.

Someone else could have set up SFI Bahamas. Tam's sarcastic comment last night was the truth: a corporation in the Bahamas practically screamed "Look at me!" at law enforcement. That and the phone calls were a pattern of sloppiness. Tamara was so much smarter than this.

Unless...unless Tamara *was* behind all of it and was setting it up to make it look like someone else was doing the embezzling. Perhaps she had it in mind that she would keep the embezzled money *and* the company by collecting insurance. What a lot of great publicity, too, a company and CEO so honest that someone went to these unbelievable lengths to discredit it. It could all be a brilliant, warped scheme.

Given that there were so many unsavory possibilities, she didn't know how any part of her could think kissing Tamara was appropriate. Yet she had done just that, last night, because part of her had concluded a kiss was the *only* appropriate thing to do.

The bank accounts owned by the Bahamas corporation were listed. She would send Buck a fruit basket or something. She was willing to bet that these accounts had received at least some of the unauthorized transfers. She could confirm that by comparing the international routing codes, and that provided one more bit of information that bolstered a prima facie case against Tam. On the face of it, she looked guilty—up-to-the-elbows-and-more kind of guilty. But it was all circumstantial.

A loud honk brought her back to the now green light. Reading in traffic was stupid, she acknowledged. She quickly veered to the unoccupied curb and was startled to hear the squeal of brakes. She glanced in her rearview mirror as a dark blue sedan swerved to the curb behind her, then back into traffic, gunning its motor to speed past her.

She caught sight of the license plate long enough to recognize the U.S. Gov exempt markings.

Her heart pounding, she finished the drive to the office in a panic. It seemed as if every car was a dark blue sedan, behind her, in front of her, passing her, just turning so she couldn't see the plate. Nobody followed her closely when she swiped her card to open the garage gate, but if she was being tailed by the Feds, they wouldn't need to follow her into the garage. Her destination was clearly her workplace. She parked in her usual row, recognizing the few people on their way to the elevators as well. At least no one appeared to be lying in wait for her.

Her imagination was getting the best of her, she told herself. She continued to repeat that until, at street level, the elevator stopped and two men got on. Blue suits, white shirts, red ties and Florsheims. Maybe on TV the FBI agents wore designer jackets and snug body tees, but not the ones who worked in Seattle.

They'd pushed the elevator button for SFI's main reception on the fourth floor. Don't panic, she told herself. Federal agents weren't infrequent visitors. After all, any one of their investigators in the building could have business with law enforcement.

They exited the elevator and went directly to the desk. A few more people exited, some entered. When the elevator's doors started to close, Kip feigned confusion and pushed the button to open the doors again. It was long enough to hear one of the agents—in that "We're the FBI and we don't have to be discreet" voice they needlessly used—ask for Tamara Sterling.

Heart throbbing in her throat, she pressed the button to close the doors. It seemed to take forever to resume the upward journey.

Someone had already pushed the button for the executive offices on eight. She rode past her own floor, not sure what she was doing, aware that her palms were sweating. She had no plan, only instinct, and it felt very scarily like the same instinct that had said, in spite of every rule to the contrary, that it was safe to kiss her boss's boss's boss.

The executive floor receptionist waved her on when she said Mercedes Houston was expecting her.

The agents could be right behind her. Tam didn't need her protection, but Kip's vision was edged with a dread black. The agents would take the evidence she had in her briefcase and she wouldn't be able to help clear Tam, which was what her stupid heart wanted her to do.

Mercedes Houston was at her desk, the picture of poised, professional courtesy. Bright, inquisitive eyes seemed to recognize her as she greeted Kip with, "How may I help you?"

"I need you to give a message to Tam. Tamara. Ms. Sterling."

One manicured and expressive eyebrow lifted though her expression remained impassive. "Yes?"

"I was followed to work. I think. I'm pretty sure. And there are FBI agents on their way to see her right now. Downstairs."

Mercedes' gaze flicked to the clock on her desk, her monitor, then back to Kip. She blinked once, then logged out of her workstation and rose. "Come with me."

Kip imagined she heard the steady tread of Florsheims on the carpet outside. Mercedes led the way into Tam's office. A good six inches taller than Kip, she moved with deliberate economy.

"Over here." She popped open a small chest on a bookshelf, revealing a keypad. A few beeps later, she leaned on the left end of the bookcase and it smoothly slid to one side, revealing a utilitarian file area. "In."

Kip had no sooner obeyed than Mercedes pushed the bookcase back into position. The beeps repeated and a soft click meant she was locked in. She'd had no idea the space was here. It struck her as a purely decorative choice because it wasn't set up to be a safe room—she could see through gaps into Tamara's office.

Mercedes had left the door between the offices open. "May I help you gentlemen?"

"We'd like to see Tamara Sterling." Voice one was surprisingly deep.

Whether the gaps in the seaming along the back of the bookcase were deliberate or not, she could see through it well enough to tell that Mercedes' rigid back was to the open doorway between her office and Tam's.

"Ms. Sterling isn't in yet. Can I make an appointment for you?"

"Where is she?"

"As her personal assistant, I'm not at liberty to tell you that."

The next bit was muffled, then the other officer finished speaking with, "So you should answer our questions."

Mercedes, in a firm but very sweet voice, said, "I see very well why you believe I should answer your questions. You've been quite clear making your point and I thank you for taking the time to explain it to me. However, I prefer requests for information about private records in writing. For example, in the form of a warrant."

"Do you have something to hide?"

"Prudence is not a sign of guilt, that's what our head of legal was saying just the other day. I'm sure I can locate *him* for you."

"Look, your boss is implicated in embezzlement and drug traffic—"

Mercedes' amused laugh drowned out the rest. She still sounded merry when she said, "Anonymous is as anonymous does, gentlemen, and the only tip I prefer is on my embroidery needle. Now please let me get back to my work. I have no time today to help you fish."

Mercedes moved out of sight, and something muffled ensued, then Mercedes, in a much louder voice said, "If you prevent me from using my phone or that door I believe that would constitute illegal detention. Now you can do that if you want, you just step yourself right out on that tree branch and wave your badge around in the breeze, but I guarantee you that the branch won't hold your weight. You can't take that tone with me, sirs."

A shadow across the light indicated someone had come into Tam's office, but they were standing in the one spot Kip couldn't clearly see. Then the second officer called from nearer to her than she expected, "There's no one here."

Kip stepped back and held her breath, but the shadow retreated.

Mercedes' voice still carried well. "Please come back out here. You don't have my permission to be in that office."

"The door wasn't shut, ma'am."

Mercedes could have closed it, Kip thought, but perhaps she wanted them to be fully aware that Tam really wasn't there. "I still want you to come back in here—David, hello. This is Mercedes Houston. I have two FBI agents in my office and they have no warrants and yet expect me to divulge Ms. Sterling's calendar to them. Oh, thank you, you're a dear."

Voice one had grown quite annoyed. "Once again, your failure to cooperate will not bode well if it's revealed that you aided and abetted a felony enterprise. You're letting yourself in for a nightmare."

"Well that will be my nightmare, won't it?" Mercedes sounded cheerful. "Right now your nightmare has three lawyers on the way."

Of all the stupid things to do, Tam thought, gingerly lifting her head. She eyed the whiskey bottle, gauging how much she'd had. Too many and not enough. Kip was still alive to her, though at the moment the thought of Kip's scathing glare at the picture Tam made—waking up after deciding to sleep on the floor—only increased her headache.

She pulled herself upright, head swimming. Her business world was falling apart and she'd decided to get drunk? Someone was doing a masterful job framing her for embezzlement and she thought she'd have a half-dozen shots of whiskey for a late-night snack?

That wasn't why she had gotten drunk, she knew that. But the compelling need for her to focus on her company and her reputation should have stayed her hand on the bottle. She'd kept drinking out of panic, panic that she couldn't put Kip out of her thoughts. The mental device of putting things in a locked room had let her lock away her childhood. It had always let her put away distractions and emotional confusions.

She forced her shaky legs underneath her and managed to make it through a shower. With each normal action her world steadied, and she could go on today as she did every day, the past at rest. She focused on brushing her teeth and planning her totally screwed up schedule.

That was when she wondered about her silent phone. Why hadn't Mercedes called to find out where she was?

Kip hunkered down in the small anteroom, wondering how long it would be before she could leave. This was her reward for loyalty? Locked in with a bunch of file cabinets, ears straining to catch as much of the drama in the next office as possible? Her only thought had been to save Tam from the FBI.

There was a whole lot of bluster going on in Mercedes Houston's office, but from what she could follow, the lawyers were winning because the agents not only didn't have a warrant, they weren't working on one. They'd gotten an anonymous tip that had excited the interest of one of their superiors and had been dispatched to make inquiries, and that was all.

Which made her an alarmist. Now she'd revealed to Mercedes Houston that she had a tie to Tam, when if she'd let things alone, Tam would have sent the agents on their way, at least for a while. She expected Tam to arrive any minute, unless Mercedes had found a way to send a text or e-mail.

One of the agents, the deep-voiced one who had been speaking less, asked if he could step into the other room to make a phone call. Mercedes agreed and a shadow crossed Kip's line of vision.

The faint beep of buttons was followed by a quiet, "Thompson, checking in. No, this is a mess."

Kip held her breath. It sounded like he was looking at the book titles on the case hiding her as he spoke.

"We might have gotten somewhere, but some assistant called legal and now Hardwell is practically measuring his dick with the lawyers. This wasn't my idea, remember?"

There was a soft rustle as a book was pulled from the shelf.

"I don't care if Sterling used to be one of us. I know—makes more money now than we'll ever see. It was too soon to demand an interview. We've got nothing. Oh yeah? Like what?"

The book slid back into place. The agent probably turned away because his words were harder to make out.

"What's she doing moving that kind of money around? Yesterday? What about before that?"

Kip stealthily got to her feet. He'd moved several feet away and his back was to her. She pressed her ear to the opening.

"Nothing? Where did yesterday's go? Oh." His chuckle was mirthless. "Well that will get us a warrant. I don't like it, though. Something's hinky."

Kip's pounding heart was making it harder and harder to hear.

"Find a judge—good luck on getting quick action. Hey, I know she was, but have you ever worked with anyone here? If SFI builds a case against you your butt is busted. Judges aren't going to jump through hoops to sign anything on some flimsy circumstantial evidence. We should pull back, get some real evidence and then move. And be prepared to be met with very clever resistance every step of the way from the staff here too."

He was pacing now, his voice low and intense. "This is your deal. I don't know what Sterling ever did to you, but frankly I had other things to do this morning. That string of bank robberies in

Oregon is trending this direction. Those guys use guns, so yeah, I think that's a higher priority. No. No. Is that an order or your advice?"

He listened a few moments more, then angrily stabbed at his phone. Whirling around to pace back to the bookshelf Kip finally saw his face—she may have met with him once or twice on a case. He hadn't done anything memorable for her to recall. So an unknown, and therefore unlikely to be any kind of ally.

"This is bullshit," he muttered. He straightened his shoulders and returned to Mercedes' office. Now his voice was unmistakable.

"I don't suppose you'd provide us with copies of the corporate filings for your Bahamas branch, now would you? A corporation your boss formed six weeks ago, and transferred one and a half million dollars in company funds to yesterday?"

There was a brief silence, then one of the SFI lawyers said, "If you had a warrant I would act on your request."

There were a few more verbal parries, then the deep-voiced officer took charge of the other one with, "We'll be back with a warrant. This is your notice that there is an official investigation pending."

"There wasn't before this? This was a fishing expedition?" The lawyer's tone was scathing. "So noted."

The door had closed behind the agents for ten seconds before Mercedes burst out with, "What was that all about?"

The lawyer almost simultaneously said, "Do you know anything about this?"

"I'm as confused as you are," Mercedes said.

"Wait." That must have been one of the other lawyers. "The guy was in there a while. It might not be safe to talk here."

"Quite right. Let's go into my office for a bit. Mercedes, lock the door."

"Okay. I need to lock Tam's private files. I was working on them earlier."

Mercedes was at the bookcase in moments, gesturing her to come outside. She pushed the case closed and opened the door of a little cabinet on a middle shelf. It turned out to be hiding the keypad on the office side of the bookcase. She pressed the buttons quickly. Still saying nothing, she gave Kip a wide-eyed look of inquiry.

Suspecting that Mercedes probably knew a lot more than she was saying, it welled up in her that there was only one thing to tell Mercedes—the most likely truth. Mercedes wouldn't want to hear her doubts, and there was no time for them. She put her mouth close to Mercedes' ear and whispered, "She's being set up. Vernon Markoff maybe."

Mercedes pulled back to give her a steady look of comprehension before hurrying to join the people waiting in her office. A short minute later they were gone and the office door pinged as the keypad locked it.

Great. She was out of the file area, moving up in the world, but locked in the office. It was a very nice office, but the locked door was a problem. She could, however, make a phone call.

Tam answered on the second ring. "What's up?"

"I'm locked in your office."

"Just when I thought this morning couldn't get any weirder. How did that happen?"

Kip explained as succinctly as she could, but when she got to the agent's phone call and that the investigation into Tam had reached official status, Tam interrupted.

"An anonymous tip, and I moved a million and a half offshore the same day? Did I tie fireworks to it and take out an ad in the *New York Post* at the same time?" She gave an unamused, scorn-filled laugh. "Come on, Kip. Damn it, I have an account in the Maldives which nobody is ever going to find. I could have moved that money and made it look like I actually used it to pay my taxes and been living in Sao Paolo before anyone could prove that's not what I did."

"Why do you have an account in the Maldives?"

Tam muttered something at another driver and Kip realized she was in her car. "I should have known that's what you'd focus on. I'll tell you—do you have any aspirin? My head is splitting.

Never mind. Here's the thing. We've got two hackers-for-hire as potential perps and a connection to Markoff to discover. This guy is good, and if we don't look now, pull records now, there won't be records to pull. I waste time talking to the FBI today and I'm probably cooked. Cooked because one of my own best agents has all the building blocks of a pretty good case against me."

"I'm sorry." What else could she say? "Tell me the truth—would you have respected any other course of action on my part?"

There was a long silence.

"I have such a headache," Tam finally said. "Meet me at the juice place down the street in five, can you do that?"

"I'm locked in your office."

Tam told her the keypad code. "Mercedes is one smart cookie. If you weren't working with me you'd still be there when she got back. If you were, I'd get you out."

Kip tiptoed through Mercedes' office to the door. "One last question?"

"What?"

"You're a big deal executive. Why on earth don't you have a private exit?"

"I have Mercedes, smarter than I am in lots of ways and better than a pit bull."

Kip snickered. "Okay, I see your point. Five minutes at the juice place? Make it closer to ten."

She listened at the door, heard nothing, then keyed in the code. The hallway beyond was empty so she slipped out, keyed the code again and walked briskly toward the stairs. She hurried down two flights, keyed her way out of the stairwell and was quickly at her desk.

Unlocking her file cabinet she squeezed all the papers she'd originally received from Tam into her satchel along with her laptop. She presented herself at Emilio's door.

He looked up from his e-mail with a puzzled expression. "I was starting to worry."

"I'm not feeling well," Kip said, aware that she was flushed, but otherwise didn't look the least bit under the weather.

"Have you seen your mail? There's some kind of freak-out about agents and Tam—"

"I've gone home sick," Kip said.

Emilio cocked his head. "I see."

She started to turn away, but he said her name.

"You're okay, right?"

She prayed she was telling the truth. "I will be."

In the elevator she could only marvel at the trust everyone seemed to have for each other, trust that she couldn't find. Emilio in her, Mercedes in Tam—even the agent on his phone had first turned to trust of past experience in the face of new, unsettling information. Though they were often quick to act and lacking in cybercrime subtleties, she could count on most FBI types to crave answers and justice as much as she did. It had been a welcome reminder, too, that whatever information they'd been fed by a tipster about Tamara Sterling, it didn't command the kind of resources that would be devoted to armed bank robberies and other violent crime. At least that's what she told herself, even as she expected an agent to intercept her at any moment as she exited the elevator on the main floor.

She could trust in the patterns of FBI officers, or her colleagues. But Tam? Her heart trusted, clearly it did. She wouldn't be carrying evidence out of the building if it didn't. Her heart didn't just trust, either. There was more, a very dangerous something more—an impossible something more. She wasn't going to name it, because if she did it would think it had found a home.

Don't believe in the impossible, she warned herself. She hurried out of the building lobby, bursting into the sunlight of the bright autumn day. The canopy of sky was brilliantly blue. She loved the way the sun felt on her face. Her feet nearly flew down the street, her body feeling light, at complete odds with her heavy thoughts, and in spite of the thirty pounds of paperwork she was carrying.

She saw Tam before Tam spotted her. Tam's dark jacket

seemed loose on her shoulders while her face was pale, all angles and sharp edges. Tam was scanning the street. Then their gazes locked and Tam grinned.

Kip found herself grinning back. "I've decided you're guilty," she announced.

Tam was clearly taken aback, but said only, "My car is this direction. Let's get some place that feels a bit safer than this and confer."

She fell into step alongside her. "I will work as diligently as possible to prove you did it."

"Okay." Tam gave her a sideways glance. "This is good news?"

"Yes." It wasn't much of a moment of clarity, but it was something. "My suspicion is an asset. I can think like Tamara Sterling, a rather inept embezzler, and possibly anticipate the next set of evidence against you. Frankly, I wouldn't be surprised if tickets to take you from here to Brazil turned up next."

"I might be able to trace back an air reservation."

"There's lot of other work to do first—I'm just saying. You're guilty and I'm here to prove it. That means I stick to you like glue."

Tam's grin froze before it was fully formed. She gestured Kip into the next store.

"What? Do you need incense? Patchouli?" Kip coughed at the other smells hanging in the air of the tiny crystals and herbals shop. Her mild allergy to sandalwood made her eyes water.

"There's a car behind my car that I think is official business."

"They can't have a warrant yet."

"But that doesn't mean I can't be detained until they do, for any number of time-wasting reasons. Right now, time is what we don't have. The tampering fingerprints are going to disappear. I was going to copy them last night but I got...distracted."

Kip wondered what that meant. "Well, the agent I overheard wasn't looking to haul you in for questioning. I think they were just going to ask you a few questions but when Mercedes stonewalled them it got more about ego."

"I'm glad there's somebody relatively calm involved, but I doubt he's in that tan sedan."

"I had a blue sedan following me." She tried to get an angle to look down the street past Tam's car, but she wasn't tall enough. Not like seeing the car mattered—white, tan and blue were standard issue.

Tam took off her jacket and relieved Kip of her heavy satchel. "Put my jacket over yours. From the back we might look like different people than the ones who came in."

"The height..."

"I know. Mutt and Jeff here. We have to leave separately. Me first."

Kip opened her mouth to protest, but Tam went on, "If they're going to seize me I don't want you taken in too on some trumped-up obstruction charge. And they can have all the evidence. I want them to have it. I just don't want them to have *me*."

Tam now had all the reports Kip had independently collected. A suspicious person might think this was a ploy to dump it. For entirely unsuspicious reasons Kip said, "Don't you dare try to ditch me."

The smile she got was lopsided. "Not yet."

As Tam left she muttered, "I'd like to see you try."

She ticked off thirty seconds on her watch. Hearing no alarm and seeing no blue-suited figures in nonchalant pursuit of Tam, she meandered out of the shop, paused to window-shop and slowly made her way down the street and around the corner. Her heart sank into her stomach until she spotted Tam sitting on a bench, face turned upward to the sun in the classic Seattle tan-while-you-can pose.

"So what do we do now?"

Tam opened one eye, still looking the picture of lunchtime relaxation. "I probably should ditch you."

"I don't think so."

"This isn't a movie, Kip."

"I know that."

Tam met her gaze. "This isn't where you defy authority and

save the planet and the audience gives you a standing ovation at the end, all crimes expunged."

"I know. And I'm not going anywhere. You're my prime suspect. It's my duty."

"You could go to the FBI and tell them what you know. Just put it out there. And walk away, because you haven't done a single thing wrong."

"And I still haven't. It's perfectly lawful for me to go into the parking garage and get my car."

Tam's eyes darkened to a steel-gray. "Will you promise me that if you're challenged, you'll cooperate? Give them every hunch and idea you've had?"

Kip swung the heavy satchel over her shoulder. "Okay, we'll let the FBI decide what I do next. But if I pull up in my car in the next five minutes, you're getting in."

Tam watched Kip's trim figure, lopsided from her heavy load, walk briskly toward the parking garage and out of her sight. In spite of her promise, she seriously considered walking away. She could probably get just as far on her own, and not endanger Kip while she did it.

She didn't want to run so far that Kip couldn't find her. Besides, she had no reason to run She was innocent. All she needed was a few more days, maybe forty-eight hours total. Just because Kip had overheard a threat of a warrant to arrest her didn't mean that a warrant yet existed, or that one ever would exist. Leaving the area wasn't a crime.

But it would surely look guilty. Because she was an ex-agent, there would be those who would make her a priority—she knew how they felt about their own gone bad. They'd sift through her life. What if someone else finally stumbled over what Kip had and brought up her lack of proof of identity? Wanted to know where she'd spent her childhood? Fine, well, she hadn't ever wanted it to be public information, but disclosure in the context of a criminal investigation was the last way she'd ever wanted her parentage to come to light. The court of public opinion took the flimsiest of suspicions and indicted a person's entire life these days. It would only take one well-financed blogger with advertisers to please to do her in, like those slimy people at SLY. Witch hunts sold ads and drew site visitors and the pay-per-click income. Throw the word *lesbian* in with those sorts of words and, oh, look at the Web hits pile up.

When Kip's car issued from the garage exit down the street and merged carefully over to the curb where she was waiting, her emotions were as chaotic as oceans meeting. When she felt like this she had always been able to calm herself, but that had backfired spectacularly last night. She would have to live with the cacophony. Pleasure wasn't hard to handle, and it was undeniably pleasurable to see Kip. But there was worry and concern, too. Excitement? Was that because she was getting out in the field to actually tackle a puzzle herself? Or was it the sight of Kip's smiling eyes?

CHAPTER ELEVEN

Kip's pulse steadied once Tam was in the car. She had expected her not to be there. "Blue suit was waiting near the elevator—just one guy and I'm not sure he was looking for me instead of you. But it wasn't on his radar that my car should stay where it was."

She glanced in her rearview mirror, noting the range of vehicles. There was at least one dark blue sedan, of course, and one black SUV, and several nondescript tan and white cars. Any of them could be official. She went four blocks in a straight line, then made a quick right turn. Several cars followed. She adroitly navigated the one-way avenue, made all right turns for three blocks, then pointed her nose toward the freeway.

Tam was looking over her shoulder out the back window most of the time. "I think we're clear."

"Me too." She accelerated up the onramp, north as it turned out, toward Edmonds. Two exits later she whisked down a ramp and turned into a gas station, circled the pumps and pulled out to follow the frontage. No familiar cars at all. "Now I'm sure."

"We can't use our credit cards," Tam said. "Not until we want to be found."

"I know. At least, not after we leave the expected radius they'd attribute to Seattle."

"If we stop now, they will see it as a trajectory toward my house, and we're not going there."

Kip nodded. "There's a branch of my bank right over there. I can withdraw cash."

"Not you. There's no reason for you to empty an account and it'll just look guilty. This is about me so let's keep it that way as much as we can. Exit west on Denny. My banks are there, and I can make a cash withdrawal that will likely see us into another car and a hotel for a few days."

"We don't need a hotel. I have something better in mind. But we'll need supplies." She followed Tam's directions and pulled into a parking space outside a local bank. "I'll have some clothes, but you'll need something more than a suit."

"Where?"

Kip decided she could be mysterious too. "You need flannel. Lots and lots of flannel."

"I like flannel."

She nearly said that she liked women who liked flannel, but thought better of it.

Tam tossed Kip a reassuring smile over her shoulder as she went into her bank. She knew where Seattle Central Savings and Loan ranked in the Federal Reserve Bank's posting order in District 12—almost last, since they were small. If she used a withdrawal slip, not her ATM card, she could get more cash and it would take hours longer to show up to those monitoring her financial activity. ATM and credit card activity were reported almost instantly.

"Off to Vegas," she told the teller when she presented her slip.

Without any special reaction, the teller asked if she wanted it in hundreds.

She did. A few minutes later she walked out the door with just under the federal reporting limit of ten thousand dollars in cash.

She paused at Kip's driver door, and after Kip lowered the window explained, "My regular bank is just across the street. I'll walk over. Why don't I meet you in the department store lot?"

Kip was clearly anxious, but agreed. "We have to get you some clothes anyway."

If Tam had wanted to, she could have pretended it was just any other day. She was out enjoying the crisp fall air, running errands, doing a little banking. On foot because it was a beautiful day and she would shortly be off on an adventure with an attractive, passionate woman.

That's the way it should have been, anyway, for some other woman. For more reasons than one, Tam had never been much like other women.

She repeated the Vegas line, accepted another stack of bills and tucked it in her other inner jacket pocket. Cash was annoyingly bulky, but it had certainly been easier to catch bad guys when it was the preferred way to move funds.

Kip was waiting at the department store doors. "I have extras of everything where we're going, so you don't need much. It's forested and gets quite cold at night so you'll need warm layers."

"And there's a satellite signal?"

"No," Kip said seriously. "No, there's no signal at all out there. We can crack this case without the World Wide Web."

"I need—oh. You make joke."

"You ask silly question so yes, I make joke."

"You sounded like Mercedes."

"Why thank you," Kip said. She was smiling.

In less than thirty minutes Tam acquired sweats, jeans and a flannel shirt, plus some long-sleeved tees and undergarment necessities. It was only another thirty minutes before they'd stocked up on basic groceries and cans of soup. A few blocks away they ducked into a large electronics store and Tam, aching over the loss of access to her beautiful laptop sitting in her abandoned car, purchased a microcomputer with high-end processors and embedded wireless. A small wireless printer and several reams of paper finished the purchase.

"That was efficient." Kip shoved the last bag into the trunk. "So what are we going to do about my car? If they get serious, they'll be looking for it. I made it easy—it's LoJacked."

"A sensible precaution, but problematic for us." She pushed the trunk closed.

"I didn't expect to be on the run from the law."

Tam settled into the passenger seat. "We're not on the run from the law. We're just avoiding finding out for sure that they're looking for either of us."

"That's comforting." Kip's grip was tight on the wheel as she backed out.

"It's not too late," Tam said.

"I'm anxious. I'm just venting."

She studied Kip's expression. The line of her lips was steady, but her fine eyebrows were drawn together by a deep crease of worry.

"I do that a lot," Kip added. "Probably from living alone. I talk to myself way too much. Do you do that?"

"No," Tam said. "Silence was rewarded when I was a kid." A major understatement, she thought.

Kip turned them southward, toward Tacoma. Finding a used car lot wouldn't be hard once they left Seattle behind. "Cell phones," she said abruptly. She fished in her pocket, one hand on the wheel and handed the device to Tam. "Pop the battery."

"I should have thought of it," Tam admitted. The GPS locator was its own form of LoJack for people.

"That reminds me." Kip turned into a strip mall. "I have to make a couple of calls. There might be a land line at that Laundromat."

Tam had no reason to think Kip was going to turn her in, but the worry crossed her mind. She wanted to know that Kip trusted her, but she was still not very good at reading Kip's expressions. "I may as well call my people, too."

There was a pay phone next to the Laundromat's change machine, and Kip went first. Tam moved off a bit so as not to eavesdrop, but there were no customers using machines so Kip's voice carried.

"Hi, Jen, I am *really* sorry to do this to you, and I hope you haven't gone to a lot of trouble, but I have to cancel dinner tomorrow night. If you already made the cake maybe you can freeze me a slice? I'm so sorry, it's... I have to go out of town unexpectedly. Please don't worry." Kip's voice trailed away for a moment. "I know you're at work. And...if... It's just that... You're the one who always says don't trust what you read in the papers, okay? Remember that, okay?"

Tam heard the tremor in Kip's voice. She wished with all her heart that none of this stuck to Kip. She was trying to do the best in an untenable situation. Once again, Tam knew Kip's best bet would be to go to the FBI right now and just tell them what she knew. Tam couldn't find the strength of will to order her to go, though. She needed Kip, for selfish reasons—she believed Kip could help prove her innocence and find where the money had been transferred. It was all about the investigation. Sure it was.

"Kim? I'm surprised to catch you."

Kip's tone was so markedly different that Tam couldn't help but listen. A bitter-edged sarcasm she hadn't heard from Kip before was pronounced.

"Lost another job? Inconvenient work schedule again?" Kip listened, her back rigid and shoulders tense. "I need you to give a message to Dad. He isn't? Oh. Sure, it'll work this time. The last dozen trips to detox worked too."

Tam was sorry she was eavesdropping. No wonder Kip didn't drink. She was doubly glad Kip didn't know about the hangover. At least her headache had subsided to a dull throb.

"Just tell him I'm going out of town. I can't tell you why and don't be surprised by anything you hear."

She turned from the phone, her expression still stormy. "All yours."

Tam had decided on her best course of action for the least amount of contact. She dialed into her mobile's voice mail, then used the group function to send the same message to Diane, Hank, Ted and Mercedes. "Greetings to all of you. I've decided that I need a mental health break. I know you will all carry on with your assignments as we've discussed while I'm away. If you're unclear on next steps, confer with each other. I don't expect to be off the grid for more than a couple of days. Mercedes, my car wouldn't start. It's at a parking meter on the four hundred block of Marion. I'd be grateful if you could have it towed to a mechanic."

"That's it?" Kip led the way back to the car.

"They'll understand and talk amongst themselves. I expect them to be the cavalry."

They were settled and heading for the southbound freeway when Tam asked, "So your sister's name is Kim? I didn't remember that from the report."

"Yes, after the Kipling book. I've often thought I should have been the one named after the secret agent. I loved that book. Read it dozens of times."

"I like Kip. It suits you."

Kip flashed her a surprisingly shy smile. "I like it too. My grandfather would call me his little Kipling, like duckling or halfling."

"He sounds like an amazing man."

"Absolutely, he was. I saw him on TV once, a few feet behind Reagan. He looked so tall and so strong. I think I was six and he was like a Knight of the Round Table. Everything noble and good."

"Maybe it's a good thing you like women. Hard for a guy to compete." Hell, Tam thought, it was hard for a woman as well. She'd already tarnished her armor with kisses that shouldn't have happened.

Kip grinned. "I never thought of it that way." She colored slightly, then went on, "He was gone a lot. We lived with my grandparents, but he wasn't home much. My grandmother—my mom's mom—kept us fed and when he died, I think it was good she had Kim and me to fuss over."

"I couldn't help but hear. Your father wasn't in the picture much?"

"Hardly at all. He ran away when my mother got pregnant with me. They never married. He would show up when he was out of drinking money. He could be charming and my mother was snowed for a while, I guess, because I've got a little sister, two years younger than me. But he took off again. She devoted herself to local causes for children. I think it was easier to deal with other people's kids than her own. After all, we both looked a lot like the man who'd abandoned her. She'd been on the path to taking religious vows when she met him. That would have been a happier life than the one she had."

From Kip's tone alone, Tam guessed her mother had passed away. "When did she die?"

"The year I went away to college. She caught meningitis and shouldn't have died, and somehow did anyway. My sister was never all that strong, but she went to pieces, and our father showed up for one of his rare visits. They've enabled the worst in each other ever since. I don't want to know how she earns money. She never keeps a job."

"She sounds mentally fragile."

"Yeah, well, it was certainly always easier to be fragile than to pull her own weight." Kip paused. "I'm sorry, I know that sounds harsh. I've always felt like I had to grow up because she refused to. I had my first job at sixteen, saved up for a car, and gave her rides to her jobs, which turned into me being the one making her go to work. So when she decided a job sucked, I sucked too. Keeping my distance has been easier on both of us."

Tam digested the information, none of which surprised her. It sounded like Kip had quickly become the adult in her household, at a young age. She could imagine what that was like, but had no experience of family life for comparison. The New England boarding school where she'd been placed after the adoption had required growing up, but she'd only been responsible for herself. "And Jen's a friend?"

Kip nodded. "If I have a best friend, she's it. She works hard at making sure I don't completely drift away. Her boyfriend is not one of my fans. My turn for a question."

"Okay." Tam felt a coil of worry form in her stomach. She wasn't good with questions, but she wanted to give Kip answers.

"The Maldives account?"

Relieved, she explained. "I received a financial reward for finishing college. I was capable of earning my living and I didn't actually want the money. I figured if I put it a long way away, if I did need it I'd have it."

"Was it from your German family or something?"

The perceptive question gave Tam a moment's pause. "Yes, relatives. Something like that."

The frown on Kip's face told her that her answer wasn't entirely satisfactory. "Another question, then—this has been bugging me all day. Why Wren Cantu?"

"She's a celebrity, I guess. She was apparently at some function the New York office put on. Maybe known for expensive tastes and illicit substance use. It's more sensational."

"But if she's an innocent bystander why single her out when her own people will refute the claim as well?"

"She's apparently a lesbian, so maybe the master planner thought some homophobia on the part of the masses would bring more scrutiny. Harassment for her, or the FBI digs into her life and finds something else equally interesting. Honest, I'd never heard of her until that reporter called."

"I have a workup on her. I never even got to read it. Maybe something in it will tell us why she was made a target. We could finally get lucky and go from why to who."

They drove for a bit talking in fits and starts. Tam found it hard to believe that some people were likely still having lunch. It was strange, too, that the vivid greens of the pines and sharp golds and oranges of maples were so bright, like the colors had never reached her eyes before. For most of her life, she'd felt on one side of a dimming pane of glass that protected her and let her be very good at her work. But clearly it had also leeched the world of vibrancy. Sitting next to Kip the separation was gone. Even the whisper of the tires on the pavement held a kind of music she'd never appreciated before.

"So where are we headed—some place a friend owns you won't be tracked to?"

Kip, who was craning her neck to see if the used car dealership they both remembered was at the next exit, shook her head. "No, it's a property registered to a little company my grandmother owned called Barb's Bon Bons. She made wonderful candies and had a little shop for a while, then sold them out of her home by mail order. After she died I thought the registered name might be useful. Plus I didn't want anyone else using it."

She laughed before continuing. "I liked making candy with her. I never wanted to be a candy maker, though. The company was a part of her I didn't have to say goodbye to, so I paid the little bit of fees to keep it open. And when I decided to invest in some property, there were some tax advantages to having the company own it instead of me. Even the utility bill goes to the company's post office box."

Tam pointed at the exit signs coming up. "I think the second one is where the used lots are."

"I think you're right."

"It does seem to me that your hideaway is much like my Maldives account. We had good reasons, but it looks suspicious to a suspicious person."

"Oh." Kip sounded genuinely surprised. "I hadn't thought of that. I guess it does look suspicious. I was practicing the American tradition of tax avoidance."

"And that's not a crime."

Her expression suddenly serious, Kip said, "I've never committed a crime if you don't count parking tickets. It makes me very dull, I guess."

"The majority of people are just like you." Tam hesitated. Kip seemed very vulnerable on the subject. "You play fair, by the rules."

"Or I don't take chances. I don't push the limits. I'm not changing the world. That's my father's point of view, anyway, when he's putting sentences together. Wanted to know why I wasn't out there barricading the streets when they voted down gay marriage."

Tam laughed. "You do what you're best at. You—everything we do at SFI—is about keeping the world in one piece, following the rules that are supposed to keep everyone honest and people's money safe. We're as necessary as the visionaries. There's a reason we don't take cases if the client won't agree to prosecution. I look at some of our own employees who planned to retire at sixty-two or sixty-five, and now they're working until they're seventy, and that's because their life savings devalued by half because a bunch of people played roulette with their money and not one of those people has been punished in any meaningful way."

Embarrassed by how impassioned she'd become, Tam lowered her voice and said, "It just kills me. I wish I had a way to right that wrong. To take a couple billion dollars worth of bonuses now being handed out to some of the same people who are going to do the same things all over again, because there's no downside for them if they screw up. Somehow spread that money around to people who lost more than they could afford. People who played by the rules, all their lives."

"Could you do it?" Kip looked half serious.

Tam snorted. "What are you trying to get me to admit to?"

"It's just a question." She signaled to change lanes for their exit.

She shrugged. "Okay, it's not like you didn't know. If I knew where the money was and where it should go, I could do it. I could pull the biggest Robin Hood ever."

"I wasn't planning on doing that this weekend," Kip said. Her eyes were shining with amusement. "Besides, that would make me Maid Marian and that's just not a role I've ever aspired to."

"Oh, you want to be Robin Hood too, admit it." She pointed at a billboard for a car dealership at the next stoplight.

"No, not really. I want to be the Sheriff of Nottingham—but an honest one."

Tam laughed and it sounded different to her own ears. Like she really meant it. Wasn't just going through the motions of expected behavior. She would have to think on it more, because something had changed. And she liked it.

Maybe, what was left of her common sense suggested, she should figure out how to get through the next few days and stay out of prison first.

Kip avoided the potholes of the dealership's lot. The cars were dusty, and some of them clearly were freshly painted taxis. It looked exceedingly seedy to her, but that was in their favor. No electronic filing of ownership papers with the Department of Licensing. She was betting someone took the day's changes of ownership forms in to be filed the next business day. With any luck no one would suspect they had a different car until Monday. They might even be back in Seattle by then.

Within minutes Tam had convinced an eager salesman her car had been totaled the day before and she needed to buy a basic replacement right away. It even sounded plausible that she was paying in cash to get the best deal. Kip noticed how smoothly she lied. It was disquieting, but it was necessary. They were only trying to buy themselves a couple of days to keep working on the case. Kip thought there was a good chance they could recover the funds, especially if Tam really was as good as she said she was.

The entire transaction took nearly two hours, with Kip expecting standard-issue sedans bristling with lights and men in blue suits to arrive any minute. But they drove away unhindered, and stopped in a deserted lot long enough to transfer everything from Kip's car to the serviceable six-year-old beige Cherokee Tam had bought. Then she followed Tam into the Tacoma business district, where she parked her car in a generic parking lot. If the FBI seriously looked for her, they'd find it using the LoJack codes, so trying to hide it more than that wasn't productive. She walked around the corner to where Tam was waiting and scrambled into the passenger seat.

A glance at her watch told her that any other workday right about now she'd have been having a fourth cup of coffee and figuring out how to skip dinner.

She decided it wasn't a good time to report to the CEO that someone else was going to have to finish numbering the exhibits for the Wyndham trial. Right then, watching Tam's hands on the steering wheel, she really didn't care. Emilio would find someone else to do it.

They grabbed a quick drive-through meal in Olympia, then Tam followed her directions north on 101 toward Shelton. The bright afternoon had yielded to low, heavy clouds. By sunset a steady rain made the road more challenging. The car was filled with darkness and their conversation lagged.

Kip couldn't tell what Tam was thinking. It was a long drive to Duckabush. Long enough for her to second-guess everything she'd done. In the dark, with all her anxiety surrounding her and telling her she could end up bitter and tainted, she knew she might well regret where she ended up. Only time would tell if it the journey was worth it.

CHAPTER TWELVE

Tam stretched as they got out of the car. Kip was already in the door of the little diner, making tracks for the restroom. The rain had turned into a light, dusting snow, unusual for the time of year. She hoped it wasn't an omen.

A young woman was wiping the counter. She smiled at Tam and said, "Kip says you're buying."

Tamara found herself smiling back. "Buying what?"

"Pecan pie and coffee. She said you were in a hurry to beat the weather." She poured a cup of coffee into a plain white mug, then watched as Tam sipped it.

"This hits the spot," she said, raising her cup in salute. The waitress continued to stare at her. "Do I have food on my face or something?"

"Sorry. Just curious. Kip's cool. I'll be back with your pie in just a minute." She drifted down the counter to pour coffee for another customer.

Kip reappeared and hopped up onto the stool next to her. "I figured we could afford fifteen minutes. You could change, too, if you wanted to get out of the suit."

"There's a welcome thought. I'll do that after we eat. I've heard we're having pecan pie. I don't know if I should have that much cholesterol," Tam said, her expression as serious as she could make it.

Kip gaped at her, then laughed. "Yeah right. This from a woman who ate a Big Mac in two bites. I didn't even see you chew the Hershey bar."

"It didn't take you too long to eat either, you know."

"It's not every day I run from the law," she whispered.

"Me neither," Tam whispered back.

Kip plucked a menu from the holder and turned it over to the back. A local map showed access to hunting and fishing areas off Highway 101. "We're going to continue north along here, then turn." She traced the path with her fingertip.

With Kip's head bent over the map, Tam caught the subtle scent of her shampoo. She bit back the gasp that nearly escaped her as she was flooded with the same breathless need for Kip's touch that she'd had on the gangplank, the same head-spinning desire she'd said no to the night before when Kip had kissed her. She didn't know how she'd find no again. But she had to. Their disappearing together to work on the case was suspicious enough. They would be asked if they were having an affair. No one would want to believe them if they said no, but at least it would be the truth.

When this was all over, she would be going back to running SFI, and she would expect her employees to live by the rules that had made their reputation. How would they respect her if she had an affair with a subordinate, with a colleague working on a case with her? And what respect would be left for Kip if she slept with a suspect?

No was the only possible answer.

Every nerve in her body was screaming yes.

It's not like she's asking. No, Kip wasn't flirting with her and hadn't in the least during the long drive. She'd just been Kip.

It worked, telling herself that, until Kip looked up. Their gazes locked. Kip's jaw went slack. Neither of them was breathing. She shivered with an ache for Kip to peel back the layers, all of them. Kip would see the truth of her, all the things that had shaped her, left their mark, that she'd found strength in. And for the first time ever in her life, the prospect didn't frighten her.

The waitress delivered their slices of pie, breaking their attention on each other. Tam hoped she wasn't blushing. It didn't help her composure to see that Kip's hands were trembling.

Several hours later, their progress slowed by snow flurries in their headlights, Kip turned off the highway onto a narrow gravel road that cut between fine-fingered aspens dusted with snow. For another twenty minutes they carefully navigated a steady climb. The Cherokee had no trouble with traction.

"Where the heck are we?"

Kip glanced across the dark car at Tam. She'd been quiet since leaving the diner. "About a mile from the boundary of the Olympic National Forest. The cabin's not much farther. This road's used mostly by Forest Service and loggers."

Kip slowed and turned left—it was a good thing she was driving. She almost missed it and she knew the way. After a few hundred feet, the A-frame came into sight of the Cherokee's high beams.

"First things first," she said. "Let's get some heat going. You bring in some wood and I'll start the stove."

Tam followed her gesture toward the woodpile, looking equal to the task in the clothes she'd changed into at the diner. Kip shook her head at herself. Since when had she begun ordering around her boss's boss's boss? Since when had the thought of flannel made her moist and weak?

She was glad to see she'd left the cabin in pristine order. As she busied herself with the kitchen stove, she tried to ignore the question that had been plaguing her for the last half hour. Where was Tam going to expect to sleep? Her objectivity was already compromised. She knew where she wanted Tam, but that wasn't going to happen. But she wouldn't have any resolve at all if Tam followed up on that naked, honest look they'd shared in the diner. Her clothes still felt too small and there wasn't enough blood in her head to power higher brain functions. Her body had plans that didn't include tracing employee financial dealings.

"Is that enough?" Tamara dropped her third armload of wood into the large crate next to the stove. Kip averted her eyes. Tam in jeans, with a white tee covered by a blue and green flannel shirt was a devastating image, made all the more worse by how easily she could picture Tam in nothing but the shirt. Was it a newfound flannel fetish? That wasn't so bad. But she suspected that wasn't the truth at all. It wasn't about the flannel.

"That'll do," she said. She'd left the stove ready to light and within minutes a hot fire blazed. It wouldn't take long to get toasty warm up in the loft, where the only bed was. She went about unpacking the groceries and heating water for coffee, then wiping out the already clean sink.

Tam was watching her from the other side of the counter that separated the kitchen from the rest of the open room. The watching made her nervous. When asked, "What's wrong?" Kip dropped the sponge.

"I—" She sighed. "I don't do this every day," she said. She wasn't used to sharing her cabin, and she felt such a fool, because it wasn't as if Tam was even asking for more than blankets and the couch.

Tam smiled slightly. "I thought you seemed fairly practiced."

"Practiced," she echoed, stunned.

"You showed a lot of aplomb." She smiled more broadly.

"That's a funny kind of compliment," she said. "I don't think I've ever aspired to being practiced at it."

"Neither have I." Tamara's smile turned wry.

Kip wiped at imaginary dust to avoid meeting Tam's gaze.

"Are we talking about the same thing?"

Kip glanced up. Tam was staring at her with a half-amused, half-puzzled expression. "What are *you* talking about?"

"Being a fugitive," she said. "Your turn."

A hot blush swept up Kip's neck and she felt her ears burn with a red too hot for her olive skin to hide. She struggled for something nonchalant to say, but her voice failed her.

"You're blushing," Tam said. "What's wrong?"

"I'm sorry," she finally managed. "I—at the moment I'm not thinking of anything but where you're going to sleep. There's only one bed. It's awkward."

"I was looking forward to the sofa."

Kip didn't dare look at her. "I think it's dangerous to ignore the elephant in the room."

There was amusement in Tam's voice. "It's a pretty big elephant, isn't it?"

"For me, yes it is. I haven't behaved typically." She risked looking up.

For a moment, it was the CEO of Sterling Fraud Investigations who was staring back at her, and in spite of the flannel, she was every inch the woman who had given her a job to do and expected exceptional results. If Tam would only look at her like that all the time Kip knew she could keep to her own resolve.

Then that look eased to something else entirely. It wasn't the same sizzling desire that had been so palpable in the diner. There was innocence, wistfulness and a passive acceptance that what was wanted could never be hers. The resignation in Tam's eyes was disquieting, and revealed a fragility that Kip hadn't known existed. Kip wanted to hold her, but not for kisses, instead to murmur, "It'll be okay."

I really don't know who she is—or was. And I may never know, Kip told herself. Even as she searched for something to say Tam turned to the table.

"I would love to read the full reports you gathered."

Kip cleared her tight throat. "I have them all, I think. There might be one or two things I'll wish I had that are sitting at home with the boxes you gave me, but I'm not sure. Why don't I heat up some soup and we'll sort ourselves out."

When in doubt, Kip thought, let work bury the personal stuff until it goes away. It had always worked before. That she suspected it would not work this time was no reason not to give it a try anyway.

Kip stirred in the downy warmth of the loft bed. She stretched and then sniffed. The aroma of something delectable was wafting up from the kitchen.

Her eyes were gritty from reading through pages and pages of computer code, highlighting strings of data for Tam. It didn't help that the fire made the air inside the cabin dry. She buried her head under the pillow. She'd made it one night without tearing that flannel shirt off Tam, so she could do it again.

The fantasy that had kept her awake last night came back in 3D splendor. She was straddling Tam's lap, naked, wet, aching, and slipping that shirt off Tam's shoulders as they kissed. Their skin was hot from the fire as her fingertips pushed the fabric down, then Tam captured her wrists, held both behind her back with one hand while the other...

There was no way her trembling legs were going to carry her safely down the ladder from the loft.

She was finally coaxed out of her warm bed by the persistent smell of bacon and eggs and an urgent need for the bathroom. Biological imperative trumped fantasy-inspired wobbles.

She wrapped herself in her grandfather's old robe and shoved her feet into thick boot socks. She didn't fall off the ladder, no thanks to her weak arms. Only one part of her body seemed to have anything like a sufficient blood supply. She'd always scoffed at people who'd claimed an uncontrollable urge was why they'd ended up in a bed they shouldn't have.

She gazed at herself in the bathroom mirror, thoroughly

disgusted with her vivid imagination. "You look like you're going to die from lust," she muttered. "You're not a politician. Show some backbone."

Resolved to find Kip Barrett, one-time candidate for the Secret Service, she padded her way to the kitchen to find Tamara sliding fried eggs onto plates next to crisp bacon and toast.

"I was going to bring you breakfast in bed," she said, looking disappointed.

Kip slid into a chair at the table. She wanted to ask, *On what planet did you think that was a good idea?* Maybe Tam wasn't feeling it the same way. She looked the picture of calm. Instead she asked, "How were you going to get a plate up the ladder?"

Tamara set Kip's plate in front of her. "Oh. Then it's a good thing you came down here."

"We've really got to stop eating like this," Kip said.

"Speak for yourself. I'm ravenous." Tamara finished a slice of bacon in two bites, then spread olallieberry jam on her toast.

"Mountain air. Is it still snowing?" Kip glanced out the window, but the shutters were angled so she couldn't tell.

"The forecast says light snow all day, but little accumulation."

"Did you sleep at all?"

"Yes. But I also copied out more code, if you're up to more sifting. Not a lot more, because I finally found what I was looking for."

Kip realized she was wolfing down her food. Apparently anxiety and an overactive sex drive made a person hungry. "That's good news. I want to poke around and see what I can learn about Wren Cantu. This has all been too clever for the choice of her to be random. The report I already have on her isn't all that interesting, though, so I'm going dig some more. And then I'll start sorting through the key card users looking for payoffs in their bank records. That is, if you'll give me that login again." Now she knew where Buck got his data.

"Sure. We'll keep going at this from all directions."

The ground felt more solid under Kip after she'd eaten. Tam

seemed so normal, so focused that her own wayward yearnings were easier to set aside. She decided a shower and comfortable clothes were a must, and they would manage a productive day of work. Finally, answers.

The moment the bathroom door closed behind Kip, Tam shuddered and put her head in her hands. Good Lord, what kind of cruel demon of sexual temptation could make an old cotton men's robe—too big and totally shapeless—so unearthly sexy? The world could keep their supermodels and stilettos. Kip was absolutely delectable in socks and hair mussed from sleep.

Watching her eat a piece of bacon with finger-licking relish had been torture.

The reason she hadn't slept much wasn't because she was working—she hadn't slept because every time she closed her eyes, Kip was there. Last night she would have given nearly anything just to sleep next to her, warm and close. This morning sleep was nowhere in her thoughts. Nothing gentle or cuddly either. She wanted to do sweat-dripping-down-the-back, still illegal in most states sorts of things with Kip, until neither of them could walk. Then start over.

It was just sexual chemistry, that's all. She'd never felt anything like it before. None of her minor entanglements could even compare. She had thought she knew what desire was and she had been wrong.

She forced herself to tidy the kitchen and return to the keyboard of the little computer. So far, its range and satellite connection were all that she needed, and she'd taken precautions to mask her IP address as she pinged from one backdoor login to another. She had to hand it to the real hacker—it hadn't been easy getting into a couple of the bank mainframes. She wasn't sure it was wise, but after copying out the code she needed, she left an intrusion marker. If she was lucky, that would trigger an automatic copy of the code as it existed and an independent copy would be available for the Feds, one that the hacker didn't know had been made. It would also shut down the other hacker's current access point.

When Kip emerged, pink-skinned and hair pulled back in her usual ponytail, Tam told her, "Copying code as soon as possible was the right priority. I just checked the last bank, and the transaction record is gone. So I went back to the first bank I checked last night, and the record is gone from there now. Someone is wrapping things up. Maybe they've played all their cards and are going to head out with the money now."

"You said you thought you knew who it was." Kip resumed her seat at the table as Tam tried not to look as if she was inhaling the clean, fresh scent of her.

"North American trained, but has some of the tools popular with the Russian programmers, which I think could mean he's a preferred contractor with the kinds of people Vernon Markoff knows and might want to help him avoid trial. It's the same fingerprints on every site."

"The kinds of stuff I'm highlighting on these printouts?"

"That's it. I'm going to look for those fingerprints in SFI's code for the key card access records and the security tests that control who can get where in our offices using their key cards."

They worked in the same companionable silence they had last night, with Kip using a ruler to scan down pages of code, marking particular strings with pink, green and yellow highlights. Getting into SFI's software protocols was easy since Tam had left herself a backdoor. A few relatively simple searches later she found the fingerprint code.

"Pretty clumsy. Basically, right now, anyone with a key card can get into the accounting file areas."

Kip didn't look up. "You'll see that the CEO was poking around in there, which seems a bit unusual to me."

Tam cleared her throat. "Are you still needling me about that?"

"Yes, of course I am."

"Oh look, one of our investigators was in there too."

"She had authorization from the CEO."

"If that's your logic, so did the CEO—from herself."

Kip looked up, one eyebrow adorably arched. "I never said the CEO didn't have authorization. I said it seemed a bit unusual."

"A world of diff—damn!" Her keyboard locked up and her screen blanked, leaving only a pop-up window visible.

"What?"

Tam studied the graphic, then laughed. "I thought I hit a trip program left by the hacker or the Feds. It's got a Yankees logo so I'm thinking it's a friendly."

She clicked the Yankee team logo and control of her keyboard came back. Once the pop-up disappeared she noticed a text file had been deposited onto her desktop. "Hank's sent me a note."

She opened the file and read it to Kip. "*Diane and I have some pandemonium from a few clients, others doing wait-and-see. Ted still has flu. Mercedes giving enemas to baby-faced agents. I've got rapport with senior agent, listening to alternatives about frame-up, suggesting they focus on M. Gathering that evidence too when it suits them, but not so gung ho since tix for you to Brazil delivered this a.m. How could you go to* Carnaval *without me?*"

Kip gave a shout of laughter. "I knew it!"

"You guessed it right." Tam was grinning. "Start thinking about what Tamara Sterling, inept embezzler, is going to do next to incriminate herself."

"Flee the jurisdiction, unfortunately. It does look bad."

"I know." Tam sighed. "What else?"

"I'm thinking some really good Photoshop images of you and that supermodel will surface."

Tam scanned the rest of Hank's note, feeling a chill. "There's more. *Not sure how Barrett involved. Sky eyes watching for both of you.*"

"Sky eyes? You mean I'm flagged if I try to buy an air ticket?"

Tam nodded. "I'm so sorry. You don't deserve that."

"Fortunately, I'm not planning to get on a plane any time soon." She didn't seem that perturbed. She set aside the last sheet of paper and reached for her laptop. "I'm going to get to know Wren Cantu, see where that leads me. Look for photos of the two of you."

Taken aback by Kip's nonchalant response to being put on the TSA warning list, Tam said, "Once you're on the no-fly list who knows if you'll ever get off it again."

Her voice quiet but firm, Kip answered, "It's a risk I'm willing to take to further the investigation."

But not one she had ever wanted Kip to face, Tam thought, though part of her was pleased. It helped enormously to know that back in Seattle her loyal colleagues and friends were supporting her and keeping things together. The quicker this was all resolved, the better.

Not certain she could get a message back to Hank without it pinging to him as an e-mail the Feds could intercept, she hoped he had left himself a way to see that the message had reached her. It had been clever of him to have figured out where she was likely to be searching for clues.

Kip made a noise of disbelief.

"What's up?"

"Here's a photo of you and Cantu." Kip turned her laptop around. "You look like you're about to speak, but I think the background has been cloned to make it look like you're in the same frame."

Tam scanned the source—coverage of the New York fundraiser posted on the New York Public Library's social page. Kip was right. "I wasn't there—a lot of people can put me in Seattle. I remember when it went off." She pointed out Nadia to one side, talking to a man Tam didn't know. "Nadia was delighted with the turnout. They raised a bunch of money for the business collection."

"So someone hunted around to find a celebrity of some kind involved with SFI, and then spliced you into the picture? That's... Well, I get why they're after you. They think they have a reason to neutralize you. But just picking an innocent person out of the crowd is pretty scummy."

"These are scummy people. They zeroed in on a lesbian celebrity, which is even more gossip-worthy."

"I know." Kip frowned. "It's possible she's not so innocent

in other ways, I suppose. The report I got on her shows a lot of debt. Using your little backdoor login, I see that she's depositing thousands in cash every week, just under the notification limit, and transferring it out."

"Drugs or money laundering for drugs. That won't go undetected for long. Banks in the U.S. are obligated to report not just literal cash transactions of ten thousand or more, but any pattern of cash transactions that might be for illicit purposes."

"Once the Feds get a whiff of this in her records, even if she can prove you and she never met, they've still got her for lots of other fun things. It's all a big messy scandal that has nothing to do with Markoff and his associates." Kip looked disgusted.

"And if I'm reputed to be dating her, and she's involved in drugs, then I'm involved by association. Cantu turns out to be a good red herring."

"One whiff of drugs and prosecutors don't want you on the witness stand." Kip tapped at her keyboard before reaching for one of the manila envelopes. "Somewhere in here... Okay, take a look at these. These are the copies of the waiver you supposedly filed with State about the foreign corporation interest."

Tam flipped through the pages. Her name, Wren Cantu's, a reasonably good job of her signature at the bottom. "These were filed in person."

"It's a proxy service," Kip said promptly. "Someone mailed the originals to the document service, who then delivered them to the right clerk. That's a lead to follow, since the proxy would have had to mail the receipts back to someone."

Tam jotted a note on her work log. There was a growing list of leads that she hoped, delivered en masse to the agents investigating her, would provide them with enough doubt that they ran some of them down before deciding she was their best and only suspect.

She turned to the copies of the applications to open bank accounts in the Bahamas, all with different banks, all of which had ties to other countries, like the Bank of Zurich of the Bahamas. That was where the first account, the one that had received the most transfers, had been opened. She ran her finger down the page and stilled.

"What is it?"

"I know this man." She turned the copies so Kip could see them. "Back when SFI was just getting started, one of the first cases was pulling back funds that had been compiled in the Bahamas at this bank, then transferred to their parent bank in Switzerland. I went there myself to establish our credentials and create a relationship that would let us open accounts quickly, make large transfers, and with their awareness that we were working for the good guys, and with the blessing of law enforcement, which was almost always true."

"So you met Robert Manna?" She peered at the signature and stamp. "Deputy Manager?"

"Yes. He would remember me very well." She held up the application copy. "We both liked breakfast in the same cafe. This paperwork wasn't even necessary. When we're on a case we'll open and close several accounts and all by remote access."

"So why would he have approved it? He'd have to have known it was fishy."

"I'd like to know the answer to that."

"Is he the kind of person you could call and ask?"

Tam's brain was spinning with possibilities. None of them were good. "I would have thought so. He's a proper, particular creature of habit who dislikes upset and is happiest when files are tidy and proper. But I have to take a page from your book—our book. I suspect he was compensated, which makes me pretty sad, because I thought he was one of the people in the Bahamas who disliked the illegal flow of money through their system. I tip him off, then the originals of this application—fingerprints and all—won't be found should anyone ask."

"At least we have copies." Kip expression grew gloomy. "But defense attorneys have a field day with the lack of originals. How *incompetent* the bank is, the investigators are, that they couldn't find a *simple* piece of paper, and they're covering their incompetence by accusing an *innocent* man of wrongdoing."

"I've heard that more times than I can count."

"So what do we do?"

"You keep looking for the inside accomplice, because a real person here in the U.S. doctored those bank statements. I'll follow up a hunch."

Several times throughout the morning Tam looked up from her own screen, trying to memorize the curve of Kip's mouth, the crease between her eyebrows, the way her hands moved over the keyboard. She caught herself watching Kip flex and shake out the muscles of her right hand, sometimes massaging it after writing a long note.

On her own screen, in addition to scanning the financial dealings of known Markoff associates, she planned a travel itinerary for only one person.

Hours later Kip said, "I have to get out for a walk." She stretched out her sides as she waited for more soup to boil. "Get my heart pounding."

Not that it hadn't been pounding most of the morning. Tam had a habit of pulling at her collar while she worked, and every time she did that Kip went through a lust spiral that included the delicious fantasy of running her tongue along the skin that was so briefly exposed.

She was disgusted with herself, leering at a woman like a hormonal adolescent. She knew better, could act better. But did she stop? No, she went right on using Tam as her personal fantasy female.

She had even tried summoning up the disapproval of her grandfather, which ought to have stiffened her backbone, but it didn't work. She didn't like herself for behaving this way, and yet there seemed no end in sight.

Tam got up from the table with a grimace. "Oh, did you hear that? I stood up and something went crack. After a mere four hours. I've done twenty-four hours without a break."

"Recently?"

"Are you calling me old?"

It sounded like Tam was heading toward her. Kip threw a glance over her shoulder. She thought that most of all, she liked that Tam's hair was pointing in all directions, giving her the look of a mad scientist. A damnably hot mad scientist.

"Never." She poured the chicken soup into mugs. "If we continue a walk up the road we won't lose our way, and it's vigorous. On a clear day a hike to the top is a beautiful view. I could really use the fresh air."

Tam appreciatively sniffed the contents of her mug. "Any new thoughts?"

"Nothing inspired." Kip leaned against the counter as she fished in the soup for the noodles. "I'm two-thirds through your list of the fifty or so people who went into the accounting file area who didn't make sense being there. None of them have suddenly paid down debts, made unexplained luxury purchases and so forth. I'm not surprised. We all know how to hide money, at least for a while. For all I know, they were paid via PayPal, and it's sitting in an account only they know how to access, keyed to the social security number of a dead relative."

Tam nodded. "You're right. It's not hard to hide a little bit of money."

"A couple of people working a couple of days could narrow it down, I'm sure, looking a little harder than I can on my own. But so far I have nothing. Except I didn't know that our head of finance is independently wealthy."

"As Cary will tell you, she works for a living. She spends all her trust fund payments on art and charity."

"For a moment I thought I had found something. But I verified the donations. She paid a huge chunk into the Hendrix museum, the Seattle Children's Museum, and so forth."

"Cool, huh?" Tam sipped at the warm broth and licked her lips. "I was glad to hire her."

There was a great deal of admiration in Tam's tone, and jealousy wasn't exactly what Kip felt, but it was close enough that she put it on the growing list of personal failings that were developing as a result of her entirely inappropriate feelings for Tamara Sterling. Kip Barrett, woman in lust, was not a good person.

She was lacing on her hiking boots when Tam commented, "My new tennis shoes are going to get soaked."

"The fire will dry them out again. Or you can stay here."

The expression on Tam's face, which had been professionally distant, flickered with something Kip could only describe as heat. "Not my first choice."

She led the way in the heavy, cold air, liking the thick sound of their shoes on the wet gravel. Her ears were tickled with motes of snow that melted on contact. The road wasn't so much snow-covered as it was muddy. In just a few steps she felt tension slipping off her shoulders.

"Further up the coast there are some scenic points. I love this area."

"Why didn't we take the Bremerton ferry? Wouldn't that have been shorter?"

"Mileage, yes. But time... Not really, and I like driving. Sometimes I take the ferry home, though, especially if I'm ending the weekend with a book I'm trying to finish. It's less stressful."

It was harder to talk as they climbed. Kip welcomed the throb of her muscles and veins with the taut chill of skin reddened by the sharp air. The cold scrubbed her eyes clean and she felt as if she could really breathe deeply again. The cloud cover didn't allow for any kind of view, but the snow-dusted trees were beautiful.

"I usually turn around here."

Tam immediately stopped walking. "Bless you." She swallowed, gasped for air, then said, "A little walk, she says."

"It's good for us."

"If I live. I had no idea I was this out of shape."

Kip smiled to herself. Tam was glowing with energy. Her breathing was already slowing and nothing about her suggested she was unfit. "It's all in your head."

She got a distinctive hand gesture in response, and after her laughter died the forest hush overwhelmed her. The wind moved the tall pines around them, a sound she loved, but there was also the whisper of the snow falling like faerie wings gliding through the air. It was a fanciful thought—snowfall was too quiet for her to hear. It didn't make sense that she thought so, but it didn't have to, either.

She stole a glance at Tam, who was gazing down the mountain. She looked as if she was thinking about something not entirely pleasant. Kip wanted to take that expression away, but that wasn't her job here. Her feelings toward Tam didn't make sense, and unlike fancies of faeries in the snow, it was essential to her that they did.

The hike down was a little more perilous. She slipped once and Tam caught her, and only moments later she returned the favor. Back in the cabin they both stripped off their wet shoes, and Tam took off her wet socks as well. Kip watched her rifle the shopping bags, then happily pull on a new pair.

"That's better." She came back for her abandoned shoes. "Oh, heck!"

"What?"

"I stepped in a puddle—now I have one wet sock."

Kip burst out laughing. Tam sounded just like a teenager.

Tam glowered at her. "I hate that. It's not funny, either."

Unfortunately, when Tam hopped back across the room to the shopping bags, Kip found it even funnier. Tam swapped out her wet sock and the look when she turned to face her sent Kip scurrying for the meager protection of the counter.

The pursuit was short. Tam trapped her against the refrigerator and Kip decided it was more dignified not to struggle.

Tam said slowly, "It's not funny."

"Yes it is. I cannot tell a lie."

Tam's fierce display of mock outrage faded away. "Neither can I."

The kiss was completely expected and it would have been a lie if Kip had protested. There was such tenderness in it that she melted, and even her suspicious, watchful mind was soothed by Tam's gentleness.

The responsive gasp of Tam's lips against hers and sudden tightness of her hands on Kip's waist told Kip the gentleness came at a price. One sign from her and she knew where they were headed.

When Tam let her go she looked as pale as Kip felt. Her eyes were glazed and her lips looked bruised.

"You hate a wet sock," Kip murmured. Desperate to derail the moment before her body had its way, she added, "Know what one of my pet peeves is?"

Tam shook her head, the beginnings of a smile lurking at the corners of her mouth.

"In a spy movie, after an hour of running about, guns drawn, leaping from speeding trains, everything stops, and people in danger decide the right thing to do is take all their clothes off..."

"I know what you mean."

"And I have a hard time respecting them after that," Kip said, even more softly.

Tam's thumb caressed the line of Kip's jaw. "I want your respect."

"It's not respecting you that worries me."

Tam stepped back, her arms dropping to her sides. "This isn't my usual MO."

"I know."

"Do you?"

Choosing her words carefully, trying not to be foolish, and not wanting to destroy something she didn't even understand, Kip said, "The woman knows. How, I'm not sure, but she does. But she's made a good living for herself being suspicious of everything. So far, she's always been right."

Tam seemed to be waiting for more, but Kip could not make herself add that this time the suspicious investigator was praying that she was wrong.

Without touching her, and in a tone only slightly edged with disappointment, Tam said, "I'm pleased to have met Kip the woman."

They went back to work. There was nothing more, really, to

be said about it, Kip thought. She kept flicking through employee banking records, telling herself that if they were ordinary people they'd be sated and perhaps even asleep in bed at the moment, and if this were an ordinary case she'd be picking over people's financial records with the blessings of law enforcement.

But really, Kip chided herself, what made them not ordinary? Just because the number of people who did what they did was relatively rare, that didn't make it more vital than teaching kids to read or tightening the bolts on an aircraft engine. But here they were, in a situation that was bizarre by any ordinary standard.

"I'm disappointed," she said aloud, "that this is all turning out to be so impersonal. It's sort of anticlimactic, you know?"

Tam blinked. "It feels a little personal to me."

"Of course." She flushed. "I meant that it's about the work, not the people. I was geared up to discover a personal vendetta. 'My name is Inigo Montoya, you killed my father...' That sort of thing." She chuckled at herself. "I guess I was hoping for a little of that spy thing. Practice my Secret Service act."

"I see your point."

"Whereas on Monday we'll probably be pushing a lot of papers at FBI agents and going back to work on other things."

"That's exactly what you're going to do," Tam said slowly. She leaned back in her chair, her expression serious.

Kip let her puzzlement show. "You make it sound like an order."

"Because that's what it is. On Monday you go back. You cooperate."

Her heart stilled. "Why does it sounds as if I'm doing that alone?"

"I have to go some place."

"Not without me."

"Kip, if you go with me you'll look guilty. You will, in fact, be committing a felony with people who have no sense of humor."

"Like what?" She put her hands in her lap to hide the sudden tremor of fear.

"I can take the risk for myself. I have more to lose. And I

want Vernon Markoff to rot in prison for the measly seven years he'll get. He ruined the retirements of thousands of people. He deserves punishment and I'm not going to roll over and let him screw up a prosecutor's case."

Kip realized that Tam had probably been smoldering with anger all along, but this was the first time it had bubbled to the surface. "What makes you think I feel any less strongly? That's why everyone I work with does their job. We're a bunch of meddling, righteous Boy Scouts—and Girl Scouts," she added. "Let me help you."

"Seriously, you want to travel under a false ID? Lie to a customs agent?"

Kip gaped. "You're going to that bank in the Bahamas! Are you nuts?"

"It's really the only way—not the bank. The manager. I need the piece of paper, not a copy, and if I wait, it'll be gone."

"The FBI can get to it faster. They'll just ask a counterpart in country, from the embassy, to do it."

"But they won't make it a priority. As fast as we think they're moving on their information, we both know if this was a violent robbery and not white-collar theft, they'd push every angle of cooperation from other jurisdictions—and that original piece of paper would likely be secured. But this case is not a priority for resolution. They'll expend resources to question and box me in so that I'm still here when they do make actually understanding and solving the case a priority. If I go there, it'll probably end up making them more interested in securing evidence, too."

Kip didn't know what to say. Tam was telling the truth. Prosecution of white-collar crimes was slow in part because law enforcement had scarier stuff to deal with. She had worked on cases where evidence had dried up because the Feds didn't get there in time, even when an SFI investigator had set up neon pointers right to it.

"You'll look like you're fleeing the country. The Bahamas instead of Brazil. Leaving Seattle unexpectedly looks bad enough."

"So be it. I'll be back before anyone truly cares."

"How will you pull this off?" Kip closed her eyes to think. Tam knew someone who could get her a fake license so she could board a plane?

"What you don't know you can't withhold."

No, Kip thought. I want to see this through to the end, she told herself. She no longer had any suspicion that Tam was guilty, but the rest of the world would think so based on the evidence that the FBI and a court would accept. "Everything you procure is going to be tainted. *My* evidence is going to be ruined the moment you touch it. This is not the part where the lone hero sends the sidekick to safety. I don't care how tall you are, *you* are the sidekick here."

Tam snapped her computer shut. "There's no point in arguing. My mind is made up."

Kip gritted her teeth. "You think this is arguing? You ain't seen nothing yet. Where are you going to get fake ID? Do you know how long it takes? I even know how they're made and how to spot them."

"What I know is that anything can be bought if you have cash." For the first time Tam looked uncertain.

"You need me and my Secret Service handbook. You need someone whose been in the field recently," Kip said, not bothering to hide the triumph in her voice. "I actually know someone who knows someone who can have two decent looking driver's licenses in twelve hours."

Okay, that was a bit of a lie. She was guessing Buck knew someone. She added, "And I know someone who knows someone who's a private cargo pilot. Flies out fresh seafood and the occasional grunge band to a gig. Would probably hop us to Boise. It's not the kind of information you've been seeing in reports."

Tam chewed on her lower lip. Kip could tell she was unhappy. "I don't want you to lose more than you already have."

Kip let the silence stretch, not sure that the truth would help. What was the point in saying that she had so much more to gain than to lose when all basis for the statement was from her irrational heart and really uncooperative body?

She opted for the other truth, the one that shouldn't have been but was vastly less important to her now. "You're still my suspect. I'm still trying to prove you're guilty...or not. I can't justify to anyone letting you go anywhere on your own. I show up Monday morning without you, knowing what I know? The FBI isn't going to want to hear a word I say until they catch you. I know I'm already guilty of bending my job more than I should. I've already violated the SFI code of conduct a half dozen ways, but deciding on a course of action and seeing it through is going to fly better than looking like I didn't have a plan. Like I let my intuition...and, and well, other feelings...run right over the facts."

"And this is your plan? Go down the drain with me?"

"If I have to." She'd go anywhere, she thought, but she wasn't going to admit it. "Don't ask me to be less than I am."

"Let's get one thing clear then." Tam wasn't smiling. "I'm not your sidekick."

Kip didn't smile either. "We each have our own agenda and needs, so okay. If you're not the sidekick, neither am I."

They went back to work in a stony silence that Kip welcomed. At least it meant her libido wasn't operating and that made it easier to think. She plunked another employee key card number into the internal database, pulled up the employee social security number and mined the credit bureau site for banking references. No brand-new vacation homes, no out of country travel, blah, blah, blah. Another dead end.

Just like with numbering exhibits, she kept at it, search after search, methodically crossing names off the list and noting every result in her work log.

She was forty-six names down and eight to go when she hit a snag. Frowning, she tried the search on the key card again.

She broke the long silence with, "I've got a key card that's not linking to an employee."

"That's not possible," was the clipped reply.

She said nothing as she rhythmically drummed her fingers on her keyboard.

"It's not supposed to be possible," Tam finally amended.

She read the key card number to Tam, who quickly confirmed her findings then muttered about the transmission speed of the connection. "Someone inserted the key card number into the database and then turned off the warning. Clumsy again—sooner or later someone issuing key cards was going to realize that the card-employee matchup safeguard wasn't working."

"Whoever this is knew they only had to hold the scheme together for about two months."

"So that's all been no help at all. Person unknown with a fake key card gets into the accounting file area and does the doctoring of the paper statements."

Kip nodded. "The time stamps of the card use are after hours—but not middle of the night. They'd look like someone working late. Of course, now that I'm looking, I see that the card was never used during working hours. So this is our insider: Jane Smith. Not a clue how we could figure out who that really is. Likely a woman, but that's little help."

"We'd have to find the card. Damn—one big fat dead end."

"So..."

Tam looked at her inquiringly.

"You got a swimsuit?"

She pursed her lips. "I refuse to laugh."

"Oh, c'mon." Kip's stomach growled. "I might not be the sidekick, but sometimes I'm the quirky comic relief."

Her reward was the tiniest twitch of one side of Tam's mouth. It was enough for now.

"Burgers, and I know where there's a land line. I can make a call to someone about the IDs we need."

She wasn't sure what Tam was going to say, but her stomach growled loudly enough for Kip to hear, right on cue. Burgers it was.

CHAPTER THIRTEEN

Listening to Kip on the phone with her sister Kim had given Tam new insights into how Kip had become the woman she was. Listening to her wrangle with some guy named Buck was another revelation—and quite entertaining.

"I know you know someone. You watch *Dark Angel* every night, same episodes. The electromagnetic pulse is coming, so don't tell me you haven't figured out a way to get out of town under another name. No, but I'll give you a finder's fee later. No, you have to wait for it." She listened.

Just when Tam thought Kip's eyes couldn't roll any further back in her head, she snorted and said, "What part of 'I need a fake ID in a hurry' don't you understand? I don't have time to drop off a muffin basket and shower you with cash. I'll make it up to you. You know that I've never not come through for you."

Kip glared at the phone. "Yes, this is a Girl Scout thing. So where is this artiste? Lake Oswego, you mean in Oregon? No, I don't know of another one. Address? Oh please—give me a break. A winery? Your *sister*?"

Kip gave Tam an incredulous look. Tam hoped her skepticism showed. "Call me back at this number. Land line of course. Who did you think you were dealing with?"

The number for their order was called and Tam returned to the car with a fragrant bag of fried goodies just as Kip got in as well.

"So he's calling his sister, who apparently is actually a winemaker, but makes a little ka-ching on the side with candid photography. If this works out, it's actually good news. The charter I was hoping we could buy our way onto flies out of Portland from the municipal airport. We have to share space with crates of shellfish."

Tam considered every word Kip was saying, weighing the possibilities, but she was somewhat distracted by the sound Kip made when she bit into the burger. Their dinner was good eats, she quite agreed, but that sound... If Kip made noises like that over good food, what would she sound like over something even more pleasurable?

Tam would hate to be compared to a bacon burger and found wanting.

Not that anything was going to happen, she reminded herself.

Kip made the noise again.

At least her worry that she was dragging Kip into a bad place had her thinking like a boss again. She was the responsible party, ultimately.

The phone rang and Kip shoved her food onto the dashboard and hurried to catch it. "Thank you for calling me. Yes, that's what I'm looking for." Kip glanced at her watch. "By eleven at the latest. Okay. Well, since I'm asking for fake IDs I'm not sure what my word is worth. Oh. I see. Well then, I swear on the soul of Martina Navratilova."

"What was that about?" Tam gave Kip an amused glance.

"Seems Buck's sister is a dyke and the only reason she's willing to do this is because her brother vouched for me as a Sapphic Sister. Like he has any way of knowing. We have to go tonight. Right away sort of tonight."

"Why tonight?"

Kip said, with exaggerated patience, "Because it's crush and she can't take any time for it tomorrow."

"Crush?"

"Grapes, wine, barefoot women stomping around in vats."

"I see."

Around a mouthful of burger, Kip said, "Soon as I'm finished I have to make another call."

"I'm impressed with the way you've handled our illegal transit."

Kip let out a choking laugh. "I'm shocked at myself. My hands aren't even shaking. Maybe breaking the rules is like smoking. You stop hacking up a lung after the first couple of tries."

Tam smiled. "I think you won't get addicted to it."

"Dunno." She chewed thoughtfully. "It's kind of fun."

"Really?"

Her expression was a funny mixture of uncertainty and chagrin. "Don't get me wrong. I do like my job. I like solving riddles and puzzles—and catching bad guys. But that's five percent of the job. The rest is slogging work. It's papers and numbers and sorting things out. It takes skill and fortitude and attention. Not everyone can do it. But sometimes it's dead boring."

"I agree with you—this at least isn't boring. It beats reading reports." Sitting in a car with greasy burgers next to Kip was easily the most enjoyable experience she'd had in a long time, and the feeling had nothing to do with work.

Her stomach appeased, Kip went back to the pay phone, digging for more quarters. She was glad when Jen didn't answer and for the first time was happy to hear instead Luke's voice.

"Jen's not here," he said promptly. "She said she was sort of worried about you."

And you're not, Kip commented to herself, but that was hardly new. "Actually, it's you I wanted to talk to. I was wondering if you could give me the name of the pilot you know. The one in Portland."

"Dave Coopersmith? You looking for a bunch of fish?"

"No, a flight. Quickly."

"Is this going to come back on me? Like—I don't know what's up, but Jen's worried and you're not answering your cell phone. I saw that woman you work for on the news."

Kip was willing to bet that by *news*, Luke meant the gossip show. She'd seen nothing on the serious newsfeeds, though every day it seemed like the dividing line between news and gossip got thinner and thinner. "I'm okay—just having to do some unusual things for a case."

His voice was gruff with emotion. "I hope so, because, like, Jen and I want kids and I can't get pulled into anything. I got friends I can't see because it's not good for Jen or me anymore, and I like the job I finally found at this recording studio. If you're not gonna be good for her then—"

"I just need the name and a number. You don't know why. You're only speculating."

"Guys like me, that's all it takes with the cops. But you're not the type to drag us down, okay, I get that. And, like, I don't help you Jen skins me alive."

Oddly touched, Kip repeated, "I just need a flight, quick."

"Here's Dave's number—and it's okay to tell him I gave it to you. He's usually happy to see cash, like, who isn't?"

She fished out more quarters and introduced herself to the sleepy sounding male voice who answered the phone at the number Luke had rattled off.

"Luke sent you? You just need a hopper? I'm going to Boise and Helena tomorrow morning. Leaving at about seven a.m. after the catch is in."

Grateful he'd given her his plans before she admitted she

had none, she said, "We were hoping Boise was on your itinerary. That'll be great. Just two people, couple of suitcases."

"Okay. Hey, I don't take credit cards."

"Cash is fine." They agreed on four hundred for the two of them and she went back to the car, very pleased.

Tam seemed impressed again. "You are the Jason Bourne of this vehicle. I bow to your connections."

"I wish I deserved credit. It's not one I ever thought of as useful. My best friend's boyfriend is someone I pretty much wrote off as a loser. Nice enough, but not going anywhere and her paycheck is the only steady one. He wants to be the next Kurt Cobain or something but I think he's getting past that." Kip was impressed by the way he'd tried to protect Jen and their future from anything untoward. Jen with kids—made total sense and a kid could have a far worse father than a laid-back musician. "I'll have to be nicer to him in the future."

Tam started the car, even though Kip wasn't finished with her food. "We have to hustle, don't we?"

"If we don't waste any time, we could be at the nearest store that carries suitcases and the like before they close. Our flight is at seven a.m."

"Ouch."

Kip licked her fingertip free of salt from the french fries. Greasy goodness. "Where's your sense of adventure?"

Tam sounded a little tense. "Not very active at that hour."

Back at the cabin they quickly tossed what they needed back into shopping bags and packed up their computers and paperwork. Thinking ahead, Kip knew they both needed a little bit of tropical weather clothing, but that was a detail that could be solved along the way.

"What I'm most worried about," she told Tam as they put the last of their things into the Cherokee, "is getting from Miami to Nassau. Customs isn't going to be easy to fool, not these days."

"I have an idea there," Tam said, following her back into the cabin. "I don't want to do customs at the airport. We can get from Boise to Miami if the IDs are good enough. Cash for our tickets isn't going to get noticed the way it will in Miami, either. But counter agents and screeners in Miami—and Fort Lauderdale—are looking for cash users, drugs and illegal entry out of and into the country. I think we'd get caught."

Kip made sure the stove was tightly shut, forcing the last of the embers to safely die, then checked the back door to be sure it was locked. The perishable food they wouldn't be able to eat she put in the freezer, knowing she'd have to deal with throwing it out when they came back.

Like that's going to happen, she scolded herself. Why would Tam come back here? Tam had a life to go return to, and so did she. Well, what passed for a life, she thought. There was nothing in it like walking in the snow with Tam. She loved her job but the past week had reminded her she loved other things too.

"So what is it you're thinking we can do?" She buckled up after making herself comfortable in the seat for the long drive. Even without stops, it was nearly four hours to Lake Oswego.

"Not so mysterious. Even if we get to Boise by mid-morning, it'll take the rest of the day to get to Miami. On Monday morning we can book a short cruise at the last-minute excursion agent at the port. They will be screening for known no-fly names and persons of interest, and that's not us. The paperwork doesn't get processed for another day or two and customs at the port is not exactly rigorous. Honest, they're focused on people carrying out cash and bringing back too much duty-free cigarettes and rum. Given the new big casino in Nassau, they're actually not all that concerned with aliases as long as cash isn't being moved. It brings in huge taxes and lots of tourism through the port."

"Won't it take a couple of days to get there? I'm sketchy on the geography." Kip knew islands sat off the Florida coast, but that was about it.

"We'll be in port Tuesday morning, pretty early. I'd rather it was Monday morning, but the only way that happens is by air."

"Okay—have you done a cruise before?"

"Years ago. A friend and I did it for fun, in college."

Kip couldn't help her curiosity. Besides, with nothing but the dark night out the car window, what else was there to do but talk? "Was it?"

"Fun? Sure." Tam was plainly smiling at the recollection. "Nadia loved it."

"Nadia? The same Nadia...?" Kip wondered why Tam didn't just say "girlfriend" or "ex"—everybody knew about them.

"Yeah. We met in college and an island getaway was one of the fun things we did. Then she met Ted and I was the maid of honor in a dress I'd otherwise not be caught dead in."

Sounded like Nadia Langhorn had done the Lesbian Until Graduation thing. Yet, there wasn't any rancor or forced nonchalance in Tam's tone.

Kip wanted to ask about why both Tam and Nadia had such odd childhood records, but she knew Tam would just shut down. Instead, she said, "On Monday, when I was visiting banks—that seems like ages ago now. Anyway, I ran into my ex. We're kind of moving out of the resentment stage. She had reason to be peeved. She thought moving in would give us more time together, but I was just as busy and unavailable as before, and meeting up in bed every night fizzled after the first few weeks. I let my hours get even longer and it unraveled. I don't blame her for being upset. I'm glad she's getting over it—she's even getting married."

"Do you think that's in the future for you?"

"It's only recently become an option for us," Kip said slowly. She wasn't going to admit that until this week the thought of marriage hadn't seriously crossed her mind. "I knew early on I wanted a career, and a demanding one. My grandfather was a rarity—happily married in his line of work. I didn't see how romance and that life could mix for a woman. I got through high school without giving boys so much as a glance, and it wasn't until college that I realized there was another reason they didn't interest me. And with a girl there still didn't seem to be a likely white picket fence thing. No marriage available, for one thing. And the Justice Department may not have an official Don't-Ask-Don't-Tell going on, but being out and proud wasn't exactly favored behavior. It was easier to do without."

"Nobody worth pushing at the limitations?" Tam now sounded too casual.

Kip tried to keep her smile out of her voice. "Nobody at all. A few dates, the occasional, um, sleepover, so to speak. I got on well with Meena, but never saw the U-Haul she had half-packed on our first date. She was looking to settle down. I was a mistake." Kip added, "I'm glad to see her happy."

Tam lapsed into silence after that, and Kip considered that she'd explained her entire sex life to Tam pretty succinctly, yet she wouldn't have said until she did that it was so simple. Nobody worth changing her other plans for. She stared at her dim reflection in the window. Had she followed the rules all her life because she'd not had a reason to do otherwise?

And now she did? Calmly and coolly planning to acquire fake identification, travel by plane without a manifest, walk through a security screening, even lie to a customs agent? It was all serious stuff, and yet the combined risks were worth it. She wasn't fooling herself that she had some future with Tam.

Kip seemed contentedly quiet, leaving Tam to watch the road and the gas gauge. Her own thoughts were far from restful. Part of her was preoccupied with the next few days and where she wanted to end up: with the original application of that damned bank account in her control and with answers from her contact in Nassau about opening the account to begin with. She badly wanted to put faces on her adversaries.

She wished, though, she could let the rest of her relax and enjoy the company of a lovely, interesting woman. Ask more questions, learn more about her past. But that was a two-way street. She'd had the feeling that Kip really wanted to know more about Nadia, and the past that Nadia and she clearly shared.

"Is this where you were thinking we could get suitcases?" She slowed and turned into a department store lot. The giant *K* wasn't lit. The store looked about sixty years old, a relic she was willing to bet had an unbeatable selection of camping and fishing gear.

"Yes—we'll find something."

Tam went along with it when Kip pointed out some utilitarian cargo shorts, swimsuits and basic tank tops. There wasn't any warm-weather appropriate footwear, but airport stores carried a lot of useful items, she supposed.

Back on the road, they were mostly silent, though comparing thoughts on movies provided some distraction for a while. She was flattered that at one point Kip dozed off. In spite of her protests, Tam was pretty sure Kip no longer thought of her as a suspect. She didn't want to get Kip into trouble, but everything was a shade of gray. They weren't doing what they were planning to further a crime, and that counted. *If* they got the proof they needed, and she was able to snatch the money back from wherever it had been forwarded, their technical violations would probably go unprosecuted. Tam didn't fear that part of it. If, however, they were stopped trying to get to Nassau it was a completely different matter. Then it looked like—just as Kip said—they were fleeing the country as part of other crimes. The day aboard ship, waiting to see what greeted her when they docked in Nassau, would be agonizing.

Kip murmured something in her sleep and Tam couldn't help but glance over at her, admiring the shadows cast by her lashes. It would also be torturous to share a tiny cabin with Kip.

Just south of Portland she shook Kip gently. "I need directions. The turnoff to Lake Oswego is coming up."

Kip scrubbed at her eyes. "Take that one, and then we bear east. It seemed pretty easy to find. I had the weirdest dream. I kept trying to call in sick on Monday and every time Emilio answered his phone he spoke a language I didn't understand. I would say I have the flu and he'd say fram-a-stat or warble-missha or something like that."

"Sounds like a typical anxiety dream. Or a warning from the beyond to speak in tongues."

Kip laughed. "I suppose. Turn right at the next signal. I do need to call in, though. I'll keep it very short, from a land line. The flu seems like a good, transparent excuse."

"Seems to be working for Ted."

"And left here—she said it was an urban tasting room. Very Gen X, I gather."

The headlights swept over a building that looked more like a garden nursery than a wine shop. The sign in the door read *Closed*, but the light was on over the parking lot. They pulled in next to a stolid Volvo, not far from a side door into the premises. All in all, Tam thought it was the most unlikely looking spot to pick up a fake ID.

Kip glanced at Tam. "This will be like every other ID photo I've ever had taken. I always look like I've just gotten off a five-day bender."

Several inappropriate things came to mind, but Tam said none of them. "Official photos are cursed."

The door opened and a woman, half in shadow, leaned out. "Barrett?"

Kip got out of the car. "Yes. And my friend."

"Come on in."

Once they were inside Tam paused to look around, making sure they were alone and assuaging her general curiosity. The tasting room was lush with plants and a curved brass and oak bar gleamed in the low light. The faint, fresh aroma of wine mingled with cheese and toasted nuts. In spite of the mountain of food she'd consumed already that day, her stomach made it clear that she would not gag on a nice malbec with a platter of antipasto.

Their silent guide led them through the tasting room to a well-organized storage and shipping area. A center table held empty boxes and both walls were lined with stacks of wooden crates. At the far end a computer monitor glowed.

The woman snapped on an overhead light when they reached the computer station. "You said you'd have cash."

Tam was taken aback by her first good look at their unlikely accomplice. She was cheekily attractive with a shock of short bright red hair and a pert nose over a sideways smile that warned of attitude. Gaydar instantly pinged—clearly a Sapphic Sister, as Kip's contact had said.

"Yes," Kip answered. "I didn't get your name."

"That's because I didn't tell you."

"I'd rather not call you Hey There, or Fake-ID-Lady."

"So call me Glenn."

"Okay, Glenn. Yes, we brought cash."

"The photos are fifty bucks each."

Tam frowned. But before she could voice her skepticism, "Glenn" pulled two plastic cards out of her back pocket.

"These are a thousand each. And yes, that's more than I paid, and no I didn't give you any kind of family discount. We live in a capitalist world and God Bless America."

They were still getting off cheaply, Tam thought, so she reached into her pocket and counted out the bills.

"Alrighty, step right this way."

A small side room was draped with white sheets, though several black sheets were slung over a chair. A covered pedestal held a trio of fluted wineglasses and a vase with roses, somewhat past their bloom. The featured wine was in a bottle with obviously feminine curves, and Tam couldn't help but smile.

Glenn set up a backdrop of watery industrial blue and switched on a large fluorescent lamp. She gestured at Kip.

"You first."

Kip delivered an anxious smile for the camera, which made Tam grin. The lighting robbed Kip of most of her coloring. When her turn came she tried for a squint and scowl.

"So while I check the photos and adjust the size, you guys should type out these details." Glenn pointed at the screen. "Name, address, date of birth, all that jazz. Don't make any typos."

"She's kind of cute," Tam whispered as Glenn left them alone.

"The apple did not fall far from the tree in their family. Aside from the red hair, she looks a lot like her brother, except it all looks better on her. Where are we going to say we're from?"

Tam was busy typing. "I picked a non-existent street address in Boise. I think we should use our existing birthdays so we don't get tripped up on our age, and for names..." She gestured at the screen for Kip to take a look.

She punched Tam in the arm. "I am *not* going to be Gracie Lou Freebush."

"Oh fine, I thought it suited you."

Kip glowered with mock offense and watched as Tam turned her into Pippa Merritt. "That's better. Pamela Curling?"

"Better chance of reacting to names that rhyme."

Glenn returned to shoo them back into the tasting room. "This is going to take me about thirty minutes. There's six laminate layers and the security strip. Go out there and wait for me."

Kip perched on one of the stools at the bar, and propped up her head by leaning heavily on one hand. She looked as tired as Tam felt. "There was an inn with a vacancy sign back toward the freeway. Do you want to stay there?"

Tam agreed. "How do you suppose someone who makes wine also does, um, creative photography?"

"Do you suppose the wine is good?"

Glenn's voice floated out of the back. "None of your business and yes, it's very good."

Kip snickered. "It's incongruous, isn't it? I mean, I'd be happy to sit here on a sunny day and see if I might like wine, one kind or another. Instead, I'm waiting for a fake ID and that's about the last thing I would have said I'd ever do."

"We'll come back, then, to sample the wine. Would you like to, really? You don't drink..." Tam studied Kip's face.

"I've nothing against alcohol in general. I have a problem with it when it's near my father."

"That must have been tough as a kid."

"He wasn't around very much to make it tough."

Tam wondered if Kip's exhaustion was why she was so much

easier to read. Her expression was nostalgic and just a bit sad. "What are you thinking about?"

"My grandfather. And my father. They didn't get on, as you can imagine. But whenever my father came back and swore he'd changed, my grandfather tried, I think, to forget the past. But it always fell apart and my father would be gone for longer and longer periods. When I was seven he left for five years, after..."

Tam waited for more, watching a ghost of a wry smile pass over Kip's lips.

"He was supposed to pick me and Kim up from school. I went to the car and Kim was already in it. She was in kindergarten I think. I don't know what I knew, or thought I knew, but I told Kim to get out of the car and come sit with me at the curb. She finally listened to me, the whole time my father was telling me to get in so we could go home. So Kim and I sat on the curb for what seemed like forever. What I remember most vividly is that my father sat in the car crying. I felt awful. I had made him cry, but I didn't want Kim to be in the car with him. Eventually my grandfather showed up and I guess I forever became grandpa's little girl, because he squeezed me hard and told me to stop crying, that nothing Daddy did was about me. Daddy was crying because he was ashamed to be drunk. I didn't understand then, but it left a big mark. That and my grandfather telling me I'd done a wonderful job of protecting my sister. Kim will tell you that I've never stopped."

Touched, Tam pictured Kip as a serious little girl. "That was really brave of you. You were so young."

"I don't know what went through my mind. Maybe I smelled the liquor and knew that whenever I smelled it my mother was also crying."

"It's a powerful trigger, the sense of smell."

Kip nodded. She looked so unguarded that Tam wondered how she had ever thought Kip was complicated—or humorless.

Her gaze sharpened in the next moment, not a lot, but Tam could see the wheels of Kip's mind turning. "I've told you a lot about me. Tell me something about you as a girl. I don't know a thing. You grew up in Germany. I've been there several times on business."

Tam strove for a neutral smile. "I remember nothing to speak of." Truthful, and exactly what she had been trained to say.

"What was your favorite food? Who was your first crush?"

"I've always liked apple fritters and I was smitten with a teacher at boarding school at the old age of seventeen. Miss Dunham had a girlfriend. My classmates were shocked and I was relieved that I wasn't the only one who liked girls way better than boys."

"That was here in this country?"

She nodded. Kip's lips parted and the question was there, Tam knew it. The awkward and somewhat irrational fear in the pit of her stomach threatened to blossom, but Kip only looked at her for a long, intense moment. Tam relaxed and the fear subsided. What was there to reveal that Kip, of all people, wouldn't understand? Nobody picks their blood kin.

Kip put her head down on the bar with a sleepy murmur, leaving Tam the freedom to study her without fear of being caught in the act.

Glenn emerged from the back room with a bang of the door.

Kip sat bolt upright, then looked sheepish. "Sorry, must have dozed off."

"It's okay." Tam gave Glenn her attention.

"These are done. Got it right the first try. I set the issue date back as far as possible. Idaho didn't have magnetic strips on the back at that time, but don't go getting yourselves pulled over."

"We won't be driving anywhere."

"Thank you," Kip said after she'd examined her new persona under the light. "This is good work."

"I have a bonus item for you," Glenn added. "It's another two hundred for both of them."

Puzzled, Tam took the cards Glenn handed her. They were cut from plain manila-colored card stock. In plain lettering it purported to be a Voter Registration Card from Ada County,

Idaho. The names and addresses Tam had concocted were listed.

"Well, there's a walking felony," she muttered.

Glenn rolled her eyes. "Yeah, that's the worst thing I've done all day. Just don't try to use it to vote."

"But what good—" Kip fell silent at Tam's gesture.

Tam had no problem handing over more cash. She should have thought of the need for proof of citizenship, but explaining the necessity to Kip would mean Glenn hearing their plans. "Thanks. Obviously, we've not had a lot of practice at this."

"Amateurs scare me." Glenn pocketed the bills. "So time for you to go now."

They were out in the chilly parking lot with Glenn's parting, "Come back when you want some fantastic wine" ringing in their ears.

"I feel like I just got back up out of the rabbit hole," Kip said. She pulled her jacket closer around her as they got into the Cherokee.

"Let's find a place to sleep, Pip Merritt."

She did finally sleep, too, but not until Kip's breathing, just audible from the other bed, had gone slow and steady.

CHAPTER FOURTEEN

"I think I'm going to smell like salmon for the rest of my life," Tam muttered.

Kip gave her an amused glance as they walked from the cargo terminal at Boise Airport to the passenger ticketing area. A sharp, dry wind needled its way under her jacket, and she was glad to be moving around instead of shivering. "Not salmon. Saltwater. It's all over our shoes."

The flight had been very low-key. Money changed hands, and for a nominal daily fee, the pilot was happy to let them park their car in the little hangar until they came back for it. He was more concerned that they knew the safety information than why they were flying to Boise under such circumstances. Kip had no trouble picturing Luke with his grunge band buddies and all their gear packed into every bit of spare space as they droned their way to Eugene or Chico for gigs.

Her suitcase bumped along on the path behind her, rapidly losing its squeaky new finish. Tam had stressed hers with dirt and dropping it repeatedly in the motel parking lot. "I was thinking that when we get to Miami we should ship a bunch of this stuff to Mercedes Houston maybe? And tell her where to find both cars if mine hasn't already been located."

Tam's nose was tipped with red and her cheeks bright in the midday sun. "Wouldn't it be just another fitting moment of this case to have our papers get lost in the mail?"

"I'd hate to have the papers with us taken by someone else. Official or otherwise."

"What do you mean by 'otherwise'?"

Kip shared the worry that had been plaguing her since her hasty shower before bolting out of the motel. "If a fraud like Markoff can hire a hacker, why wouldn't he hire someone else to keep us from finding the evidence we need? Maybe it's not just the FBI we should be afraid of finding us."

"You mean muscle? Guys with broken noses?"

"Yeah." She glanced up at Tam, who was frowning.

"Well, I suppose that's possible. Fortunately I have an almost Secret Service agent with me."

"Tam..."

"I know. Here's how I see it. The entire campaign against me has been discredit, distract and harass. Even if we find the evidence, and even if we're given an all clear by the authorities, it'll be several weeks before life is anything like normal. The rumors will go on forever, too, thanks to the Internet."

Kip knew that. "It's just that the FBI is worried about what we're running from, not what we might be running toward. So I wondered who would be thinking more like we are."

"I was working out motive and other factors on the plane. I thought about what exactly Markoff hoped to achieve. To permanently neutralize me, or for only a little while? Permanently, well, Markoff could have afforded that, too. But he's a white-collar thief, not a killer."

"Okay." Kip felt foolish for having been fixated on the good guys who wanted to talk to them to the point of not realizing that bad guys could want them not to talk at all. "So this is a lot of time and expense for a temporary outcome?"

"Markoff's at the limit of continuations. His attorney keeps asking for and getting them, though after the last one the judge said no more. The trial is at the due process limit. If it doesn't go to trial in two weeks he walks for lack of a speedy trial. So the prosecution can't ask for a continuation to wait until I'm available and cleared of suspicion. They would have no choice but not to use me as a witness. Without me, and likely without anyone from SFI, the case is harder to stitch together and a lot of evidence can be challenged because one of his accusers—me—isn't there to validate the chain of evidence. Markoff is the person with the most to gain from all of this, and all he needed was me out of the picture for about three weeks and in a way that doesn't track back to him for new charges. He's already gotten one of those weeks."

Kip thought it over. "That all makes sense to me," she admitted.

"As for who else is thinking like us, Hank and Diane in particular will be ahead of them, too. They've likely anticipated where I'm going."

Kip nodded and took a deep breath. The passenger terminal was only the length of a football field away. "It's about time for you to move ahead."

She gave Kip a steady look. "I'll see you at the gate."

"Promise?"

"Promise, ma'am." It was Tam who gave a mocking salute as she used her long legs to slowly outdistance Kip. It was best for them not to be seen together, not to buy their tickets together, not to go through security close enough together to be seen in the same camera shot. Tam had found them an itinerary from Boise to Miami, through Denver. They only had to get past the security here. Until they got to Miami they were strangers.

She didn't really have time to appreciate the gleaming Rockies to the west, which ended the long flat of desert. When they'd landed she'd seen forested land to the north and a river splitting the populated area in two. As Tam's distance increased with every step the wind's edge felt colder and the sky's span loomed larger.

Her nerves jangling with fear of discovery, Kip presented herself at the ticket counter. It went like clockwork, just as it should. Kip was braced for a dark-suited figure to fall into step alongside her at any moment, right up until she boarded the flight. But it didn't happen. She received her boarding pass and at security the driver's license passed scrutiny.

Her anxiety was eased by the sight of Tam seated in the boarding area, reading a newspaper. She stopped at the convenience market to buy a magazine and some M&Ms. She boarded before Tam, and as Tam passed her on the way to open seats in the back of the long, slender craft, one hand brushed her cheek.

She was immeasurably comforted. She might have spent the whole flight fussing about whether it was right, or ethical, or moral to feel the way she did, but instead an unexpected sense of safety welled up inside her. She tried to tell herself she was losing her edge, that worry and suspicion were her basic survival skills.

She kept repeating that until she fell asleep just after the plane leveled off and turned south toward Denver.

Feeling refreshed for a frozen yogurt, Kip nevertheless had trouble shaking off the effects of the brief nap on the flight. Denver's airport featured huge panoramic windows in all directions, but she favored the one that faced west. In Denver's mid-afternoon sun the Rockies in the distance were towering and nearly black. She tried to talk herself out of the sense of isolation that continued to grow. Finally, the useful aspects of fear began to make headway with her errant common sense.

Maybe, she scolded herself, she felt isolated because she was.

And why was she isolated? Because she had chosen to stick

with a suspect and a primary source of more information, without going to the authorities. Now, forty-eight hours later, she was totally dependent on that suspect unless she surrendered herself. Her inner devil's advocate reminded her that she could summon federal agents in two minutes or less in an airport.

She hoped—prayed—that she wouldn't have to explain to anyone why she hadn't done exactly that.

Reflected in the glass, several feet behind her at a narrow WiFi station, Tam was tapping away at her little computer. Last night she had very much wanted to ask Tam about her childhood. Why was it such a secret? Every time she was about to bring it up she could see the wariness in Tam's eyes. Her shoulders and stance tightened, as if braced for a fight, and it made Kip's heart ache. She kept thinking about getting Kim out of the car with their drunk father at the wheel and she wished she had been able to take Tam away from whatever it was that had shut down that part of her life.

That protective impulse could be exactly what Tam wanted. She could be on the receiving end of masterful manipulation, she reminded herself.

That inner voice sounded pathetically uncertain and weak—no help whatsoever. All through the boarding process she tried to fan the flames of suspicion and perk up her paranoia, but it just wasn't working. Instead of sleeping she thumbed through the in-flight magazine. The Sudoku was no real challenge and took only a few minutes, so she turned to the crossword. One across was a six-letter word for "One is born every minute."

She penciled in "s-u-c-k-e-r." It was going to be a long flight.

From the Miami airport they took a shuttle to a nearby convention hotel, carefully sitting some distance from each other. A couple of frat boys sat far too close to Kip, trying to engage her in conversation, and Tam watched, annoyed by their presumption and amused as Kip's Secret Service face eventually silenced them. The hotel was large and impersonal, and it was still bustling at nearly eleven o'clock at night. They registered for separate rooms but Tam slipped Kip the sleeve where the clerk had written her room number. They'd agreed to rendezvous and share a room service meal to plan their tight schedule for the next day.

She'd already logged onto the Internet when Kip quietly knocked on the door. It was all Tam could do not to hug her—so much of the day had been spent apart. She restrained herself, but it became doubly hard when she realized Kip's hair was wet. She'd showered. Even with hotel products, Kip smelled like Kip.

"I hope I didn't take too long. My eyes were so dry that I knew a shower would help."

"No problem. I haven't ordered food. I wasn't sure what you wanted."

"Considering I ate a house yesterday and snacked on M&Ms and chocolate frozen yogurt all day today, maybe something light we could split?"

Tam pointed out the room service menu on the little side table in front of the window. Kip suggested several options and Tam tried to pay attention, but a preoccupied part of her was picturing Kip not demurely seated in the utilitarian side chair, but half-naked on the king-sized bed, still damp hair spread out over the pillow.

They agreed on a grilled shrimp and mango salad and a bowl of Cuban ajiaco stew. Tam noticed Kip looked longingly at the desserts—the photo of a seductive hot fudge sundae practically crooned from the top of the page—but set the menu down without asking.

I could love her for that alone, Tam thought, just for being so completely human.

The moment the thought was complete blood roared in her ears. She masked the wave of vertigo by gesturing at her computer. "There's an upscale shopping mall not far from here. We can probably get the last things we need when they open."

"And then we go to the port?"

She nodded. "To the last-minute purchase office. There are berths available on two cruise lines, both going first to Nassau. We book, then when asked for our passports, we explain they were stolen and present our licenses and voter registration cards. The cruise line staff gives us an affidavit to fill out wherein we attest that our passports are unavailable, we are who we say we are and we're not intending to immigrate illegally or commit any crimes." Tam felt steadier for dealing in the mundane details. "We're not in any more trouble for signing the affidavit than we are for using the fake identification to begin with. This is all routine for the port. It won't really raise an eyebrow."

"How do you know all this?"

"I read it at soyoulostyourpassportandstillwanttogoonacruise dotcom."

Kip laughed. "You did not."

"Seriously. Same place you land if you query 'what do I do if my folks lost their passport on the way to the ship' on Google."

Kip's laughter faded and she looked suddenly wan. From the desk Tam thought she detected a glimmer of tears, but that might have been the light. "Sorry," she muttered.

"What is it?"

"Scared. Tired. Trying to figure out how it made sense that we're here."

Tam sat down on the bed. "I think we're going to be okay."

"You really don't think there are bad guys with broken noses out there looking for us?"

"I could be wrong."

"But you're not often wrong." Kip's expression was rueful. "When you said earlier that you had the protection of an almost Secret Service agent? Well, that almost agent's gun is locked up in her apartment, three thousand miles away. Pretty stupid place for it."

"You couldn't have brought it on the plane anyway."

Kip shrugged. "No matter. Do you really want to know the reason why I'm an *almost* agent and not a *bona fide*?"

Tam blinked. The mystery had annoyed her, true. She realized, though, that she knew what mattered about Kip. It was the truth when she said, "You don't have to tell me."

"It embarrasses me. Most of the time." She shrugged. "I failed the final simulation run. Tried it several times, but was never going to pass. I did great up until the end. You can't imagine how loud it was—big warehouse, almost like a movie soundstage with set after set. One minute I'd smell smoke, the next pizza, then sewage. There was fog everywhere and buses honking, and the sound of an overhead train never stopped. And I did great. Stalked, ducked, covered, rolled, shot the bad guys. Kept moving. The mantra, it's a rhythm. It gets in your heart. *Protect POTUS. Protect POTUS.*"

Her gaze was far away, and Tam had no doubt that for Kip, the memories were close, real and painful.

"I finally got to the limo. Everybody's down, just the President and the driver. Driver can't get out—that's his orders. So it's up to me when a figure appears out of a side alley. Luck of the draw, I guess. Nine times out of ten it's a woman with a bomb. I might have fired and I wouldn't be here. But I got the one time out of ten it was a baby, not a bomb. Didn't fire—which is fine. But right behind her, a few seconds later, woman with a bomb."

She was silent long enough that Tam gently supplied, "You didn't fire?"

"I did—but in a simulator four seconds is a lifetime. Enough time for the dummy to light up twice as having detonated. And when I did finally fire I missed. So that's your protection."

Tam didn't know what she had expected, but that hadn't been it. "How could I fault you for a women and children first philosophy?"

"I don't know if it's because I'm a lesbian and part of me just refuses to believe that women can be so fanatical and venal. It's not rational, because I know that it might be rare, but it's real. Women can do anything. But I froze—and it didn't help to have my trainer screaming in my ear to 'blow the *bitch* away.' But the Service rightly held it against me."

"So you started over."

"At the time it was the Service or nothing for me. Then I heard about Sterling Fraud Investigations and..." Again, her smile was rueful. "And here I am."

"A new life and career built."

"Not if we get caught tomorrow." Kip appeared to be studying the faded laminate surface of the table.

There were a lot of things she could have said, but what she might have chosen went out of her head when Kip abruptly scrubbed at her eyes.

"Please." Her voice broke. She took a deep breath and started again. "Please don't be the woman with the bomb. Please don't leave me wishing I'd pulled the trigger the moment I walked into your office."

"Oh Kip..." Tam slid to one knee next to her, gazing up into her face. Taking one hand between both of hers, she said simply, "I'm not that person. I promise you."

Her eyes glittered with unshed tears. "So there you have it. All my secrets."

I'll tell you mine, Tam wanted to say. Kip had put all of her past on one side of the scales. It was time for Tam to match it. She couldn't make her mouth move. She had no practice at the subject. Where to start?

A knock at the door was followed by a cheery, "Room service."

Kip sighed and pulled her hand from Tam's grasp. "I'll wait in the bathroom."

Pressing a washcloth to her eyes, Kip told herself she'd done all she could. The ball was in Tam's court now. She heard the clatter of the room service cart and had the irrelevant thought that she hoped her only choice in swimsuits wasn't a butt-floss bikini.

None of which mattered. Gun or not, she was on a case. She

had a client who expected results. Utterly convinced Tam wasn't involved, in spite of no confirmation by the facts, Kip knew her responsibility now was protecting her client. She couldn't do that if she was weeping over lack of parity in their honesty with each other.

She had felt so naked, and hoped that maybe Tam would share something, anything. It was clear who didn't trust who. At least she thought so.

Pull yourself together, she thought. *I'm sure as hell of no use to anyone if I'm worried about a swimsuit making my butt look like a barn.* Personal and professional weren't supposed to mix. That was why there were rules at SFI about exactly that conflict.

She patted her eyes dry and gave herself a scolding look in the mirror. Imitating her grandfather's voice, as best as she could recall it, she said, "You've got a job to do, little Kipling. Your only choice is how well you do it."

"All clear," Tam said from the other side of the door.

"That smells good," she said as she emerged.

Tam had put the plates on the table and was just transferring a small vase of wildflowers as well. She draped a white napkin over her sleeve. "Your midnight buffet awaits, madam."

Kip decided to keep the light tone. There wasn't really anything else to do. "Thank you, *garcon.*"

The stew turned out to be delicious and heartier than she had anticipated. Spiced chunks of chicken were in a rich gravy, redolent with roasted and fresh peppers. The other ingredients included different tropical taro, a South American sweet potato Kip recognized, and roasted plantain both in the stew and on top, crisped and in slivers. By comparison, the salad, when they traded plates, was pedestrian, but still tasty. They discussed food adventures as they ate. Tam's experience was much broader than Kip's, but none of the disclosures came close to the moment when Kip had thought Tam might finally explain the mystery of her childhood.

Calmed by the banality of talking about their meal, Kip wasn't sure she had a right to know. A couple of kisses didn't mean anything these days. She had no reason to think Tam knew that kisses weren't casual to Kip, not in the least. And even if she did, why should something so painful to Tam be any of Kip's business? Did Kip's not knowing interfere with their investigation? Did not knowing keep Kip from doing the job she had to do? If not, it was none of her business.

The dishes empty, Kip said, "We should be at the stores when they open at nine, shouldn't we? Then back here to check out and take a cab to the port?"

"That seems right," Tam agreed. She might have been pale, or maybe it was just the lighting. But her air was as professionally distant as Kip's. "There's still enough time to get a good night's sleep."

A good night's sleep, right, Kip thought, once she was in the elevator. It didn't seem likely to her.

CHAPTER FIFTEEN

"Are the expenses of being a fugitive tax deductible?"

Kip answered in a matching droll tone. "I don't see why not. They *are* job-related." The basic Speedo looked just dandy on Tam. Scrumptious even. But Tam looked as if she'd rather be seen in a potato sack. "You can stick with the board shorts and a tank top. Totally acceptable women's pool gear these days."

Tam frowned into the full-length mirror. "I think I will. This looked good on you but me... It's so tight."

"You obviously didn't have gym class in a public school in the U.S."

"You're right. I went to a boarding school in Connecticut, and swimming was not on the list of activities." Tam disappeared into the dressing room again.

Kip leaned on the wall next to the door, glad they were alone. At this hour on a Monday morning, the department store was nearly deserted. She might never shop on weekends again. "Did you sleep okay? You look really tired."

"Remind me not to have Cuban food at midnight."

"Oh, I'm sorry it bothered you. I slept like a baby." She had, too, much to her surprise. As conflicted as she was emotionally, her body seemed not to have a worry in the world. It knew something she didn't, or it was just besotted and happy to be so. She'd been relaxed until she'd seen Tam in the shorts and a tee they'd bought before leaving Washington. Then her body had been something completely opposite of relaxed, and aside from the worry that she wasn't worried, the feeling was very... pleasurable.

The last of their purchases made, they walked back to the hotel, agreeing to meet in the hotel's business center again in fifteen minutes. Kip put her heavy walking shoes into the suitcase and slipped on the new Keen sandals. They were perfect for the muggy, heavy air outside. It wasn't as humid as she had expected. Under other circumstances, she would have found sunny Miami a refreshing change from Seattle's impending winter.

At the business center, she added her papers to Tam's in a box the center supplied. Taped and wrapped, Tam labeled it for shipping to Mercedes Houston at her home address. Once the fee for shipping, tracking and insurance was paid, Kip had to admit it was a relief to leave their accumulated evidence behind. All she carried with her was her work log and her laptop.

After a quick stop at the lobby pay phone, where she faked up a raspy cough for the benefit of Emilio's voice mail, they could finally leave.

Having evaded any detection so far, it didn't seem useful to avoid being seen together any longer. At the port they were planning to pose as a couple. From the fast-moving cab she could see palm trees lining the main boulevard of the port district, and feel a light breeze blowing in from the sea. The broad saw-tooth leaves stirred lazily against the cobalt sky. Impossibly, the air smelled of coconut, if she ignored the underlayer of diesel fuel. Through gaps in the buildings Kip could see cruise ships, mammoth white floating hotels, all with streamers snapping in the rising wind.

They waited in what seemed to be a short line, not talking much. Kip was amused by several little old ladies reminding each other where they'd put their papers and who had seen them last and asking if someone remembered to bring the sanitizing wipes for the slot machines. Kip decided when she was old and gray she wanted to be the kind of little old lady who turned up for a last-minute cruise, in sensible walking shoes and a hat.

She realized, too, that she didn't want to travel alone. A much taller little old lady as a companion would be nice.

When they finally reached the counter Tam told her rambling tale of woe to the pretty blonde. "We lost the packet with our passports and the marriage license—"

"Our marriage license!" Kip echoed. She'd never thought much about getting older, but the idea of Tam going through those changes with her was welcome. Far too welcome.

"We went to Iowa, being from Idaho, starts with an I, it didn't take long, we've been wanting to get married for ages, you know."

The clerk, obviously thoroughly trained in customer service, passed over forms. "Just fill these out. You only have fifteen days to report a stolen passport, so you have to do it the moment you get back. It'll take forever to get replacements if you don't."

"Sure, sure," Tam said.

"Our marriage license, too..." Kip bemoaned again as she rapidly filled in the blanks on the affidavit. "I told you we should have booked this ahead of time."

"This saved us so much money, sweetie. Otherwise, we were having a honeymoon in Des Moines."

Kip gave the clerk her most sincere look. "Des Moines is nice. I like Des Moines. But this is better than Des Moines."

The woman laughed. "It sure is. So let's see what's available right now on the four-night itineraries."

While the agent pecked at her keyboard Kip tried not to look guilty for playing so broadly on the woman's natural empathy.

She hoped the agent didn't get in trouble for helping them out, even though it was her job to sell them the tickets.

She did exactly that, too. They walked out of the office ten minutes later with their boarding packets, stamped waiver for lack of passport to show customs and luggage tags for the *Blue Sky of Sweden*. Boarding began in three hours. First stop, eight thirty tomorrow morning, was Nassau, Commonwealth of the Bahamas.

The clerk had suggested they spend some of the next few hours at a nearby coffeehouse instead of the bleak embarkation waiting area.

Crossing the street, Kip said, "I feel like we just used up about ten years' worth of gay marriage karma."

"I thought it was nice that she didn't even blink. Let's get some coffee."

Tam used the time for one last check of the SFI mainframe. "I was hoping to have another note from Hank, but no such luck. Thankfully, there's nothing on the business blogs about any of this. If we can grab that application, and find out a few more clues, we could even go public ourselves before we leave Nassau, with our theory of the crime."

"I'll be really happy when that happens," Kip said.

Tam gave her a look she couldn't decipher. "And the weather in Nassau looks wonderful. There's a little store that sells the world's best mango sorbet. Interested?"

Tam showed her a map of the small port town and for an hour Kip let herself feel like a tourist. Maybe even let herself think it was the start of a honeymoon, that it wasn't the last time she'd ever travel with her boss's boss's boss. The arm around her shoulders might have been to accommodate the tiny table, or just to look the part of women in love, but Kip found herself relaxing into it, as welcome as if she had known its comfort for years.

There were no snags of any kind as they made their way up the switchbacks of the boarding ramp. The customs officer had asked the purpose of their travel and waved them on. Kip was grinning as she studied the ship's map and found their room.

"I should be shocked that it was all so easy."

"There's low relative risk here, especially leaving." Tam tried not to sound as relieved as she also felt. She had known it could be this easy, but she hadn't been sure that it would be.

Their mid-ship upper-deck cabin was already cleaned and available. Tam's first "uh-oh" was upon opening the cabin door.

Of course the steward had made the bed up for a couple. "We can have the bed changed," Tam said.

Kip didn't sound worried. "It might look suspicious if we did."

The space was tight but they quickly stowed their suitcases after removing the essentials to shelves in the tiny bathroom, all tucked safely behind each shelf's safety bracket.

Finally, the bustle of settling in over, there was an awkward silence. To Tam, the single bed was seductive. The tiny couch was equally beguiling. She felt somewhat dizzy, and her largely sleepless night, mostly spent ping-ponging between worrying about her company and totally inappropriate fantasies, wasn't helping with her composure.

Kip snatched something small and black out of a drawer. "There's only one thing to do." She ducked into the bathroom.

"What?"

She stuck her head back out the door. "We're on a cruise ship. Guess."

Okay, Tam thought. She had a point. All the worry in the world would not change the fact that until eight thirty tomorrow morning there wasn't a danged thing she could do about diddly.

She quickly pulled the new board shorts and a skimpy tank top out of the drawer. When Kip emerged in her swimsuit Tam's stomach did a full roll of delight. The suit wasn't a cleavage and butt cheek style, not at all. But it was filled with woman, all woman, a cute, trim woman with strong arms and soft curves. Clearly, they had to get out of this tiny cabin *now*.

"Last one there gets thrown in," Tam said.

"I'd like to see you try." Kip took off, already in her sandals.

"Oh hell," Tam muttered, realizing she hadn't a clue where one of hers had ended up.

Kip had made good use of her lead—enough time to secure two tall, frosty glasses of passion fruit iced tea. "No tossing me in the pool, okay?"

"Okay. One-day truce."

They found deck chairs in a mix of sun and shade and listened to the live band blasting island music across the pool area. When the ship pushed back from the dock, taking on the merest hint of rocking motion, Tam finally relaxed. Fifteen hours of needing to do nothing more than breathe was ahead of them both.

Kip covered Tam's legs with a towel, not wanting to wake her but also not wanting her to get a sunburn. Maybe it was the mild rocking motion or simply the awareness that they were out of the reach of the world for a little while. Whichever, Tam's face was utterly relaxed. She was almost smiling in her sleep.

She thought some exploration was in order. The way the ship moved was soothing and yet exhilarating. The coast of the mainland slipped into the distance until it was just them and hopeful seabirds following in their wake. Her favorite part quickly became the forward deck, in front of the windbreaks. She imagined a lot of people tried to reenact that Titanic scene. It wasn't on her list of things to do. But the ship's forward motion through the cool sea air was exhilarating. The buffeting of the wind was almost as good as a sailboat. Her hair was a tangled mess, but she didn't care. Her head was clear.

As the deck departure party started to wind down she decided it was time to wake Tam. Tomorrow would likely be a stressful and potentially unhappy day, if Tam's banking contact decided to resist Tam's request, or was more deeply involved than they knew. Tam would need a good night's sleep and much more of a nap might have her sleepless later.

As for herself, she wasn't sure how she was going to sleep with Tam's body only inches from hers. But she'd slept well the night before and right now, lungs filled with nothing but ocean air, she felt composed and steady.

She wasn't expecting Tam to be gone, though. The towel was still there. Kip turned toward the elevators, thinking perhaps Tam had gone to the cabin, when a hand slipped around her waist.

"How's the missus?"

Kip grinned and leaned into Tam's grasp. "Surprised you woke up. You were really out."

"I was looking for you." Tam offered her one of two plastic cups filled with ice and something that was amber in the sunlight. "Plain iced tea?"

"Thank you." She was thirstier than she had realized. "Did you have a nice sleep?"

"Yes—and thank you for the cover. I'd have cooked. You look like you've been forward."

Kip put a hand to her wrecked hair. "It's really wonderful up there."

Tam held out her hand and Kip took it. They explored the forward area again, breathing in the air together, then circled down the ship on the exterior decks, one at a time, peeking into bars, the casino, the gym, even the library. They scanned dinner menu choices and decided on Italian, giving themselves an hour before the reservation to clean up.

It was so awkward navigating showers and modesty in the small cabin that Kip knew she was blushing, and brightly enough that her skin didn't hide it. She hoped Tam thought it was the hot shower. At one point, to let Tam pull her suitcase out of the closet, Kip climbed up onto the bed, still only wrapped in a towel.

"These cabins are cute, and I really like the shelves and how they keep things from sliding off, but the floor space is a little limited."

Tam, kneeling next to her suitcase, looked up at Kip. "I can't say I mind the interior view at all."

Well, that wasn't helping. "You're dressed already. I'm at a disadvantage."

"How about I step out for a few minutes and you finish up?"

Relieved, Kip agreed. Tam, in new tailored black slacks and white blouse, looked poised and elegant and confident and... everything that Kip wasn't. The moment the door was closed Kip abandoned the towel, scrambled into her undies and attacked her hair with brush and blow-dryer. She had brought clothes from her stash at the cabin—nice enough but not very elegant. She could have bought something this morning, but when they were possibly only going to be on the ship for one evening, a little black dress hadn't seemed necessary.

At least she had brought along a wrap blouse in a vibrant purple that she'd left at the cabin one weekend. Her jeans would have to do, but they had only been worn a few times and the indigo dye was flattering. She wished she had slinky, strappy slides or her tallest pair of heels, though. Even as she brushed some color onto her cheeks she told herself that she wasn't going on a date, but that message got lost in the one from the mirror. It said she was dowdy. Uninteresting. And short.

Tam knocked, then opened the cabin door. "Ready?"

"Yes." She abandoned all the paraphernalia that wasn't helping her ego in the least and busied herself finding her cabin key card. When she turned to look at Tam, she was warmed by the admiration in Tam's eyes. Maybe, all in all, she didn't look too bad.

"That blouse is a crime," Tam said. She pulled the cabin door all the way open and stepped aside to let Kip out first.

Kip was feeling better by the minute. Over her shoulder she asked, "In what way?"

From behind her Tam said, "The front way and the back way."

Kip laughed.

"Sorry, that sounded stupid, didn't it?"

"No." She slowed so they could walk side by side in the wider main corridor. "Thank you. You look so elegant I was worried I was frumpish next to you."

"I think it would take you a while to achieve frumpish."

"Okay, that's one of the more unusual compliments I've ever received, but I thank you."

Tam again reached for her hand as they walked. Kip told herself it was just to maintain their cover as a couple, but when she looked around she saw a thousand people who simply didn't care about them in the least. She tightened her grip and received an answering squeeze from Tam.

The restaurant was quiet and largely occupied by couples. Tucked along the starboard side of an upper deck, they had a spectacular view of the darkening sky and endless expanse of rolling ocean. As they discussed the menu it wasn't appropriate to compare Tam to Meena, but what else was new? She couldn't help it. Some of the differences were subtle. Tam was attentive, but Meena had seemed smothering. Tam showed concern that Kip enjoy her food, even when she was picking red onions out of the salad. Meena would have kept asking. Something about Meena had made her feel like a child being coaxed to let mummy make it better. Tam treated her like a competent woman. After asking if the salad would be okay, and Kip's assurance that it would be, Tam didn't ask again. But when they ordered their main course, Tam asked the waiter if Kip's dish contained red onions. It didn't and all was well. It was so foolish, her heart, as was the part of her that felt seen and treasured. Foolish and wonderful heart that simply didn't hear the part of her that knew these feelings couldn't possibly be allowed to thrive.

Dessert—a trio of cheeses with a trio of chocolates and fresh berries—had arrived when Tam put a small jeweler's box with the ship's logo on the table. Kip's heart flipped over. No way. Stupid assumption. It wasn't...

"What's this?" Her voice sounded perfectly natural, she thought.

"A very belated birthday present. I really messed with yours."

Fortunately, she had the presence of mind not to blurt out "I had the best damned kiss of my life on my birthday." Instead she opened the box.

Twinkling silver earrings set with rainbow stones gleamed at her. "Oh... They're lovely, thank you." She hurriedly took the simple gold studs she wore every day out of her ears and replaced them with the new pair.

"How do they look?"

"Lovely. I knew you would object to something... Let's just say they had a genuine stone version and that's not what you're wearing."

Kip laughed, knew she was blushing and didn't care. "They're perfect. Thank you."

"My pleasure."

They agreed to walk off dinner with a stroll around the deck. The foredeck seemed the best place to go, and was well worth the stairs. Above them the sky was a dark bowl studded with stars. As they stood in the protection of the windbreaks, the air was still and refreshingly cool.

Kip found herself at a loss for words. She wanted to say so many things, none of which she could, and they crowded out every other thought in her head.

She didn't object when Tam pulled her close. She nestled her ear to Tam's chest. So comfortable and warm, so familiar, like home.

Tam said softly, "I was thinking that if I kissed you now I wouldn't be tempted later."

Kip had to look up at her. "Seriously?"

Her face was in shadow, but she could see lights reflected in Tam's eyes. "No, I'm lying through my teeth. I'll want to kiss you later."

"Please now," Kip whispered.

Their lips met with the quiet sizzle of starlight, both of them almost still. Then Kip put her hands in Tam's hair, felt Tam grasping her hips possessively, and the kiss deepened into exploration, not gentle, but not harsh. Intentional, careful and focused. With a shared gasp, there were more caresses in a leaping fever, opening layers of aching in Kip for something she had never known before.

When they parted Kip again put her ear to Tam's chest, as much for steadiness as for the pleasure of the pounding she heard. She was frightened by how much she wanted to give Tam, and Tam's racing heart told her that she had some power over Tam as well.

"I think," Tam said in a low voice, "that it would be best if we said good night now and you went to bed. I'll wait and join you in a bit."

Kip nodded and caught herself before she rubbed her cheek against Tam's breast. All she would have to do was turn her head slightly.

Instead she stepped back. "Good night, Tam."

"Good night...Pippa."

It did make Kip laugh and she retreated to the cabin, more than a little dizzy and parts of her sodden beyond any experience in her life.

She brushed her teeth, changed into a T-shirt and put her beautiful new earrings on the bedside table. She tried to only take a third of the bed, but her body felt swollen and awkward.

Sleep was impossible.

Tam doubted she would sleep a wink. She was tempted to find a chair in one of the lounges to see if she could doze. Maybe a shot of whiskey would calm her nerves. Or eight or nine. In the end it was weariness and the hope of at least a few hours of rest that made her decide to see if Kip was asleep.

She moved about the cabin stealthily, leaving the bathroom light on because without it the room was almost pitch-black. She quickly changed into a T-shirt, brushed her teeth, washed her face, hung up her clothes, and couldn't think of another thing to do. So she switched off the light and managed to crawl into bed without stubbing her toe in the dark or making contact with Kip's body.

Kip's breathing was steady. She hadn't moved at all. Tam

suspected she was awake. The ship's motion rocked the bed gently from side-to-side, and that ought to have lulled her into at least some kind of calm.

Instead, the dark was her undoing.

"Kip..." She said it softly. She simply meant to say "It'll be okay. You can sleep." It started out that way, but she only got as far as, "It'll be..."

Kip stirred.

Crossroads, Tam realized. Rules only mean something if you follow them, even when no one is looking. Kip was a capable, honest, principled woman and if she touched Kip right now they'd be officially lovers in thirty seconds. It would cost Kip twice over—her self-respect and the respect she held for the woman Tam no longer recognized, Tamara Sterling, CEO. That it would cost her her own self-respect didn't matter as much to her. This was bad for Kip.

"Are you okay?" Kip's whisper held concern, but was at a pitch that Tam didn't think Kip realized was a tantalizing half-purr.

Her fingers twitched. She wanted to feel the velvet of Kip on her hands, her lips. *Anything* was preferable to hurting Kip and that's what her touch would do.

She had a diversion to offer and so she asked, "You've heard of David Koresh, right?"

Kip wasn't sure she'd heard Tam correctly. "Who hasn't?"

"Koresh was another of those breed-my-own-cult, not the first, not the last, unfortunately. But I bet you've never heard of David Halley...hang on."

Tam sat up and the bedside lamp came on, leaving Kip blinking.

"I've never told anyone about this," Tam said slowly. "I don't really know how to go about it. It seems a ridiculous thing to hide but honestly, it was a good idea then, and I think is still a good idea. Thing is, you found holes in my citizenship paperwork.

Those holes used to be filled. I presume the hacker did that. But if it had been left alone, you'd have never known there were questions to ask. I doubt I would have ever told you."

"Why is it such a secret? So you were born in Germany. So maybe you don't know who your parents are—"

"I wasn't born in Germany. That's the cover. I was born in a wide space in the road in Pueblo County, Colorado. At the time, it was known as House of Zion City. Long gone—never really was a real place on the map."

Kip brushed hair out of her eyes. She'd listened to Tam getting ready for bed and steeled herself to feign sleep for however long it took. She hadn't really expected Tam to decide that it was the right time to fill her in on those mysterious blanks in her background. Now she pieced together what she knew, which wasn't much. "I guess I assumed that you were being hidden. I don't know from what, but the timeframe was when the Berlin Wall fell. I guessed it was political or something."

"There was so much confusion over records after the consolidation of the two countries that I think they took advantage of that. But we—me, Nadia, about twenty-five children in all—were moved out of Colorado after David Halley's family had the tent town destroyed. That was his parents and two brothers who did that—the real family and apparently one with a lot of money. We weren't real family, but we surely were an embarrassment."

Kip scooted back so she could lean on the pillows, the sheets pulled up over her breasts. Tam was so calm about it and yet if she was talking about what Kip thought she was, it was weird and terrible. "Halley—had he died?"

"Killed himself before the local sheriff could haul him in for child abuse, tax evasion, welfare fraud, bigamy... I only remember that police cars pulled up and all the mothers were scared."

"And that left a lot of children with no...father?"

"A lot of children with no father and a bunch of brainwashed women all claiming to be his wife. My mother was fourteen when I was born. She died in the process, or that's what I was told. Nadia's was twenty-four or twenty-five at the time of the raid.

They've never located each other again. Like I said, there was money. Lots of it. The mothers signed us away in what I'm sure wasn't any kind of legal agreement and they probably got a nice chunk of change to start a new life. But we were all too young to protest or even be sure what was happening. Life wasn't great, then it got a lot better. I was grateful."

Kip didn't even know where to start. "Are you telling me that Nadia and you weren't..."

Tam gave her a wan smile. "You thought we had been together?"

Kip nodded.

"That rumor never quits. No, we were never lovers. Eww." Tam let out a long sigh. "But we are half-sisters. Nobody but us knows that. I suppose it gives us a certain air of intimacy that people misinterpret. Mercedes probably thinks that's why I always take her calls." Tam repositioned so she was sitting cross-legged under the covers.

Kip said, trying not to let her tone rise too much, "What a horrible thing to do to a bunch of kids. Separate them from their mothers after they'd already been traumatized."

"Yes. And no. Some of them were as crazy as he was. And a few more were broken—hardly functional. Others were children in their heads and never grew up. I was just a kid, but looking back, I don't know if there was a fit parent among them."

"If yours was alive, wouldn't you want to find her?"

Tam stared down at her hands. "I have to tell you that this is the most I've thought about any of it in years. I guess—if she was alive I'd have probably tried to find her. Whatever agreement she signed wouldn't have been binding on me. But it's moot. Nadia never said she was looking for her mother and I think she would have told me. She was younger than I was. Fortunately we were both "not ripe" as that crazy man put it. There were a couple girls, just a bit older than me who'd been turned into wives."

"Oh my God," Kip said. She touched Tam's hand, just for a moment. "I am so sorry. What an awful, awful thing. And I understand why you really don't want to talk about it. I can see some people getting obsessively fascinated by the whole thing."

"Who wants to be a Wikipedia article like that? Not me. The Halley family gave us a good education. I got a new name and an orphan's bio. If I finished college I would get a bonus. My life was turning out pretty good."

Kip connected that dot. "The Maldives money?"

"You guessed it. I should give it away to a shelter or something."

"What were you called before Tamara, then? Do you remember—never mind. You don't have to tell me."

"It's okay. Rebekkah. They made our first names our middle names."

Kip decided not to say that she thought it did suit her, but she liked Tamara better. "You never have nightmares? I think I would." She wasn't sure she wouldn't have a nightmare later anyway. The cruelty of such a sick man using all those teenaged girls to build his own little cult was inhuman. How could Tam be so calm talking about it?

"I did have nightmares for a while, but once I got to boarding school and started learning, they stopped. My mind was finally occupied. We'd only read the Bible. I used to know chapter and verse. But I did really well in boarding school, learned fast, then tested high for science and math and here I am. I always felt blessed for having been rescued."

"His parents are lucky they haven't had grandchildren showing up on their doorstep," Kip said.

"Maybe they have. They are very good at keeping things quiet."

There was a long silence, then Kip said softly, "Thank you. I will not tell a soul. I promise you that."

Tam nodded. "I know."

"Do you think that's why you do what you do?" Tam's father, after all, had been a coward—victimizing defenseless girls and then killing himself to escape the mess he'd made. She hoped he'd ended up in the burning hell she was sure he imagined existed—it was what he deserved.

"What?"

"Well—he evaded justice. You make sure some people finally get some justice."

Tam's eyes clouded and her face stilled. "I never thought of that. I don't think I want to see myself as doing anything in relation to him, certainly not my life's work as a form of rebellion."

"I didn't mean that. I'm sorry," Kip said quickly. "That was thoughtless of me."

"No, you're probably right." Tam's eyes rimmed with red. "It's pretty obvious that your father shaped a part of you."

"Absolutely. And I like who I am. But I'm not going to be grateful to his alcoholism for that. I hate everything it's done to him and my sister and mom, too."

Tam bit her lower lip. "I just—he was never my father. He doesn't even get enough status in my life to be worthy of rebellion against him." She gave an unamused laugh. "I'm not sane because he was crazy."

Kip felt so helpless. "Your mother must have been from an amazing line of women because you certainly didn't get your strength and intellect from him."

"I've tried so hard not to let it matter." Tam's voice broke and Kip wanted in the worst way to hold her. "It was all a long time ago. It's almost a dream. It's not about who I am."

Tam drew herself up and though tears shimmered at the corners of her eyes, they didn't spill over. "You're right, the women in my family must have been strong."

"I'm sorry I asked about it, and pushed."

"I know why you did. Those holes weren't supposed to be there for you to see."

The silence stretched long enough to be awkward. Kip sensed that if she offered to hold Tam, Tam would agree. But her rigid posture and faraway look weren't asking for comfort. Kip could almost hear her thinking that she had gotten through life on her own and wasn't about to start getting weepy on someone now.

Kip slid back down into the bed and adjusted her pillow. "Do you think you can sleep?"

"Even if I can't, it's fine." Tam quickly turned off the light. "The dark is restful. It'll be okay."

Oddly reassured by the rocking motion of the ship, Kip was glad to find herself drowsy. She was aware of Tam but she didn't ache the way she had earlier. She felt inside Tam's life in a way she hadn't expected or believed in. For the first time in days, sex was not simmering right below the surface. She felt...trusted.

She woke once in the night to feel Tam snuggled against her back. She burrowed until she could hear Tam's steady, slow breathing and went back to sleep.

CHAPTER SIXTEEN

Kip stirred in the wee morning hours to find herself still in the circle of Tam's arms. The heat of Tam's body was not bringing out feelings of safety and comfort, however, and Kip slipped away to visit the bathroom and school herself into a professional frame of mind. Today they hoped to finally have a concrete piece of evidence in their possession that proved someone other than Tam was involved in the embezzlement. She needed her instincts at their sharpest.

She also couldn't forget why she was here. And who she was. The dim display of her watch said they would be docking in two hours. She knew Tam wanted to be among the first to leave.

When this was all over, when the FBI was satisfied, and any rumors quashed by the truth, SFI still wouldn't allow for relationships between employees. Tam couldn't enforce a rule she didn't follow herself. So whether she was part of Tam's life, what she could have, according to the rules, was something she couldn't live with. She didn't want to be a mere friend. She didn't want Christmas cards and birthday gifts and "how have you been" a couple of times a year because they didn't dare see each other more often.

Her image in the bathroom mirror shimmered as her eyes filled with tears. Yippee, Meena would think it hilarious. Kip Barrett had finally lost her distance and over someone she couldn't have.

Finally feeling a little more calm, she went back to bed, not sure if she should wake Tam yet. It was moot, however. Tam stirred and pulled her close again, but it wasn't to sleep. She trembled as they fell into a long, slow kiss, the first of several. She should have said stop, should have rolled away, should have gone in search of an early breakfast.

She didn't do any of those things. Instead, she let Tam pull her on top for more kisses, for caresses. She felt like a candle, her edges soft and melting and a flame burning inside. She wanted to feel Tam's naked skin. Nothing had changed, but her heart and body were taking charge.

She was breathless and dizzy with desire when Tam finally pulled her close, hands no longer stroking her thighs and back.

"I'm sorry." Her voice was hoarse. "One bed, bad idea."

"We start disembarkation in about ninety minutes," Kip whispered. She desperately cast about for a reason to make her heart and body obey her.

Well, there was the truth—at least part of it.

"We have something really very *extremely* important to do and I would like a shower and breakfast before we disembark."

"Know what? You're always hungry."

Kip wasn't about to admit that being in lust was very tiring. She ran her hand along the wall above the head of the bed until she found the light switch.

Tam flung a hand over her eyes. "Warning next time?"

"Sorry." Kip had thought that Tam's revelations would show, but she still looked like Tam. A little puffy around her eyes, but the same face, same brow, same mouth...

Tam peered at her through her fingers. "You have no right to look like that."

"Like what?"

"Edible."

"Oh." Kip flushed.

Tam moved her hand from her eyes, blinking at Kip. "And I know that was a good line and I ought to go back to kissing you, but..."

"But you know it's not a good idea."

"No," Tam said seriously. "You're on my bladder."

Kip found herself tumbled unceremoniously to one side and she was left laughing into the pillows. When Tam emerged, she said, "Keep your distance."

"You wound me." Tam gave her a slow, open smile that dazzled Kip's eyes. Clearly, some care had washed away.

"That's what I mean. Stop that." Kip pulled her knees up to her chest, hoping to look a little less edible even though just about all of her was tingling at the compliment. "We do need to see to that really very *extremely* important something, and now isn't the time to forget all that."

"I know," Tam said. She leaned against the tiny vanity, her legs crossed at the ankles.

Kip was deciding how long it would take to kiss her way up those legs when Tam coughed. She felt herself blush again. "Breakfast."

"And showers." Tam didn't move.

"Don't make me be the one who has to find all the willpower."

She shifted into action at that. "You're right. I don't know what's wrong with me today."

"Nothing's wrong. Why don't I shower?" Kip scrabbled under the bed for her suitcase, not sure what the professional woman wore in Nassau. Whatever it was, she didn't have it. The suit she'd been wearing when they'd left Seattle was a wool blend. She'd last two minutes.

Obsessing about her clothes was better than thinking how

she'd measure Tam's inner thigh with her tongue. She discovered, too, that a cold shower was the biggest old wives' tale ever. It made not one bit of difference.

Tam had never arrived in Nassau by ship, and she found it far more pleasant than by air. The cruise lines had taken great care to make the dock area welcoming, and the moment they stepped from the gangplank to the shore the smell of the island filled her head. Music from the not-too-distant straw market drifted on the wind toward them. The sun was hot and it felt wonderful on her face. Buildings and awnings in sharp white stood out against the blue skies and green, mounded hills.

Kip in dark glasses, a crisp short sleeve button-up shirt and cargo shorts was easy on the eyes. Tam also recognized Kip's natural tendency to draw herself up to an almost regal stance when she was working. In spite of her height, her bearing and the impenetrable sunglasses were more than a little intimidating.

"We walk through the market and then we'll find Robert Manna. If he hasn't changed his habits, he's having coffee at a local place near his bank. There won't really be any place for him to hole up and call security. If he's uncooperative, we can bring in the higher-ups at the bank, hopefully before he has a chance to get to the paperwork first."

"Got it."

She was so adorable, so... Tam made herself stop thinking about Kip that way. Not right now, she told herself. Right now she had to think of Kip as the kick-ass investigator she'd hired to get to the bottom of theft at SFI.

She led the way through the cacophonous, crowded pier market and onto Bay Street. They passed kitschy T-shirt shops and then more refined jewelry emporiums, interspersed with banks from all over the world. Like the rest, the Bank of Zurich's doors were still shuttered. After several blocks of ducking around shoppers, they turned onto a quieter, less traveled side street.

The Balcony House Cafe was a few steps up uneven rock stairs. The entry was crowded with bougainvillea which had attracted its share of bees, and Tam guided Kip around them. In the U.S. the stairs would have been leveled, the plants trimmed back and the bees exterminated. But here such things were regarded as part of the atmosphere, and anyone who couldn't cope was welcome to leave paradise for a sanitized city any time they liked.

There were times, like now, when island life definitely appealed to her.

The cafe's dining room had a distinct tilt, and she spotted Robert Manna almost immediately, ensconced in a sunny corner, tea brewing in front of him as he scanned the morning paper. At first glance, he was the picture of a European expatriate, snow white hair, a thin mustache, meticulous white tailored slacks and shirt. His figure was more trim than most. She knew that he was well over six feet, though the last time she'd seen him he'd adopted a silver-tipped cane to give him "a spot of steadiness for the old knees." She called up what she could remember about him. Had served in the Swiss Army, was married with children and grandchildren. Had served the bank all over Europe until settling here, where he had declared he intended to end his days, even if he was frustrated by the illegalities that were commonplace. That he had helped their embezzler didn't fit his profile, but given the temptations that crossed his desk every week, maybe it wasn't a surprise that he had finally succumbed.

Her heart pounding, she approached as casually as possible, letting her shadow fall on his newspaper. When she didn't move on he looked up.

"Tamara Sterling!" He leapt to his feet to seize and enthusiastically shake her hand. "I was half expecting you."

"You were?" It was not the response she had expected. There was no sign of dismay in his face.

"Yes, I was thinking about you just last week. We'll talk business at the bank. Let me get you some breakfast."

"Tea is fine," Tam said. She introduced Kip, and Robert gave a casual wave at the waiter, who promptly retreated to the kitchen. Once they were seated, she said, "I'm afraid I can't wait for the bank. My business is quite urgent."

"I was hoping you were on holiday." His gaze flicked to Kip, mildly speculative.

"No, on business I'm afraid. It's about the account SFI opened about six weeks ago."

"That was why I was thinking of you. We had so many transactions pass through, and last week it was such a flurry that our internal monitors tagged it. I authorized them, of course, but it was odd I hadn't heard from you directly."

Tam was nonplussed. Robert sounded as if he hadn't a clue that Tam had known nothing about the account.

Kip, her face like steel, asked, "Who did you hear from?"

"Ted of course."

Tam tried to breathe in. She was glad her hands were under the table so no one could see them shaking.

If Kip was surprised, it didn't show. "Ted Langhorn? He set up the account? How?"

"What's wrong?" Robert's brows came together. "Ted brought me the paperwork himself. I explained it wasn't necessary, but he assured me that you felt that we did so much work by computer contact that it was time to see the whites of someone's eyes again. Plus, that pretty wife of his was wanting a vacation, and why not put the two together."

Tam was dazed, and incredibly grateful to have Kip with her. This was why she'd hired a professional.

Following the playbook of always asking questions and never giving answers, Kip continued, "Did he indicate why the account was necessary?"

"Some inside job you were worried about, but the account was for recovery not outbound. Though I've only seen outbound." He paused while the waiter delivered two pots of hot water, delicate teacups on saucers, and a selection of British teas.

Once the waiter departed, he said in a low voice, "I thought about calling you, Tamara. Not that it didn't seem all spot on, it was just unusual. We had a system and it wasn't like anyone at SFI to divert from it."

Tam finally found her voice. "I knew nothing about the account. That's why I'm here. I need the application preserved, fingerprints and all. I had no idea Ted... Kip has been tracking an internal embezzler. That much was true. Apparently, Ted is the one."

Kip shook her head. "No, not him. It can't be. He travels too much. He simply isn't in Seattle often enough to be doing the work there." She turned her attention to Robert again. "Did you talk to anyone else about this account?"

Clearly perturbed, Robert shook his head. "No. I used the usual procedure."

"I'm not suggesting you didn't," Kip said quickly. "But could you tell me what that procedure is?"

"I established the account with the contact information provided on the application. Had there not been an application, I'd have used the contact e-mails that I always used. But since this was supposed to be an internal matter, it made sense that a different e-mail was being used."

Tam couldn't help a noise of self-disgust. "The e-mail account. I never thought of backending the e-mail account on the application copy we already have. It would have probably traced back to their contract hacker, eventually."

"What is this all about?" Robert lowered his voice further. "Ted Langhorn is embezzling?"

"I don't think so," Tam said, in spite of Kip's warning gesture. She was not following investigation protocol, but she trusted Robert more than ever. "He's helping someone who is. It's not about money. It's about me."

Robert Manna gave every appearance of being honest and trustworthy, but Kip remained vigilant as Tam and Robert talked, their tea forgotten. Tam was too involved to keep her distance, but Kip listened closely for equivocation and any sign of rehearsed answers. She heard none, though. Adding to her impression of innocence was Robert's lack of alarm at seeing Tam again. In fact he seemed almost delighted. If he'd been complicit some dismay ought to have shown.

"It's highly unusual," Robert was saying as he got to his feet, "but not unheard of. Our largest clients are sometimes given access before and after hours, for the sake of discretion. We'd best be going."

Kip followed Tam and Robert back through the increasingly crowded streets of Nassau. The Bank of Zurich was still closed, and Robert took them around to a side door which he opened with a key. They were all inside when a guard challenged them, but Robert explained and signed them in. Once inside, the security was more stringent, requiring a key card and numeric input to open doors.

Without customers there was a regal hush over the marble floors and heavily draped walls and windows. The air was cool and still. Kip saw that there were a few employees at their stations already, though it was still twenty minutes until the bank opened.

"Please have a seat." Robert opened the blinds of his neatly appointed office situated just off the top of mezzanine stairs. Rich blue carpet and drapes whispered of old and new money, and the heavy antique desk was clearly of European import. Behind him, photographs of family and dignitaries were clustered on shelves, adding warmth to the room.

"I have a copy of the transactions in question, with the routing numbers," Tam said. She put the sheet of paper on Robert's desk, turned toward him. "I'd like to try reversing them. At least see if the money is still at the destinations, just as we've done before on SFI cases."

Robert nodded. "As soon as the manager is in I'll ask for the four of us to go and remove the application and secure it..."

Kip saw him frown as he studied something on his desk. "What is it?"

"I have an urgent request. It must have arrived after I left on Friday evening. I had a Governor's tea... Friday afternoon your embassy conveyed, with gratitude for prompt response, a request from U.S. authorities for information related to recent dealings with Sterling Fraud International, a corporation of United States registration, details provided below... Oh dear. I'm in a bit of a pickle. I can't ignore this." He gave Tam a look of concern.

"If part of what they would get is your statement that I didn't open this account, and the original application for their own testing, then please respond," Tam said quickly. "My priority is that they know I'm not involved and preserving Ted Langhorn's fingerprints on that application. If they take me in, we'll never get the money back. That's why I took the risk to travel here, yes, under an assumed name."

Kip interjected, "I want to know the original still exists. That it's here." She wasn't sure how far Robert would bend, but she played her hand anyway. "I'm the official investigator into this matter from SFI. I won't interfere with law enforcement requests, but I have a need to see evidence with my own eyes whenever possible. That's why I'm here in person. And I also used a false name to get here undetected. After that, by all means, accommodate law enforcement. I assure you, the real culprits would rather you didn't do that."

Robert scratched his neatly trimmed mustache as he sat down in his desk chair. "This is all really most irregular, but I understand your needs, Miss Barrett. However, under the Mutual Legal Assistance Treaty I am required to respond in an urgent manner and attest as to who and how this account was opened, plus supply copies of our transaction records." He picked up the phone before Kip could say anything more.

"Dahlia, yes, it's Robert at Bank of Zurich. Martin, is it? Is he in yet? What luck." He gave Tam a droll look. "Martin, I've got the request here, will do right away. I was out Friday afternoon. There is?" He swiveled around, putting his back to them. "I just saw her this morning. Yes, I met Miss Barrett as well. There is? No, Sterling didn't open this account. I haven't had any contact in about three months before this morning. If I see her again, I'll tell her to visit you promptly."

Kip's nervous energy wouldn't let her sit still any longer. She went to the window, wishing they were getting that piece of paper right now. She listened to Robert explain who had opened the account while she studied the crowded street below her. Everyday tourists looking hot in the morning sun mixed with local police in their unmistakable white uniforms. Strange to glance down the marquees and see Dicky Mo's and Conch Bakery next to Burger King.

"Sterling told me that she was being falsely implicated, and Miss Barrett, as the SFI investigator, was most interested in seeing that application for herself. This is all a proper mess. What a way to start a Monday. So indeed, yes, this account was opened by Theodore Langhorn, and not by usual protocol. No, I've not seen him since. He could be anywhere."

Kip blinked. She knew where he was. She was staring right at him. He appeared to be making a beeline for the bank.

Tam's focus on Robert's one-sided conversation was broken by an urgent gesture from Kip. She crossed to the window and followed Kip's pointing finger.

Son of a bitch. And that was Nadia with him. She was willing to bet that Ted—Ted of all people—had assured Hank and Diane that he'd get to the bottom of things in Nassau while they held down the fort. But Ted didn't know where Robert took his morning tea, and that had made all the difference. How could Ted do this? What possible gain could be worth the risk of prison and loss of his personal honor?

She scrawled the news on Robert's notepad and waved it to get his attention. She knew he'd been trying to evade telling the embassy that he was actually in her presence, but there was no time.

Robert peered at the note, then put on his glasses and peered again. "Martin—you know, I think all in all, it would be wise for you to dispatch some representatives quickly." He sighed and gave Tam an apologetic look. "Yes, Sterling and Barrett are here. And, apparently, so is Langhorn. It would be most efficient if you were prompt and discreet. Our doors open in fifteen minutes."

He hung up the phone and got to his feet. "Miss Barrett, come with me. Tamara, I am quite sorry about all this, but you'll have to stay here."

Just like that, Tam was alone in Robert's office. It was disconcerting, but not unexpected, to hear a key turn in the office door lock.

All this way, all that worry, and she was caught. She suspected the windows wouldn't open and the high transoms that let the island air circulate were too small for her to climb through. Besides, she wasn't going to go leaping about rooftops and swinging through trees. It wasn't necessary and would only make things worse.

Ted, of all people, and Nadia helping? She thought over the past week. Maybe Ted hadn't had the flu and they were covering preparations to run? Maybe Nadia didn't know anything about it, actually. She had no proof... With a sinking heart she realized that it had to have been Nadia who guided their hacker to Tam's passport and background information, who had to have been the one who explained what to remove. She had deliberately exposed *both* of them to the scrutiny of curious and hostile eyes. Everything she'd told Kip she'd have to tell again, and not to anyone she thought had any damn right to know. After their years of unspoken support for each other, behaving somewhat like the sisters they might have grown up to be, this betrayal was in a place she was only just realizing might have never fully healed.

She sank into a chair to put her head in her hands. Vernon Markoff, a fraud and embezzler, had hired Ted and Nadia, or both, to derail her. They had really put their heart and souls into it, and found insidious ways to wound and distract her. She was wondering now if Ted was the hacker she'd been stalking online. He'd been so good at software design in school—had an aptitude that matched her own. But he never pursued it seriously, saying it was too much hard work. Life was easier if you were handsome and glib. But if he'd kept up, knew or bought the right access, he could probably figure out how to carry off the entire scheme. He could do that anywhere he traveled. Nadia , with the mysteriously issued employee ID card that Kip had discovered, would be available when necessary to doctor the statements.

She'd been a fool. It had been right under her nose, the whole time. She'd distracted Kip with bad information; otherwise, Kip might have seen it.

Through her shock she chafed at the inactivity. Robert's office was excessively quiet. She couldn't hear anything but a low whir. She paced once around, then paused to listen again. Clicking, whirring, clicking... She opened a door to what she had assumed was a closet and discovered Robert's computer desk. It looked like they were using UNIX, or an equivalent.

She trailed a finger across the keyboard. UNIX. It had been awhile. She went back to Robert's desk for the list of transactions she was hoping to reverse. She might as well make use of the time.

Robert's employee login had security nine ways from Sunday. It would take her too long to crack. But like most people, he had a personal login for access to basic, nonsecured tasks, like web browsing. And really, he ought to know better than to use his wife's name as a password. Once past the sign-in she looked for the programmer's backdoor exploit.

Kip tried not to dance with worry as Robert conferred with the bank manager. He, too, looked like a Swiss expatriate, but didn't appear to have started his day quite yet. Robert repeated himself and then, after an elaborate search for the right keys which had allowed time for the delivery of spiced coffee, they proceeded in due haste to the file rooms in the basement. It was more damp than Kip liked down there, but the manager explained that records were only temporarily domiciled on site. In another week, the paper in question would have been transferred to a secure storage facility.

With the two bank officers slowly thumbing through the cabinet in question, conferring in low tones, she had no choice but to wait.

"Here we are." Robert pulled out a folder. "Miss Barrett?"

She stepped closer as he opened the folder. Using a pencil, he separated the pages. "Is this what you're interested in?"

"Yes, it looks exactly like the copy I was given as a valid digital duplicate. May I add a mark to the page?"

"I'd rather we all did, then I will put it in the sleeve for your embassy people. They have to sign for it."

Kip was glad her hand wasn't shaking as she initialed the two sheets. Robert and the manager added their own initials and she watched it transferred to the document sleeve, which the manager sealed with a strip of tamperproof tape. Her heart rate slowed. If Robert was telling the truth—and why wouldn't he be?—Ted Langhorn's fingerprints were all over it. Tam's contention that she had known nothing about it was far more believable. They might, just *might*, be able to walk away from the whole issue and let law enforcement focus on Langhorn.

She wished she could tell Tam that the papers were here, that they were secure. She could only imagine how worried Tam must be.

"What about Langhorn?"

"Well, I am hopeful that your embassy staff will ask him to assist with inquiries."

Kip had always known she would have to turn herself in. "And they'll likewise want to talk to Tam—Ms. Sterling—and me as well."

Robert put a gentlemanly hand at the small of her back as they walked up the stairs to the main lobby. "I believe they consider that a priority, yes. I am quite sorry about that, but I have no choice if I wish to preserve a good relationship with your embassy."

"I understand," Kip said. Like Tam, she would soon have a locked door between her and the world. Well, it wasn't as if she hadn't known that was coming.

"The doors are just opening now. Clients are arriving," the manager said. "Can I leave this to you, Robert? So much to do this morning..." He signed the sleeve and handed it to Robert before making his stately way in the direction of his office.

They were standing in an alcove at one end of the large marble and plush carpet interior. Bank staff were arriving at their desks and windows, meticulously groomed, all moving at a measured, graceful pace. It had been a long time since Kip had been in a bank that was so...bank-like. There was a hush like a library and even the arrival of customers didn't add much to the noise level.

Kip shrank back when she picked out the top of Ted Langhorn's sandy-haired head. His lanky frame wasn't quite as relaxed as she'd last seen it, and he appeared to be looking for someone—probably Robert. To his left was his wife, as carefully coiffed and ostentatiously elegant as one of the Real Housewives. The body and tan were flawless. Kip was sure the ankle-wrapping high heels had cost a small fortune, and she wasn't thinking the jewelry was fake, either.

"He'll recognize me," she murmured to Robert. "And probably cause a scene."

She didn't know if Robert heard her, though, because he strode forward to greet Langhorn and his wife with a jovial but restrained air. "Ted Langhorn, what a surprise to see you this morning. And Mrs. Langhorn as well."

Ted began to speak, but Robert continued talking in the same congenial manner. "I must make introductions." He gestured to the men now assembled right behind the Langhorns. "Martin LeRoi, this is Ted and Nadia Langhorn. I spoke to you about them just a few minutes ago. Mr. and Mrs. Langhorn, these are members of the United States Embassy staff. They have inquiries and believe you can assist them."

Kip had the satisfaction of seeing Ted Langhorn turn as pale as the uniforms the embassy officers wore. For the first time since she'd taken on the case, all her instincts screamed that she was looking at someone guilty of *something*.

Ted blustered, and Kip turned her study to Nadia Langhorn, who hadn't moved. She gave the impression of unshakable composure.

The officers moved forward as Robert invited everyone to his office. Ted fell into step, but there was a small amount of jostling. Nadia gave a little cry, stumbling on her high heels. Several arms shot out to keep her from falling, then she was back on her feet, offering smiles and apologies.

From where she was Kip saw something in Nadia's hand she hadn't had before, and she was slipping it into her oversized designer bag. She glanced at Robert, who was patting his pockets and looking down at the floor as if he'd dropped something.

Kip gave up her hiding place, but had no sooner started forward than Nadia simply dashed for the nearest doors.

Nothing for it but to make a scene, Kip thought. She thanked her sensible sandals for plenty of traction on the marble floor as she sprinted forward to yell, "Nadia!" Her mind flicked through the thousands of papers she'd reviewed and zeroed in—more loudly, she yelled, "Rachel!"

Nadia skidded to a stop, pivoted in place, eyes wide.

Everyone in the bank stopped what they were doing, except Kip.

With a sudden gasp, Nadia shook herself into motion again. She scrambled toward the door, elegant heels finding poor purchase on the polished marble. She was reaching to push the doors open when Kip clamped her hand around one diamond-adorned wrist.

So she couldn't pull the trigger on a woman and child. She had far more practical skills. How much of a challenge could pampered Nadia Langhorn be?

The elbow strike to the side of her head told her, and left her ears ringing. The price of overconfidence, she told herself. She clung to Nadia's other wrist, ducked another strike and went for the basics, sinking one hand into Nadia's very expensive hairdo while tangling the woman's arms in her own designer bag. Nadia let go of Kip in an attempt to free her hair. They twisted against each other until Kip hooked one of her sandals around Nadia's ankles and they both went down with Kip's elbow in Nadia's solar plexus.

From the gasp, she was pretty sure Nadia's stomach felt like her head.

She rolled back to her feet and the embassy officers were around them. One quickly handcuffed the still struggling Nadia. Kip was dazedly trying to keep her balance and realized, too late, that handcuffs were also being ratcheted around her own wrists.

CHAPTER SEVENTEEN

Tam rose when the door opened. She had expected something to have transpired, but was still taken considerably aback by the sight of Ted and Nadia Langhorn in handcuffs along with a half-dozen white-uniformed guards. Nadia looked somewhat the worse for wear with a heel broken on one shoe and her hair lopsided.

Robert looked both disconcerted and satisfied, though his tone sounded as if everyone was concluding an ordinary transaction. "Let's just settle our paperwork, shall we?"

Finally, dwarfed by the embassy muscle, she caught sight of Kip—wrists cuffed in front of her and something strangely wispy and yellow in her hands. Kip gave her a wan but encouraging smile. The papers were secure maybe?

Kip cleared her throat and handed the blonde wad of hair to Nadia. "Sorry. I didn't mean to ruin your weave. I was hoping it was real."

Tam managed not to laugh. She ought to have been worried sick but right then all she could think was that she wanted Kip there always to make her laugh, to make life less of a grim business. How had she *ever* thought her humorless?

"Ms. Sterling?" One of the embassy officers had stepped forward. "With the permission of the government of the Bahamas, I'm detaining you on behalf of the United States of America. We'll transfer you to U.S. soil in a few minutes."

Tam held out her wrists—it was a first.

Handcuffs were heavier than they looked. She supposed she should argue that being detained didn't mean she should be manacled, but it was only a minor detail at that moment.

"I have the paperwork." Robert pulled a crumpled document sleeve from a large purple bag—had to be Nadia's. "I know Mrs. Langhorn was eager to get rid of it, but it's here." He held it up. "Your mark Miss Barrett?"

Kip eased her way past her escorts. "Yes, that's my mark. Those are the papers you removed from your files downstairs."

With a huge sigh of relief, Robert handed the document sleeve to Martin LeRoi. "Please take charge of this. It's vital evidence. All the other copies you requested will be made as soon as possible and carried up to you. Of course, I'll be available for any deposition you may wish to take from me. That's all our business, I believe."

Before Tam could point out that there was one more matter to resolve there was a knock at the door. A wide-eyed clerk stepped into the room, a printout in one hand.

"I need a signature for these transfers, Mr. Manna."

Robert glowered. "I think it can wait."

"No," Tam said. "It can't. You should sign off on them. All of them."

Robert gave Tam his attention. Without the least bit of surprise, he asked, "Why Tamara, have you been using my computer?"

Behind her Tam heard Kip stifle a laugh.

"I'm so sorry. I did borrow it."

"Nearly seven million dollars? How enterprising." Robert initialed the paper and then asked the clerk to bring back a copy right away. "That adds to the considerable sum that arrived on Friday."

Tam hadn't yet been able to meet either Ted's or Nadia's gazes, but she steeled herself for it. What else was there to say but, "I don't understand why. You didn't even get the money."

Ted looked guilty but not the least bit chagrined. "It was never about the money."

"It was about making sure I wasn't credible for Markoff's trial."

"At first." Ted looked not the least cowed or worried. In fact, he looked every inch like he had the world by the short and curlies. "Nadia is the one who saw the bigger opportunity when Markoff's people approached her."

Nadia shrugged and said nothing.

"You told Ted to tamper with my immigration record, my passport verification... I think out of everything, that surprised me the most."

She gave Tam a direct look, with none of her usual coy evasions. "That's how they got to me. I don't know how they found out. They offered me papers, contracts, faked adoption records—they had copies of everything. They thought I would do anything to keep the past a secret when they'd just handed me all the evidence I'd never been able to piece together about my grandparents. The ones who farmed me out like the accidental mongrel offspring of their thoroughbred son. I agreed to facilitate a crisis for you in exchange for the box of documents. I knew what Ted could do with a little focus. And I knew what a little well-placed gossip could do."

"Why Wren Cantu?"

Nadia looked like she wanted to ignore Kip, but her satisfaction with her own handiwork kept her talking. "She was supposed to be one of the big headliners at the New York Public Library benefit. She shows up an hour late and spends the night being rude to everyone and with a spoon up her nose. But she can get an invite to any party in that town. I spent the last five years doing all those fundraisers, all that charity work. I watched porn stars and politicians' mistresses trump me and realized I was going about it all wrong. If I can't have celebrity, I'll take notoriety. It's a bigger paycheck in the end."

Now that they were talking, Ted had the air of a professor propounding on a pet theory. "You just don't get the new world order, and you were never going to. Our whole business model is a relic. Rich enough, big enough, you can't fail today. You can steal *anything*, ruin a natural wonder, profess ignorance as wisdom, and go on getting richer and richer. All you have to do is blame anything and everything *except* a corporation for oil on beaches, cancer clusters in school kids, whatever the crime. Toss the public a villain and protect big business and you can be rich, famous and respected."

"You've been rehearsing that speech," Tam said, her numbness finally giving way to anger. "Did it take you long to believe it?"

"You can be pissed all you want. But Nadia and I are going to be thanking you all the way to the bank. I *knew* you'd catch us. You were incredibly predictable. You even brought in a staffer. Barrett was one of four I had already identified. Only time you surprised me was running for it on Friday morning. I thought the Feds would wind you up enough to keep you in town. Instead, you dropped off the planet. Still, I was pretty sure you'd get here this morning."

"You're going to prison." Kip sounded about as angry as Tam felt.

Nadia favored her with a pitying look. "We're heading for minimum security and with good behavior, ankle bracelets. It'll give me a chance work through those documents they gave me and write my exposé of my father's cult and how his parents covered it up. How much do you think his family would pay me not to publish it? I'm betting there's a house on Star Island in it for me."

Tam didn't know what Robert and the embassy agents were

making of the conversation but she had been aware of Martin LeRoi's discreet voice recorder from the beginning. Tam said, "So this really *was* about money. I was just collateral damage."

Ted laughed. "It's always about money. All it takes is being wildly successful, and I just was. I hacked six banks and embarrassed the premier fraud detection company in the country. Once my book hits the shelves I'll be doing commentary about corporate hijinks and the failures of big government, and making more in a week than I do in a year now. *Life on the Dark Side: One Man's Corruption by the System.* Catchy, isn't it? And I have the other necessary ingredient—a smokin' hot wife with brains."

Tam shifted her gaze to Nadia. She wasn't serious when she asked, "And you get your own reality show?"

Nadia's reply was dead serious. "Or a talk show, or my own column at the big blog sites where I get to decide who's hot and what's news. We'll have many friends, and they'll respect our resourcefulness. We'll be welcome at Martha's Vineyard."

My respect, obviously, means nothing, Tam thought. "The people you worked for—did they know you expected to fail?"

"Those people, they're not the forgiving type," Kip added. "They expected results for their money."

They both shrugged, with a shared, half-amused glance between them. Ted answered, "Here's the ironic part—Vernon Markoff doesn't know anything about it. We were brought on by one of the sons trying to score points with Daddy. This works, he's a hero. It doesn't work, Daddy never knows he's a failure."

So much for hoping that this mess would further incriminate Markoff and give him more time in jail. "But you're going to tell the world all the details so you can get famous."

Nadia rolled her eyes. "Why on earth would we tell the whole truth? It's Ted's book. He's not under oath."

Tam couldn't help the glance she shot at Kip. She shrugged in defeat—she would never understand people who could exist in such a moral vacuum. Sadly, she considered that they could be right about where they ended up. Maybe she could preempt some of their notoriety with an exclusive interview for that sleazy reporter. The very thought repelled her.

Robert had been watching their exchange with a weary smile. Apparently, the Langhorn point of view was nothing new to him. Nevertheless, his understanding nod at Tam helped her feel that the world hadn't completely turned night into day. To Martin LeRoi he said, "I believe we've complied with your urgent information request. I'll be sending over the additional details."

"You've been more than helpful, and the United States thanks you," LeRoi responded.

All the courtesies observed, they were urged to their feet. Though their escort was not even touching them, there was no way to walk through the bank discreetly. Handcuffed ducks in a row, they drew raised eyebrows from the bank staff and outright gawks from the customers. Tam hoped nobody had a cell phone camera.

They were all separated during transport, each of them in a separate car. Tam's was last and she was relieved to see all three ahead of her pass through the embassy's tall wrought iron gates. She had only the briefest glimpse of the colonial portico of the main building, brilliant in whitewash and choked with crimson bougainvillea. Her head was spinning—Ted and Nadia were utter strangers to her. How could they believe they lost nothing if they took the path to wealth through notorious crime and false, public penance?

They were marched—firmly but not discourteously—into a small side building behind the main structure. Tam suspected it was a holding area for U.S. citizens waiting to leave the country by diplomatic escort, and she wasn't wrong. Nadia and Ted went directly into separate rooms of their own. It was satisfying to hear the locks click into place.

Expecting the same treatment, Tam was surprised instead by the interjection of a middle-aged man in a suit that said he'd arrived from a colder climate and hadn't had time to change.

"Elliot Druckerman," he said. "I'm counsel for Ms. Sterling and Ms. Barrett." He looked like he'd been on a very, very early morning flight.

Martin LeRoi was very reasonable, immediately offering them a private place to confer. He said to Kip, almost apologetically, "I need to search your belongings first."

Kip eagerly said, "Go right ahead. The sooner this is over the better."

Tam also gave permission and wasn't surprised when LeRoi found and confiscated their identification as Pippa Merritt and Pamela Curling.

"Are these the papers you used to enter the Bahamas?"

Druckerman said, "You don't have to answer," but hardly got that out before Kip and Tam in stereo said, "Yes."

Kip added, "That's the only thing we used them for—to book the passage on the cruise ship so we could get here."

Druckerman sighed. "Let's confer before my clients make any more spontaneous confessions."

"That's all there is," Kip said. "We sent all the evidence we gathered to Tam's assistant. She'll have it tomorrow, or know where it is, and will I'm sure happily surrender it."

Elliot Druckerman sighed again.

Tam shrugged. "She speaks for both of us."

LeRoi didn't smile, but he lost some of his stern glare. Whatever FBI request he'd been given to fulfill, it hadn't included treating them like criminals. Tam could only hope that the only order he'd been given was to detain them if found.

In no time at all she and Kip were in a private room with Druckerman, who had successfully argued to have their handcuffs removed after LeRoi confirmed that indeed, there were no charges filed against either of them, at least not yet.

Once the door closed, without any further preamble, Druckerman said, "I have a message for you from Mercedes Houston. She says this is what happens when you keep secrets from her."

"We're really done?" Kip couldn't believe she and Tam were

standing at the embassy gates, waiting to be released. She had followed and agreed with every argument that their lawyer had made with the embassy staff, but still... Was it really true? She lowered her voice. "We broke the law."

"No one at the FBI is going to push that through inter-departmental headaches to press charges for flying with a fake ID alone. The case will end up dismissed in someone's crowded docket because there's no other crime to pursue." Druckerman looked half-wilted in his suit. "I expect the next you'll hear about any of this is depositions for the case against the Langhorns."

"And if the rumors haven't hit the financial press already," Tam said. "That's my last worry. If we beat that cycle, then this was all worth it."

"You should manage the press," Druckerman advised. "Quickly. After all, that's a key staff person back in there, waiting for transfer to jail in Miami. They won't have immediate access to the press. You do."

Kip watched the light in Tam's eyes dim as she nodded. "Yes, I think I need to get out there and talk about it, make sure our clients know that we did what was necessary to the criminals in our midst, and we will prosecute to the fullest extent of the law, just as we insist on from them." She tapped her temple. "I made some mental notes for a press release while we were waiting in there."

"Don't forget that we made full recovery." Kip grinned and was glad to see Tam smile as well. She knew it had to hurt. Ted—and certainly Nadia—had been more than colleagues to her. "I can't believe they think they're going to be reality TV stars, or pundits, cashing in on their crimes to be richer than ever. Like people who crash state dinners or weep their tales of remorse in front of millions."

Druckerman shrugged. "I turn on the TV every day and see financial advice being doled out by people who've been tried and fined or jailed as SEC rules violators, so maybe they're right. No bad deed goes unrewarded in this world."

"What a depressing thought," Kip said. She would much

rather live in SFI's world—Tam's world.

Once Druckerman showed their passes to the guard they were let out onto the elegant Nassau Place. From their vantage point at the top of the hill the port shimmered in the mid-afternoon sun. The *Blue Sky of Sweden* gleamed at her moorings and Kip wondered if maybe...just maybe...

"We sail at six thirty," Tam said to Druckerman. "Can I buy you the best conch fritters in the Bahamas, and a cold beer?"

Kip's heart did a pleasurable slow roll. They were going to go back aboard, to that tiny little cabin and the soothing, rocking bed.

Druckerman blinked. "I had thought we'd all be flying back to the mainland. There's a flight late this afternoon I had hoped to catch so I can make a connection to New York. I'll fully brief Hank Jefferson as soon as I get to the airport."

Tam's lips twitched, then creased into a full smile. "Ms. Barrett has earned a night of relaxation given what her client has put her through."

Kip saw the speculative look in Druckerman's eyes before he assumed a more lawyerly mask of disinterest. It wasn't right, the way it looked. Tam was no longer her suspect, true, and she was no longer actively working evidence. But Tam was still her boss's boss's boss. Nothing had changed. She should go back with Druckerman.

The three of them began the walk down the sloping hill toward the ocean. Kip knew she should tell Tam to fly home. They should both fly home. If they went back aboard ship there was no way they'd make it through the night without compromising their signed statements of ethics. She didn't know if she had a future with Tamara Sterling, either, so ultimately what would she get for breaking faith with herself and with her employer? Possibly nothing but heartache and unemployment checks.

Really, she told herself, there's only one thing to say that can make any of this right. It was going to hurt.

"Tam," she said, pulling her to a stop. Druckerman hesitated as well, though he continued to scan the traffic for the taxi he needed. “Mr. Druckerman, I think as my attorney, I want you to hear this.”

“What is it?” Tam took both her hands. “You look so serious.”

“There’s only one right thing to do here. I have to say it. It’s wrong if I don’t.”

Druckerman and Tam both wore the same expressions of confusion.

She took a deep breath. She had not a clue what the future would bring. Her heart and her body had been right all along, though, and right now they told her that she was doing the right thing. She would probably regret it, at least a little. There was no getting around it, but sacrifice was a part of life. It was a big risk, but a potentially big payoff.

“I quit.”

“I can’t let you do this,” Tam said again. They’d left Druckerman to find his cab and Kip was walking steadily down the hill toward the port.

“There’s no letting me. You can’t stop me. I don’t have to work for you. I get to quit if I want.”

“But Kip... I don’t care what the Langhorns say. The world isn’t theirs or anyone else’s to plunder. You love your job. You love what we do.”

“And,” Kip said, “I love you. So which would you rather I quit? The job or you?”

Tam stopped walking. She could think of nothing to say.

Kip only continued a few paces before she stopped and slowly turned back. Behind her the ocean was sparkling under the afternoon wind and someone close by was roasting pineapple. Tam opened all her senses. She wanted to remember everything.

Kip’s expression changed. “Okay, maybe you’d rather I loved the job.”

“No,” Tam finally managed. “You took my breath away, that’s all. Not the first time, either.”

With an amused and slightly annoyed look, Kip prompted, "And so your answer would be?"

"I want you to love me more than any job. Any job ever."

"Was that so hard?"

"I don't have a lot of practice at this."

"You're going to have to get some. With me. You only get to practice with me."

Tam pulled Kip to her, gazing down into her lovely face. "What would you like to practice first?"

Kip shivered and Tam felt a matching echo in her body. But she answered, "I would like to practice you keeping promises. I was promised mango sorbet."

"Upstaged by your stomach. I'm wounded."

"You love it."

Her spirit unbelievably light, she said it with a smile because it was so easy. "I love you more."

Kip snuggled her head against Tam's chest. She fit so perfectly there. "I need you to say that again."

"I love you." Even easier. She wanted to float.

"Again—later. And tomorrow. And next week."

"Every day, Kip."

"Good." She raised her head to find Tam's gaze. "Where's my ice cream?"

Laughing, she took Kip's hand and they strolled the streets like any other lovers, peering in windows and finally in possession of two cones of mango sorbet. A bench on the pier was the perfect place to enjoy them. The cafe behind them was playing steel drum music that danced on the wind.

"I suppose I should call Mercedes." Tam focused on her own cone, not daring to watch Kip for the moment. "Give her a press release."

"This is delicious." Kip wiggled closer, and draped Tam's arm around her shoulders. "And yes, you probably should."

"I think when we get to Freetown tomorrow we're going to have to head home."

"I know."

They enjoyed their sorbet in silence for a bit. Tam surreptitiously watched Kip lick her cone. It was adolescent to get all warm and anticipatory and moist. She really didn't intend to stop feeling this way. She wanted to feel like this most of the time. Whenever Kip was near, in fact.

"I think I feel sort of let down," Kip said. "Nothing about you or us or this case has led me in expected directions but in the end it all resolved so easily."

"You call that *easy*?"

"You know what I mean. For all the risk it felt like we took, it seemed easy."

"It's supposed to be like that." She took Kip's hand in hers. "Most of the time, that's exactly how it's supposed to be. I'd like to think it was easy because we were together and everything we did together was right."

Kip flashed her a brilliant smile. "You're not so out of practice after all."

"C'mon. There's a hotel here."

"Why go to a hotel when we have a cabin?"

Tam laughed. "Pay phone."

"That makes more sense." Kip blushed and let Tam pull her up to her feet.

It might have been that her relaxed tone showed, or that the steel drum music was audible, but Mercedes was not the least bit pleased to hear from her.

"I nearly didn't accept the charges. I thought that can't possibly be my boss, she wouldn't wait until an *hour* after her lawyer called me to say everything was resolved. That must be someone else having some fun, but I took a chance."

"I'm sorry, Mercedes. I hope I didn't give you too big a scare."

"Me scared? Never happened." Her ire seemed to be abating and Tam more clearly heard the concern.

"Your timing was impeccable. How did you know to send a lawyer?"

"It was because of that model, that Wren Cantu. By the way, I worked all weekend. Was thinking someone might get in touch some super stealthy way, or just, maybe, call, so you've got a hundred file closures waiting for you when you get back here from your ordeal, which I notice, has dance music."

Tam laughed into the handset. "What about the model?"

"Wren Cantu called last night just as I was about to leave. It rang over from your private line and I thought it might be you. She was really upset. She didn't mind the reporters, but the FBI was simply too much. She didn't know what kind of game you were playing, but... What was it she said? I think it was *screw you.* I asked her how she got your number and she said Nadia Langhorn gave it to her, saying you two were perfect for each other. I found that very interesting. I couldn't reach Diane, but Hank was home—really, you should send his wife a gift. I think I woke her up."

"And Hank told you that the Langhorns were heading here to clear my name."

"Nobody ever tells me anything until it's nearly too late."

"I'll tell you something." Tam grinned at Kip, who had been patiently listening to her half of the conversation. "We have an Internal Audit Specialist vacancy. It seems Ms. Barrett has quit."

Kip grinned at her.

"Has she now? To do what?"

"I don't know, but hopefully whatever it is, it'll be near me."

Mercedes laughed, all her pique dissolved. "Congratulations on losing a fine employee."

"Why thank you. I do have a spot of business."

"Really? You've only been completely out of touch for three full days, so I can't imagine what has come up."

"So far, there are rumors swirling but nothing in the press yet about this, is there?"

"Not that I've found. I have a press release drafted. Diane approved the language, pending details from the lawyer, and I can send it on to our public affairs officer to do those blasts or whatever it is she calls them. She's e-mailing me every three minutes. Just so you know."

"I am grateful to all of you," Tam said seriously. "I trusted that you would all know what to do and I was right. Why don't you read it to me?"

She listened and smiled at Kip to let her know all was well. As much as Ted's and Nadia's betrayal hurt it allowed for the loyalty and good sense of other people to shine.

The release was fine, worded as an early warning to clients that a criminal investigation of one of their own had been concluded with a successful recovery. With simple modifications, it would go out to press contacts as well.

Disaster averted. She knew that she didn't have to tell Hank to get back with Big Blue and see if they wouldn't reconsider the cancellation. He knew what to do. There was a thought—she was essential to the company, but maybe not quite as essential as she liked to believe. There was perhaps time in her day, in her weekends and in her life.

They chatted a little bit more, and Tam agreed they'd be returning home the following day. After she hung up, she filled Kip in on the details that hadn't been obvious from Tam's half of the conversation.

"What a relief," Kip said. Hand in hand, they went back out to the crowded street where the heat was getting intense. "What shall we do until embarkation?"

Tam gave Kip a wide-eyed look. "There's no rule that says we can't go back aboard early."

"Really?" Kip turned on her heel and made a beeline for the straw market. "I'd have skipped the ice cream."

Tam hopped along behind her, dodging tourists and barkers. She was having a little trouble keeping up. She hoped, sincerely, that it wasn't a portent of the ways things would always be.

By the time they reached the cabin door, Kip's hands were shaking so badly she couldn't get the card key in place. Tam needn't have smirked, but once the door was open she didn't care in the least.

She'd given up her job and dragged Tam at a breakneck pace down the long pier and now she didn't know what to do.

Tam pulled her close and the door swung shut.

So what if her brain still didn't know what to do, she told herself. Her body knew.

Tam's kiss was tender and brief. "Your hair," she murmured, pulling the tie off the ponytail. "I have been aching to touch it." Tam's face was buried just above her ear.

"We have all afternoon, all night."

"We have longer than that."

Kip experienced that same dizzying sensation of melting, losing her edges against Tam's heat. She untied her shirt, her heart beating hard and fast. It was intoxicating to be free of guilt, to be free of all her suspicions.

She didn't have to dig down to find a no.

She could be all yes.

The hastily stripped bed was firm, the sheets cool, Tam's skin like silk. Clothes scattered, she explored Tam's legs with her hands, smoothing up and down their length. She let Tam draw her up for a kiss and was shocked with a pleasure deeper than any she'd ever felt the first time her breasts touched Tam's. The wonder of it spread throughout her body. It was nearly as intense to feel their stomachs touch and their legs tangle.

The daylight that streamed from the porthole over the bed lit up Tam's body, leaving no shadows. Once again Tam pulled her on top so that she was straddling her. Her unbound hair swept around them as they kissed. Only that morning Tam's hands had stopped at the hem of her T-shirt, but nothing was in the way now and she moaned as Tam's hands cupped her breasts. She was dissolving into Tam's touch even as her blood roared in her head.

Her fingertips had never seemed so sensitive to texture, but she could savor the difference in skin over Tam's collarbone and her chest. She was so lost in the newness of Tam's body that she didn't feel the change in Tam's touch until her hand had slipped between her spread thighs.

She groaned and momentarily stilled. Gazing down into Tam's face, she sought for her reflection in Tam's shining gray eyes. Then she kissed her with yes, her needy yes. She begged with kisses and spread herself on Tam's hands. All that electricity, the yearning, shadowed glances, the confusion of wanting, all swirled through her body in a rush like a waterfall. She spilled over and she breathed out a nearly inaudible, "More."

Tam's eyes were fierce with passion. She pulled Kip down to her for more kisses, saying against her mouth, "More. All you want."

Finally, when Tam rolled on top of her, Kip felt a wave of surrender. Until then she had been taking what she needed, but now she gave. Tam's fingers were deep inside her, her mouth at her breasts was demanding and rough. She had never felt stripped bare like this before, so enjoyed and savored. She had never felt like she was giving so completely what was wanted.

She moaned Tam's name. Exhausted, only the edges of her desire sated, she leaned over Tam to watch her eyes as she finally explored the exquisite velvet and wet of her. There was only love there, bright with need and wonder. Her fingers caressed and she followed the light in Tam's eyes. How far, how deep, how much, it was all there in eyes she had thought would never be open to her. There were no secrets, no shadows, and she was wanted.

She abandoned Tam's eyes to love her with her mouth, tasting passion, letting it paint her lips, roll over her tongue. She could feel Tam's response and adored the mirror of their passion. She loved doing this and clearly Tam loved feeling it. She could have laughed with delight at the surging of Tam's body, but saved it until the long arms pulled her up again and she was held close.

Tam pulled a sheet over them, and Kip realized she was shivering with emotion, exhaustion and release all rolled into one. She kissed Tam with her wet lips, which drew a responsive shudder. If resting had been in Tam's mind, she abandoned the thought and Kip found herself again loved, again wanted.

"We're underway," Tam murmured.

Kip listened—she was right, the engines had changed. "Did we leave early or something?"

"No, love. We've been in bed for hours."

Kip's disbelieving eyes found the bedside clock, then she ducked her head sheepishly.

Tam tipped her face up. "I'm not done with you."

She shuddered and felt so wanton, so undone. She could say nothing but "yes," with her lips pressed to Tam's.

"Do you suppose they're still serving dinner?"

Tam smiled sleepily against Kip's hair. "Probably. If you can get up, I'll join you."

Kip's soft laugh flowed around Tam's ears. "Okay, you got me. I can't move."

"Warm enough?"

"God, yes."

Tam was almost asleep when Kip said her name.

"We go back to the real world tomorrow."

"Mm-hmm."

She shifted and Tam opened her eyes. The last of sunset painted Kip with orange and gold.

"I want this—" Kip touched Tam's lips with her fingertips, then brushed them tantalizingly over her nipple, drawing a gasp. "I want this to be the real world. The one that counts most."

"So do I. It'll only be that way if we work at it."

Kip nodded and settled again. "I like the rocking."

Tam gathered her close. "I'll take you sailing the next possible day. We'll dine in the sunshine."

Kip murmured something else and Tam didn't know which of them fell asleep first. It didn't matter.

EPILOGUE

"The marina confirmed. The hamper will be delivered by four o'clock. I did that much. It's up to you to get the boss off my back and onto the boat." Mercedes' tone indicated that she thought it an impossible task.

Kip leaned against the wall in one of the less traveled corridors of the Federal courthouse. "Once sentencing is over I am kidnapping her. The weather is supposed to be spectacular—a genuine summer weekend in Seattle. Who would have thunk it?"

"From what I hear, you're the one who needs the break."

"Nah. It's good to be fully occupied again. Oh, Tam's waving. I think we're going back into session."

Kip clicked her cell phone shut and turned it off. She wasn't going to get caught by a bailiff with her phone on. It would earn her a dressing-down from Judge Warren, an experience anyone with sense would avoid.

Tam took her hand with a tense smile. “What were you plotting? You had that look.”

“I don’t know what you’re talking about. I was just chatting with Mercedes.”

“Great. The thought of the two of you in league is too much to contemplate.”

They found seats in the crowded courtroom. Kip felt a thrill of satisfaction when Nadia and Ted were brought in. Before their guilty verdict they’d been in carefully chosen, sober suits. Now that they were officially felons, she had to say that orange didn’t become either of them. Nadia was no longer perfectly tanned. It must have been the shock of her life when Judge Warren had agreed with the U.S. Attorney that they were a flight risk and denied them bail.

It was the first of many shocks—poor Ted and Nadia. They’d not looked the least concerned during Kip’s testimony, even though their attorney had failed to undermine or rattle either of them by revealing their now-public relationship.

The Langhorn defense had been greatly bolstered when the recording of their confessional conversation with Tam had been ruled inadmissible, so their own incriminating words couldn’t be used against them. They hadn’t been read any rights, or advised they were being recorded. But dear Robert Manna, who had given incredibly detailed testimony, had been challenged by the defense for his claim of exact recall. How could he possibly remember exactly what was said nearly nine months later? Why, to be fully prepared he’d requested a copy of a recording he knew had been made. It had, after all, been made on his employer’s premises in the Commonwealth of the Bahamas, and in the spirit of cooperation, the local embassy staff had provided it to him. So he’d listened to the recording to refresh his memory of what he and others had said he’d answered, an allowable rebuttal to the doubts raised about his memory.

Neither of the defendants had looked quite as confident after that. Guilty on all counts, bank accounts drained by a series of attorneys of decreasing skill and the only bright spot was possible grounds for appeal over the recording, if only they could afford an attorney good enough to make their case.

The recording had of course fallen into the hands of reporters as well. Their bald-faced decision to buy their way into celebrity had not endeared them to the very people they had hoped to impress. The Langhorns were regarded as the type of wannabees that would crash a State dinner. Them that had weren't sharing with grasping posers.

The final blow had been the court's decision to gag all mention of and seal the records concerning the cult where both Tam and Nadia had been born, forwarding the matter to Family and Juvenile Court for investigation. Nadia would eventually get her evidence back, but the undoubted sympathy she'd hoped for from the jury hadn't come to pass either.

Fortune was being awful slow to smile on them.

Kip whispered in Tam's ear. "I want Judge Warren to rule the world."

Tam nodded and whispered back, "I'm sorry, honey, but I fell for her hard when she gave Vernon Markoff fifteen years."

Kip gave her the look that remark deserved but didn't say anything because the bailiff announced the judge's entry into the courtroom. The charges were read and the judge finally spoke. Kip covered Tam's hand with her own.

"In considering the facts of this case," Judge Warren read aloud from her prepared notes, "as well as the nature of the crimes and the motivation behind them, I have taken into account that no weapons were used in the course of the felony acts. Therefore the maximum sentence is proscribed by law. I have considered the statements of contrition by the defendants, which would suggest that a long rehabilitation would be unnecessary."

Kip felt Tam's hand twitch. It wasn't sounding like a heavy sentence so far—the Langhorns could get as little as seven years, with half that sentence served on probation.

"Prison, however, serves more than one purpose. Rehabilitation is one. Punishment is another. In spite of the defendants' belief that prison is little more than a sequestered writing retreat, it is supposed to punish, as long as it's not in cruel or unusual ways. In my years on the bench I have seen many defendants who were motivated by greed and ambition, and even a desire for notoriety. In most of those cases, the defendants perceived no other option when they chose a criminal act. What I find disturbing in this case is that the defendants had choices and opportunities of many legal kinds. From dozens of lawful options, they elected to commit their crimes as if choosing the right suit for a job interview."

Kip squeezed Tam's hand and held her breath.

"Having been found guilty of all charges against them, I hereby sentence both defendants to serve the maximum sentence of twelve years—"

Pandemonium erupted. Bloggers rushed for the doors in a race to be the first to report on the outcome. Kip couldn't hear what the judge was saying, but Nadia had put her head in her hands. Maybe she'd done the math. Even if they got out halfway through, with the rest to be served on probation, six years was twice what Nadia had counted on. Six years without Botox was a long time.

She had moments of feeling sorry for Nadia, but they were brief. Her childhood had been a nightmare, but she'd put together a good life. There had been no reason to gamble that life to try for something more. Nadia didn't have to be like Tam—after all, Tam was an exceptional woman—but she could have stayed Nadia Langhorn. Now she was nobody.

Tam squeezed her hand hard. Stealing a glance at her face, Kip saw a triumphant relief. The system worked, at least in this case. Everything they'd done then and since mattered. Though it wasn't always so, justice had been served this time.

Poor Ted and Nadia. Kip thought bitterly that if she worked at it real hard she could shed a half a tear for their fate.

Finally finished giving reaction interviews and able to make their escape, Tam was still stunned as they got into Kip's Camry. "Twelve years," she repeated. "It's more than I had hoped, even."

"I admit I was worried for a moment there. But it's okay if you're in love with the judge. I am too, now."

Tam's mobile chimed. She checked the display. "It's Hank. This won't take long."

Even though she didn't intend to gossip, it was impossible not to give Hank her impressions of the sentencing. The call took longer than she had intended. It was Friday evening, and she tried very hard not to work on Friday nights. They didn't always get Date Night, but it was still a shared goal.

After she hung up she beamed at Kip. "It's been a great week."

"It has."

Tam prodded her gently in the side. "You got your last two clients."

Kip gave her a mega-watt smile. "I did. God bless rock and roll."

"Are you really happy?" Tam had meant it to sound like a joke, but it came out as a serious question.

"Yes, silly. How many times do I have to say it?"

"One more, I guess." She looked happy, Tam thought. Her lovely blue eyes were full of light and joy. She smiled deeply and often. The creases of worry and stress had all but gone. Still, Tam needed to be reassured from time to time that her wife had no regrets for the unexpected turn her career had taken.

Kip took her gaze off the rush-hour traffic long enough to give Tam a serious look. "I have you. I had time for lunch with Jen the other day. And I have some really fun work that, at the moment at least, doesn't involve numbering exhibits or filing reports for the court. Just a handful of highly strung recording artists who want to be sure their managers, agents and promoters aren't robbing them blind." She bounced in the driver's seat. "I am expected to suspect *everyone*. They love it when I'm paranoid on their behalf. I get to put on my mirror sunglasses and ask people questions, and they have to answer me or risk losing their star client. I don't even have to read people their rights. It's a dream come true."

Tam laughed. "Your grandfather would approve?"

"Well, I'm not looking out for POTUS. But there are shockingly large sums of money involved and I'm trying to keep people honest. I'm still floored that Jen's boyfriend Luke, of all people, recommended me to that first band when they were complaining during a recording session."

Tam finally took in their surroundings. They weren't anywhere near home and she'd been planning a memorable evening in front of the view with Kip that included, when they were exhausted by other things, watching the summer sun set over the Sound. They were skirting the edge of Lake Union, which was shimmering under the cloudless sky. "Why are we headed this way?"

"Part of our original deal was that you keep your promises, and you've been promising me a honeymoon for months."

A shiver of pleasure mixed with anticipatory butterflies left Tam breathless. "This is what you and Mercedes were concocting?"

"Unlike you, I know when to ask for help. Besides, I ask for her help and that means your cell phone won't ring for the next forty-eight hours."

Kip took one hand off the wheel to lace her fingers around the tie that held back her ponytail. She stripped it free and then shook her hair out around her shoulders. "You've also been promising me a night of lovemaking on the lake for months."

Speechless, Tam watched Kip unfasten the top two buttons of her blouse, revealing an undergarment that made Tam's mouth water.

How had she ever thought this woman straitlaced and humorless? She was grinning at Tam now, her eyes sparkling with mischief and delight.

"I take it I have your full attention?"

Tam nodded.

"And your full cooperation?" She turned into the Gas Works Marina lot.

"Indeed."

"Excellent." She idled at the dock manager's office. "There's a hamper with your name on it inside."

Tam would have leapt out of the car but Kip undid another button. Then another.

She wasn't sure how she made her legs and arms work, but she did manage to fetch the hamper. It was large, heavy and awkward and she wondered what all Kip and Mercedes had deemed necessary for their weekend.

Back in the car it took only one look at Kip, with her blouse open to reveal the delicious round curves of her breasts and her hair down around her shoulders, to make her feel faint.

"What happened to the Kip Barrett who never broke the rules?"

Both serious and flirtatious, Kip asked, "Is there a rule against this? I've seen swimsuits that cover less. And besides, do you want to live in a world where there's a rule against me driving you crazy?"

"I see your point."

Kip parked near the *Emerald Petral*'s docking and Tam found the will to gather the hamper and—as instructed—an overnight bag from the trunk.

Kip, however, didn't immediately get out of the car. Tam gestured at her to roll down the window.

"Aren't you joining me? This weekend won't be nearly so fun without you."

"Yes, I...."

It was delightful to watch Kip blush. It wasn't always easy to tell, but there was a definite red tinge to her cheeks. "What?"

"Oh hell." Kip hurriedly buttoned up her blouse. "I thought I could do it, but I can't."

"I adore you," Tam said, comparing the vision of Kip in front of her, blushing at her own boldness, overcome with shy propriety, to the incisive, unflappable witness with nerves of steel she'd been during the trial. "You are exactly my kind of femme fatale."

Blouse tidied, she gave Tam a sheepish smile and got out of the car. "Some femme fatale I am. I mean—what if someone saw me—"

Delighted and laughing, Tam backed Kip up to the car and kissed her. Thoroughly.

"We're never going to set sail at this rate," Kip finally murmured.

"Sweetheart, I've been at sea since the moment I met you."

Kip grinned. "Good. Let's keep it that way." She lifted one handle of the hamper Tam had abandoned.

Tam happily took the other. It was an easy load to manage together.

Publications from Bella Books

The best in contemporary lesbian fiction

P.O. Box 10543
Tallahassee, Florida 32302
Phone: 800-729-4992
www.bellabooks.com

MILES TO GO by Amy Dawson Robertson. Rennie Vogel has finally earned a spot at CT3. All too soon she finds herself abandoned behind enemy lines, miles from safety and forced to do the one thing shenever has before: trust another woman.
978-1-59493-174-1 $14.95

PHOTOGRAPHS OF CLAUDIA by KG MacGregor. To photographer Leo Wescott models are light and shadow realized on film. Until Claudia.
978-1-59493-168-0 $14.95

SONGS WITHOUT WORDS by Robbi McCoy. Harper Sheridan runaway niece turns up in the one place least expected and Harper confronts the woman from the summer that has shaped her entire life since. 978-1-59493-166-6 $14.95

YOURS FOR THE ASKING by Kenna White. Lauren Roberts is tired of being the steady, reliable one. When Gaylin Hart blows into her life, she decides to act, only to find once again that her younger sister wants the same woman.
978-1-59493-163-5 $14.95

THE SCORPION by Gerri Hill. Cold cases are what make reporter Marty Edwards tick. When her latest proves to be far from cold, she still doesn't want Detective Kristen Bailey babysitting her, not even when she has to run for her life.
978-1-59493-162-8 $14.95

STEPPING STONE by Karin Kallmaker. Selena Ryan's heart was shredded by an actress, and she swears she will never, ever be involved with one again.
978-1-59493-160-4 $14.95

FAINT PRAISE by Ellen Hart. When a famous TV personality leaps to his death, Jane Lawless agrees to help a friend with inquiries, drawing the attention of a ruthless killer. #6 in this award-winning series. 978-1-59493-164-2 $14.95

NO RULES OF ENGAGEMENT by Tracey Richardson. A war zone attraction is of no use to Major Logan Sharp. She can't wait for Jillian Knight to go back to the other side of the world. 978-1-59493-159-8 $14.95

Women. Books. Even Better Together.
www.BellaBooks.com